P9-CLE-858

THE PERFECT SUSPECT

Berkley Prime Crime titles by Margaret Coel

BLOOD MEMORY
THE PERFECT SUSPECT

Wind River Mysteries

THE EAGLE CATCHER
THE GHOST WALKER
THE DREAM STALKER
THE STORY TELLER
THE LOST BIRD
THE SPIRIT WOMAN
THE THUNDER KEEPER
THE SHADOW DANCER
KILLING RAVEN
WIFE OF MOON
EYE OF THE WOLF
THE DROWNING MAN
THE GIRL WITH BRAIDED HAIR
THE SILENT SPIRIT
THE SPIDER'S WEB

THE PERFECT SUSPECT

MARGARET COEL

BERKLEY PRIME CRIME, NEW YORK

THE BERKLEY PUBLISHING GROUP
Published by the Penguin Group
Penguin Group (USA) Inc.
375 Hudson Street, New York, New York 10014, USA
Penguin Group (Canada), 90 Eglinton Avenue East, Suite 700, Toronto, Ontario M4P 2Y3, Canada
(a division of Pearson Penguin Canada Inc.)
Penguin Books Ltd., 80 Strand, London WC2R 0RL, England
Penguin Group Ireland, 25 St. Stephen's Green, Dublin 2, Ireland (a division of Penguin Books Ltd.)
Penguin Group (Australia), 250 Camberwell Road, Camberwell, Victoria 3124, Australia
(a division of Pearson Australia Group Pty. Ltd.)
Penguin Books India Pvt. Ltd., 11 Community Centre, Panchsheel Park, New Delhi—110 017, India
Penguin Group (NZ), 67 Apollo Drive, Rosedale, Auckland 0632, New Zealand
(a division of Pearson New Zealand Ltd.)
Penguin Books (South Africa) (Pty.) Ltd., 24 Sturdee Avenue, Rosebank, Johannesburg 2196,
South Africa

Penguin Books Ltd., Registered Offices: 80 Strand, London WC2R 0RL, England

This book is an original publication of The Berkley Publishing Group.

This is a work of fiction. Names, characters, places, and incidents either are the product of the author's imagination or are used fictitiously, and any resemblance to actual persons, living or dead, business establishments, events, or locales is entirely coincidental. The publisher does not have any control over and does not assume any responsibility for author or third-party websites or their content.

Copyright © 2011 by Margaret Coel.
Interior text design by Laura K. Corless.

The prayer on page 283 is based on an Arapaho prayer found on the monument to fallen Arapaho warriors at the Battle of the Little Big Horn.

All rights reserved.
No part of this book may be reproduced, scanned, or distributed in any printed or electronic form without permission. Please do not participate in or encourage piracy of copyrighted materials in violation of the author's rights. Purchase only authorized editions.
BERKLEY® PRIME CRIME and the PRIME CRIME logo are trademarks of Penguin Group (USA) Inc.

ISBN 978-0-425-24348-0

PRINTED IN THE UNITED STATES OF AMERICA

For George

ACKNOWLEDGMENTS

I want to thank the following persons for taking the time to read this manuscript and suggest the changes and corrections that would allow my fictional world to reflect the real world more accurately: Mike Fiori, retired detective, Denver Police Department; Sheila Carrigan, former judge and deputy district attorney; Karen Cotton, features/entertainment reporter. I also want to thank my good friends and astute readers for their excellent, as always, comments: Karen Gilleland, Bev Carrigan, Carl Schneider, and of course, my husband, George Coel.

THE PERFECT SUSPECT

1

She never meant to kill him.

Shooting David was not a premeditated act. There were no plans, no blueprints, like the detailed drawings of a grand building. Nothing like that. It had happened in an instant, the loud retort of the gun that had shattered the quiet and shocked her as much as it shocked him. She had seen the shock and disbelief in his eyes before they went glassy and he started stumbling backward, grasping at the cord of a table lamp. The lamp had crashed on top of him.

Ryan Beckman pulled herself over the steering wheel and flexed her fingers. Her hands had gone numb, she had been gripping the wheel so hard, staring at the oncoming headlights on I-70, taking the curves around the mountains too fast. She needed to put as much distance between herself and David Mathews's house as possible. Still she forced herself to let up on the gas pedal. It would never do to be stopped by the state patrol when everyone at headquarters thought she was in Breckenridge. She could see the lights of Denver glowing in the rearview mirror.

Not premeditated? Then why did you bring the 9mm Sig 226 Tactical? That would be the first question the detectives would ask. She knew exactly how the questioning would go. She had been a detective almost fourteen years, the last three years with the Denver Police Department, and before that, eleven years in Minneapolis. She was inured to surprises in investigations, hardened and experienced. She knew how to anticipate questions and turn them away from her. But her colleagues were the type to pound and push, refuse to give up. How could she make them understand? She had carried the gun to get David's attention, that was all. Make him look at her and see what he had done. Destroyed her life, her peace of mind, her future. All of it disappearing like smoke out of a burned house that once had been beautiful and filled with promise. David was her life. They were perfect for each other, he had said so himself. Destined to go on together, be old together, sit on the porch and hold hands and laugh about how close they had come to losing everything. But David was likely to brush aside anything she said, just as he had done two weeks ago when she had pretended to bump into him in the hotel lobby downtown. Telling her not to make a scene, telling her to get over it. Shrugging and smirking, with that ugly way he had of dismissing unimportant things. The valet had brought his SUV around, and he had left her standing in the lobby, the upholstered sofas and chairs, the thick wood tables, the Oriental rugs and chandeliers blurring around her. The SUV had peeled away, the engine roaring in her ears.

So she had brought the gun to force him to listen.

There won't be any questions. The sound of her own voice over the noise of the tires and the hum of the engine made her feel calmer. The tension began to drain away, her fingers relaxed around the wheel. She had to remain logical and in control, not let the situation get away from her. She had signed out for a long weekend. Three days in Breckenridge she'd told Sergeant Crowley. Hiking, a little fishing. "You fish?" he'd said, barely swallowing the amusement and incredulity in his voice. "It's very relaxing," she'd told him. He knew she deserved a little relaxation, time off from the madness. The last case had shaken her—the bludgeoning death of a seventy-six-year-old woman by her beloved grandson. Crowley had called in the department therapist to talk her and Martin Martinez, her partner, through the images and nightmares. When she told the sergeant she needed a few days off, he had balked only enough to remind her that she had used most of her vacation time, which she knew. All those weekends and stolen hours with David.

You left town. Booked a condo in Breckenridge to give yourself an alibi, drove back to Denver and killed David Mathews.

"Stop it!" She heard herself shouting, felt her fingers squeezing the wheel again. *Stay calm! Stay calm!* There was no reason to suspect her, and there would be no intimidating interviews. In any case, it was an accident, a horrific, unanticipated event. She had never planned to kill anyone. She had discharged her pistol before, it was true, but only in the line of duty. Only to save herself or another officer. She had been exonerated, even commended for her quick-thinking actions. There had been other tense standoffs, once with an Indian at the end of an alley, standing up practically comatose, gripping a knife, ignoring her orders, poised to rush her. "Drop the knife!" she had shouted. She was close to pulling the trigger before the knife clattered onto the concrete. That had brought another commendation—for restraint under stress.

Something had changed. It was as if she were driving underwater, and she realized she was in the Eisenhower Tunnel beneath long tubes of fluorescent lights. Red taillights blurred ahead. She realized something else: she was crying. David had been as quiet as that Indian, comatose on his feet, looking straight at her and not seeing her.

"This isn't a good time," he'd said when he opened the door. He blinked hard as if an unwanted apparition had appeared on his porch.

"Why is that?" She could see herself standing under the light on his porch, her straw bag hung off one shoulder, the black night folded around her. "Are you expecting someone?" She had brushed past him into the marble-floored entry with the staircase that curved upward and wound overhead, then into the warm, soft lighting in the living room beyond.

She had walked straight into the living room, sensing the exasperation and barely controlled anger that rolled off David like perspiration. "Can I have a drink?" she'd said.

"You have to leave." His voice had been hard and cold.

"One drink, David? Surely you have time."

He had stepped over to a cabinet and poured two fingers of bourbon into a crystal glass that danced and sparkled in the light. An ice cube tinkled against the crystal, and hope had washed over her. He remembered her drink: bourbon, neat, a little ice. She smiled at him as she took the glass. "We have to talk," she said.

"Look, Ryan." He held out both hands, as if he wanted to pull her toward him, even hug her. Her heart had pounded with anticipation. "What we had was very good, but it's over. It no longer works." She had tried to interrupt because it wasn't true, but he had kept on, always the politician, as handsome and charming as JFK, cajoling and soothing different factions, searching for common ground. "Let us go forward together" was his campaign slogan. He was sure to be the next governor of Colorado.

"The timing's all wrong, for starters," he said. "Sydney has agreed to work things out. Polls have me thirty points ahead, but the election is two months away. Any scandal, rumors of an extramarital dalliance could destroy everything. I can't take the chance."

He had gone on, saying other things, but she hadn't heard. Her mind had stuck on the word dalliance. A year of her life, and that's all she was? A dalliance? "You don't know what you're saying!" She had heard herself shout over whatever political platitudes he was still spouting and struggled to sound calm, rational. "We can work it out," she said. "All you and Sydney have to do is put up a front until the election. Then you settle into office, get a divorce, and we'll be together. Until then, I'll stay in the background. No one knows about us. No one will suspect . . ."

"Listen to me," David had said. "It's over. How many times do I have to say it?"

"But that's all wrong. Try to understand, David." She could hear the hysteria working back into her voice.

"You have to go now."

"Please don't do this." She had been holding the glass. She couldn't remember whether she had taken a sip of bourbon, but her mouth felt dry, her tongue as thick as sandpaper. She must have set the glass on the lamp table, because she realized she had taken the gun out of her bag and was holding it on him, pleading with him, issuing orders. "Listen to me. Listen to me." *Drop the knife!*

"For godssakes, Ryan. Put the gun down." She had heard the tremor in his voice, so unlike the candidate renowned for his cool demeanor, his control of every situation. "Don't do anything that . . ."

It was lost, all lost, in the explosion of the Sig. Her own life crashed around her, as if the beams and the plaster had fallen from the ceiling and she was left standing in the debris, staring at the lifeless body of David Mathews. You had to be ready to pull the trigger—that had been drummed into her from her rookie days. If you take out your gun, you must be ready to fire.

She had been shaking, her hands trembling so hard that she had difficulty shoving the gun back into her bag. She made herself step across the living room, searching for the casings. My God, there were three. She had shot him three times. Maybe she had fired off even more bullets. She managed to extract the gun and check the magazine. Three bullets missing. She stepped back to the lamp table and picked up the glass. She hadn't touched anything else, she was sure. She had been careful. David had let her inside, and she had walked past him without touching the door.

She had to get away. A neighbor could have heard the gunshots. People could appear out of nowhere. She backed across the living room and into the entry, not taking her eyes from David's body, so still and helpless and complete. There would be nothing more for David Mathews. She slid the glass inside her bag and used the front of her jacket to turn the doorknob. Still using the jacket, she pulled the door shut behind her.

She saw the woman then, halted in mid-step on the sidewalk next to the curb, a shadow swallowed in the darkness except for the white slacks billowing and shimmering.

Ryan swung sideways, out of the porch light, ran along the front of the house and rounded the corner. She kept running, slipping on the lawn, catching herself and finally throwing herself inside the gray Ford parked a half block away. *Never park in front.* She could hear David's voice in her head. *Park down the block so no one will connect your car to my house.*

The street was quiet, wide and lined with oaks. The thick, heavy branches nearly obscured the mansions behind the deep swaths of lawn and curved walkways. She had pulled into the lane and forced herself to maintain a slow, steady speed, a resident returning home after a late night, not wanting to disturb the neighbors. She had felt the shaking deep inside, as if her heart had gone into free fall.

The woman on the sidewalk had seen her! In that instant, when she had looked in the woman's direction. An instant was enough for a witness to pick someone out of a lineup. She had seen it happen. Every instinct told her to drive around the block, find the woman and kill her. It would be obvious what had happened. Someone had gone to David Mathews's home, shot him, then shot the woman outside who must have been a witness. Logical, unsurprising, the kind of act homicide detectives would accept. She would have accepted it. A killer, wanting to make sure no one could identify him. Or her.

Instead, she had turned onto the thoroughfare that ran through the neighborhood west to the highway, on automatic now, her hands glued to the wheel, the straw bag with the Sig and the crystal glass tossed onto the passenger seat. Still calm on the outside, she thought, her heart pounding against her ribs, probably driving like a drunk, the slow, cautious turn, the effort to keep from swerving into the next lane. She kept going, the highway somewhere in the darkness ahead pulling her forward like a magnet. She was not a killer. It had been a horrible accident. The case could even be made that what happened was David's fault. Anyway, the shadow on the sidewalk would never connect the woman under the porch light of David Mathews's house with Detective Ryan Beckman.

She had followed the entrance ramp onto I-25 and forced herself to concentrate on merging into the traffic that curved to I-70. She drove west, the dark, ragged shapes of the foothills floating ahead for a while. Then she was climbing into the mountains, barely aware of the uphill pull on the engine, her heart still hammering, the image of David, shocked and surprised, thrown off his own game, running through her head. At one point, alone on the highway with no oncoming traffic and nothing but the enveloping darkness behind her, she had rolled down her window and thrown out the crystal glass.

She followed the exit to Frisco and drove through town. Moonlight traced the waters of Lake Dillon outside her window. Twenty minutes later she was in Breckenridge heading up the mountain toward the ski area. The condo she had rented was hidden in clusters of lodgepole pines, and the smell of pine drifted inside the Ford. She parked in the garage underneath, a voluminous cavern lit by dim overhead bulbs and bisected by rows of parked vehicles. The sound of her door slamming bounced around the metal and concrete. She rode the elevator to the third floor, let herself into the condo and leaned against the door a moment. She was safe. No one had seen her driving into the garage, making her way upstairs. Had she planned all the details, they could not have worked out so well. She turned on the table lamp, then slumped onto the sofa, giving in to the crushing sense of exhaustion.

The ringing of her cell cut through the silence.

Ryan blinked into the light flaring from the lamp a moment, trying to get her bearings. The night came back to her in a rush, like photos flashing in front of her. Finally she managed to pull the cell from her bag, and check the readout. Headquarters. She waited for two more rings, trying to still her breathing and control the erratic rhythm of her heart, before she answered. "Hello," she said. Her voice sounded mute and thick.

"Ryan?" The sound of Crowley's voice drilled into her. "Did I wake you up?"

"What do you think?" Her heart had started up again. "What time is it?" She tried to bring the face of her watch into focus. 5:45 a.m.

"Sorry, your vacation's over. I need you here."

"What are you talking about?" My God. The woman on the sidewalk must have gone inside David's house and found his body! But how had she gotten in? The door was locked. Maybe she looked through a window, saw David on the living room floor, and called the police.

"High-profile shooting," the sergeant said. "David Mathews shot in his home last night."

"Mathews, shot?" She clasped the cell hard against her ear. "Is he dead?"

"Two bullets in the chest, one in the thigh. Somebody made sure he was dead. I need you here."

She managed a gulp of air. She felt as if she were in a race, trying to stay ahead of the man on the phone. What was he saying? She should investigate the case? It was so absurd she had to jam her fist against her mouth to keep from laughing. After a moment she heard herself say: "I have a three-day vacation, Sergeant."

"Williams and O'Keefe are tied up with a shooting in Montbello. Bustamante and Greeves are still in L.A. investigating a possible connection to the gang shooting and the muggings in LoDo. I don't expect them back until tomorrow."

"What about the other detectives?" The sense of absurdity expanded around her, as if she had stepped into a funhouse and was surrounded by an array of mirrors that reflected distorted and grotesque images. "You can find somebody else."

"Not with your experience. This is the highest profile homicide we've handled in ten years. The press will be all over this, and that includes the national press. Television, radio, bloggers, you name it. We can't have any mix-ups. I need an experienced detective in charge, and you are it. How soon can you get down here?"

"I'm in Breckenridge," she heard herself saying. The grotesque images in the funhouse mirrors seemed to be closing in. "I need a couple of hours."

"I'll expect you in an hour and a half," Sergeant Crowley said.

2

Catherine sat up with a start, her skin cold and prickly. She flipped the switch on the bedside lamp and blinked into the circle of light, trying to banish the blackness of the nightmare. The heavy noise of an explosion, the rise of wailing sounds in the distance and the sense that she was spiraling downward into an abyss—the nightmare was always the same. She had thought it was over. There had been almost six months of peaceful nights without the horror that had previously crashed over her for months and left her weak and disoriented in the mornings. But now the nightmare had started again. A dull wine-ache spread behind her eyes. She pulled her legs to her chest, leaned against her knees, and waited for the spasms in her stomach to stop. The warm, musty smells of early September drifted through the opened window. Rex was still asleep on his pillow in the corner, and for a moment, she thought it strange the golden retriever hadn't heard the noise and gone into a barking fit, the noise had seemed so real. Finally, she slid out of bed and spent ten minutes in the steaming shower with hot water pounding her shoulders and back. She began to feel situated again, the tile solid beneath her feet, the glass shower door cloudy, and the familiarity of the small bungalow gathering her in.

She wandered into the kitchen, dressed in a white cotton blouse, tan skirt and high-heeled sandals, her black hair still damp on her neck. Rex waited at the back door. She let him into the yard and watched him circle the lawn, stretching his muscles in the soft newness of the morning. The sky was pale blue with wisps of clouds rolling past and spears of sunlight falling through the leaves of the elm tree and scattering about the lawn. The pansies, daisies and petunias she had planted in the narrow garden near the back door seemed to be wilting with the end of summer. In the near distance, like a massive wall looming over Denver, were the silvery blue peaks of the Rocky Mountains.

She closed the door, started the coffee brewing, and turned on the little TV at the end of the counter. Leaving the volume low, she stared at the movie-star-handsome couple seated on sofas in a studio in New York almost two thousand miles away. An anchor woman interviewing a young Broadway actor who kept tossing his head to clear the mane of dark hair from his eyes. Catherine thought about the way people opened up to complete strangers—someone sitting next to you on the plane, or standing in a line, or tossing interview questions across a table—and divulged the most important parts of their lives. They were divorced, had lost a child, had a debilitating disease. It was as if they were compelled to divulge the information. Otherwise no one would really know them, or even see them. She wondered what she might say in that studio in New York: "Hello, I'm Catherine McLeod. Investigative journalist with the *Denver Journal*, forty years old and divorced. Last summer, I killed a man."

She turned away from the TV and poured a mug of coffee. The almost empty bottle of Burgundy sat on the counter, a reminder of last night. What had she been thinking? Alcohol had only fueled the nightmares. Self-defense, the investigators had ruled. She had killed the man before he could kill her. There was no blame; and no charges had been brought. Yet she had relived the incident night after night, the horrible explosion and wailing, the spiraling downward, the feeling that she was disappearing, until she realized that, in the horrible instant when she thought she would die, she had experienced her own death. Except that, in the end, she wasn't the one who died. She had spent months in counseling. She had quit drinking, except for an occasional glass of wine with dinner, and gradually the nightmares became less frequent. But last night, when she'd gotten home, the bungalow had seemed so vacant and quiet, even with Rex jumping about, welcoming her. She had felt limp with loneliness.

She was accustomed to being alone, she had told herself. She had made her own way for two years since her divorce. For the last ten months, Nick Bustamante had been in her life. Hardly long enough to dent old habits of independence. So what if he had been in L.A. for ten days interrogating gang members about a gang-related murder and random muggings? Marie—she had always called her mother, who had adopted her when she was five, by her first name—was in New England visiting a cousin, but Catherine had gone to dinner several times with friends. A couple of times, she had gotten together with Dulcie Oldman, who had been helping her understand her Arapaho heritage, ever since she had discovered last year that she was part Arapaho. She had called Dulcie and gotten her voice mail, and at some point, she had dragged the wine bottle from the back of a kitchen cabinet.

She had just poured another cup of coffee when she glimpsed the name "Mathews" in the crawl on the TV screen. She moved closer, sipping at the coffee and trying to block out the muted TV voices. The crawl started over. "Police report body of man found shot to death at home of David Mathews, candidate for governor in Colorado. No further details available. Stay tuned to Channel 9 for breaking news."

She set the cup down and went looking for her cell phone, which she found on the table next to her bag. A feeling of unreality washed over her, like the feeling she'd had when she awoke, as if the world were rearranging itself in inexplicable ways. She had covered David Mathews's campaign for the *Journal*, the rallies and speeches, the photo-op visits to retirement homes and veterans' halls and Little League ballparks. Rumors swirled about the candidate—financial improprieties, shady business deals, extramarital affairs. She had never succeeded in running down any of them. They were like the dull throbbing in her head, elusive and maddening and persistent. Mathews ran a well-organized, efficient campaign, and if there was anything to the rumors, the evidence had been buried so deeply she doubted it could ever be uncovered. All she'd had were notes, conjectures and innuendos, nothing she could write that wouldn't invite a libel suit. But all of her investigative reporter's instincts told her that something about the perfect candidate was not quite perfect. Now someone had been shot to death in Mathews's home.

She punched the button for Marjorie's number. It was still early, a little before seven by the silver watch that dangled on her wrist. Marjorie Fennerman, *Journal* managing editor, would not be in yet, but calls would be transferred to her home, and Marjorie would decide which to answer and which to ignore. After three rings, Marjorie's voice said, "I was just about to call you. You've heard the news?"

"What exactly is the news?"

"The night editor heard the police radio and recognized the address. All we know is what you've seen on TV. Dead body. Male."

"Mathews?"

"The police aren't saying until they have an ID. Jason is on the way over there."

"Jason? I've been on David Mathews's campaign since he announced he was running. This is my story."

"Jason has the police beat."

"He doesn't know anything about Mathews."

Catherine listened to the slow, thoughtful breathing at the other end, finally broken by Marjorie's voice. "God, it's too early in the morning for this. Gubernatorial candidate, thirty points ahead in the polls, certain to be elected, has either been shot to death or could be involved in somebody else's death. The national news will be all over it, but it's our story, and I have no intention of being scooped by some carpetbagger from the *New York Times*. We're the experts on Mathews. No doubt the campaign and party hacks will issue a lot of stupid press releases. I want you to get the facts behind the releases, work in the background stuff on Mathews and the campaign. Jason will stay on the police investigation. Oh, and I want to see you when you get back from Mathews's house."

David Mathews lived in the kind of glass and steel residence featured in architectural magazines, spread across a double lot with walls of windows that peered through the tall pines and elms planted after construction vehicles had destroyed the original landscape. The whole neighborhood had been transformed from the intimate, brick bungalows that had given Denver neighborhoods a distinctive charm for a hundred years into blocks of modern, impersonal structures. It had taken Catherine twenty minutes to drive across town from her own brick bungalow in Highland, an old residential neighborhood that straddled a bluff above the Platte Valley. Mercifully, Highland had escaped the modern makeover, a fact that left her giddy with gratitude every time she passed the Victorians, duplexes and bungalows sheltering under century-old elms and cottonwoods. An old cottonwood shaded her front yard, and a gnarled elm kept the sun off the back of the bungalow.

From a block away, Catherine spotted the police cars, TV vans and other vehicles along the curb in front of Mathews's house. A small crowd hovered just outside the yellow police crime-scene tape that wrapped across the yard and driveway. Little groups of people sauntered up and down the sidewalk, and gawkers stared out of the vehicles that inched down the street. She pulled the silver Chrysler convertible into a small vacant slot and walked a half block, bag hooked over her shoulder, notepad and pen in one hand. The faint odor of exhaust from the stalling traffic mixed with the smell of the morning dew on the lawns. Despite the hint of autumn in the air, the coolness of the night had evaporated. The glass blue sky promised a still, hot September day.

She shouldered past the crowd on the front sidewalk and went over to the TV and radio journalists and bloggers who had managed to hear the news before she had. Didn't these people ever sleep? Camera people from the TV channels had positioned themselves close to the yellow tape, black, rectangular boxes hoisted on their shoulders. They motioned to one another, nodding and blinking in some silent language. She slid in beside Jason. Through the enormous front window, a chandelier glowed in the entry of the glass and steel house.

"What are you doing here?" Jason Metcalf was short and barrel-shaped with a thin spray of brown hair combed over a pink scalp. He had been at the *Journal* eight years ago when she had started as a general assignment reporter. But he had stayed on while she took time off to work on a marriage that had headed downhill from the beginning.

Even before her divorce, she had grabbed at the opportunity to return to the *Journal* as an investigative reporter. By then, Jason had racked up a wall of congratulatory plaques, which, she suspected, led him to believe he had squatting rights on any major story.

"What am I doing at the biggest story of my career?" she said.

"It's my story."

"I'm on background and context," she said. "Campaign, future of the party. I'll be filling in around the investigation."

"That's just great." It was barely audible.

"Has the body been ID'd?"

Jason took a moment, checking the screen of his phone and slipping the phone back into his shirt pocket. "Coroner's been here awhile." He worked his lips silently for a moment, as if he were wondering how much he should tell her. Finally, a mask of what passed for acceptance dropped over his face. They were on the same paper, after all. "It's Mathews," he said, "but it's not official. Unofficial word is he was shot around midnight."

"Who's in charge?"

"The B team, you ask me. Your boyfriend's out of town, and the other first-rate detectives are tied up. They brought in Ryan Beckman and Martin Martinez. Beckman's okay, I guess. At least she has experience."

Catherine glanced around at the crowd ebbing and flowing along the sidewalk. Newcomers moved in closer, others walked away, tense, unresolved looks on their faces. A muffled sputtering of voices cut through the air. "Who found the body?" she said.

"You're full of questions. Maybe you should've gotten here earlier."

"Come on, Jason," she said.

He rolled his eyes and stared at the sky a moment. Then he let out a long, sour breath before he said, "Housekeeper arrived at 5:00 a.m., like usual. Found the body, ran to the neighbor's house and called 911, according to my police source, who is, of course, anonymous since he is not the official spokesperson."

"Any witnesses?"

"You mean, other than the killer and the victim? Quiet, ritzy neighborhood like this? Midnight?" He tossed his head toward the houses running north. "Who's gonna be out and about?"

"A neighbor walking the dog."

"This isn't TV," Jason said. "My source said nobody's stepped forward, so nada."

Catherine turned away and looked out at the crowd that seemed to be growing. It might have been a street fair, people milling about, cars trying to get through. The houses behind the groomed lawns and shaped trees looked like cardboard props set up for the fair. She was vaguely aware of the dull ache at the back of her head. "Did your source mention which neighbor?" she said, turning back to Jason.

"Next door. People by the name of Kramer." Catherine followed his gaze to the two-story gray stucco house with big, rectangular windows and a brass door. Standing in the yard, probably along the invisible line that divided David Mathews's property from theirs, was a middle-aged couple with a rumpled, hurried look about them, as if they had thrown on the tee shirts and shorts dropped on the floor last night and combed their fingers through their hair.

A white Cadillac pulled into the curb in a space that didn't look large enough to hold a motorcycle. The driver's door flung open and Sydney Mathews, reed thin with bony shoulders poking out of a sundress, and reddish hair that fell like a veil along her face, ducked out of the car. Little cries of alarm broke from her as she threw herself through the crowd toward the yellow tape. Two police officers appeared out of nowhere. Catherine watched the woman jab at them like a boxer, as if she could knock them aside and pull away the tape. "Let me pass," she screamed. "This is my house. He's my husband."

Another uniformed officer, a woman, moved in close, took hold of Sydney's arm and urged her over to a police car. Catherine heard the officer say something about arranging a viewing later, that no one was allowed at the crime scene. Sydney was sobbing, shoulders shaking as the officer helped her into the rear seat.

"Interesting the Mrs. didn't happen to be home last night," Jason said.

Catherine told him the rumor she'd heard that David and Sydney Mathews had separated two weeks ago. Why they had separated, what was going on, what it meant for the future were questions that had been met by blank, controlled stares from Mathews's campaign staff, along with assurances that whatever nasty rumors she may have heard were lies spread by the opposition. Funny thing, Mathews had no opposition. There had been no challenger in the primary, and Monty Bond, the sacrificial victim nominated by the Democrats, had all but conceded the election. A recent *Journal* poll showed that the majority of Colorado voters couldn't even remember his name. Yet Mathews's campaign insisted on keeping a lid on the separation rumors. Nothing was allowed to slow the victory express.

On two occasions, the campaign had given the press access to Mrs. David Mathews. But not alone. Mathews himself had hovered over his dutiful, supportive wife. At least that was the image Sydney Mathews had managed to convey. Three weeks ago, Catherine had requested another interview, and to her surprise, the media director had agreed. She had come to the house late in the afternoon and was shown into the living room beyond the entry. Sydney Mathews, in a subdued designer suit with a double strand of pearls and hair that looked glued into place, sat on a sofa that bisected the large room. David had stood behind her, tall and silver-haired, with a square jaw and steady gaze, and the manner of a man accustomed to commanding others and eliciting obedience. He invited Catherine to take one of the overstuffed chairs across from the sofa.

Throughout the interview—a total of ten minutes—Sydney had seemed composed, impossible to rattle, until Catherine had asked about the rumors of her husband's infidelity. The woman's face closed down, frozen into a blue-eyed, red-lipped mask, and David had cut off the interview. He ushered Catherine into the entry. "We had agreed, no personal questions," he said, but he had been rattled. She had felt the anger churning beneath his calm exterior. He had yanked open the front door, and as she walked out, Catherine had glanced back at Sydney Mathews, posed on the sofa like a mannequin, wearing the same placid expression.

The black police car maneuvered out of the tight parking space and lurched into the street, the reddish hair falling forward over the woman's hands, pressed against her face.

"Where will they take her?" Catherine said.

Jason shrugged. "Probably their Evergreen house. Doesn't look like she's in any shape to drive. Soon as they get the body in the morgue, they'll arrange for her to come in and ID him. They're gonna look at her real hard."

Catherine could hear Nick's voice running through her head. *Homicide investigations always start with those closest to the victims, then move out in concentric circles of friends, neighbors, acquaintances and finally strangers.* She tried to imagine the mannequin with the perfect hair and perfect posture rising off the sofa, pointing a gun at her husband and pulling the trigger.

"I think I'll try the neighbors," she told Jason. Then she threaded her way through the bystanders to the couple huddled on the property line, gazes fixed on the house. "Excuse me," she said. Both heads snapped around in her direction. She was struck at how much they looked alike. The same brown, flat hair, the narrowed, suspicious eyes and the chins that folded into their necks. She told them her name and said she was from the *Journal*. "Did you happen to see anything last night? Anyone outside?"

The woman looked away and pulled a hand across her eyes. "She's such a nice woman," she said.

"You mean, Mrs. Mathews?"

"What a shock," the woman said, a distant tone in her voice. "So unexpected."

The man stepped sideways, nudging the woman behind him. "We've already spoken to Detective Beckman. We have nothing to say to you people." He gave a dismissive wave toward the TV reporters and photographers, the little group of bloggers and Jason. "We don't want anything to do with this. Nobody's been arrested, so far as we know. Whoever killed David is out there someplace. Like I said, it's none of our business. I don't want our names in the newspaper, you got that?"

"I don't know your names," Catherine said. She knew the last name, and the first names would be easy enough to find. She had the address.

"That's how it's gonna remain. Detective Beckman promised we'd remain anonymous. Come on, Carol," he said, turning toward the woman. "Let's go inside."

"I can't help thinking how sad it is for her," Carol said as her husband nudged her across the lawn toward the gray stucco house.

"It's not our business," Catherine heard him say. She cupped the notepad in her hand and jotted down the address and the woman's name. Carol was obviously affected by whatever had happened next door.

Just as Catherine started back, the front door of Mathews's house opened and two officers stepped out and came down the sidewalk, waving people aside. A gurney topped by a gray bag with the lumps and edges of a body visible under the plastic bumped down the front step, across the porch and down another step. There was a man at each end, and another man ran alongside, all in gray slacks and blue jackets that flapped open. They guided the gurney to the white van that had backed into the small space vacated by the police car. Black, block letters were painted on the side: Denver City and County Coroner. Photographers shadowed the gurney, cameras clicking.

Catherine looked back at the house. Several people were moving about inside, lab techs, she thought, gathering evidence. Then, for an instant, a woman appeared in the doorway, as if she had paused on her way across the entry. She wore beige slacks and a navy blazer over a white blouse with a collar that stood up at her thin neck. Probably in her late thirties, with shoulder-length, blond hair cut irregularly about her face and a sense of intelligence and competence in the way she moved.

So that was Ryan Beckman, Catherine thought. Nick had mentioned the detective once or twice. Possibly more times than that. Nothing other than the fact that their paths had crossed on some case. He had neglected to mention how beautiful she was.

3

Kim Gregory took a long draw on the cigarette, leaned into the window and watched the wisps of clouds trailing across the sky. The glare of snow on the mountains in the distance made it seem as if the clouds had draped themselves over the peaks. Her heart thumped in her ears. This was her second cigarette, but she couldn't shake the tenseness, the sense that she was coiled around herself like a spring. She should run away. Get in the BMW and drive until she was . . . where? Where could she go that the police wouldn't find her? David Mathews wasn't just some poor slob shot to death in the middle of the night by an intruder. He was a local celebrity. His handsome, smiling face stared out of newspaper photos and TV screens, his silver hair reflected the light. He was going to be the next governor. The police would drag in everybody he knew.

They would question her. She flinched at the rough laugh that erupted from her throat. They would already have the answers. Telephone records, statements of busybodies who had spotted her BMW in the neighborhood. They would ask when she had last gone to David's house, and would wait for her to lie and concoct a story, knowing she had been there Saturday night and that David had asked her to come around midnight last night. She could feel the panic rising inside her; her thoughts were zigzagging off course. She had to stay focused. How could the police possibly know about last night? She and David hadn't spoken since Saturday when they had made plans. But the police could guess. They would hammer her. *Isn't it true, you often went to Mathews's house in the middle of the night? Isn't it true you were there last night?*

Her heart was leaping so hard against her ribs she feared it would turn over. She had seen David's killer, that was the thing. A woman. How many women had he invited over last night? What was she, just another knot on a long rope of conquests? Hurrying away one lover before the next arrived? The woman under the light on David's porch had blond hair, tapering about her face, trailing onto the shoulders of her dark jacket. She was beautiful, with high, prominent cheekbones, fine features and eyes that had narrowed in her direction. A quizzical look had come into her expression, as if she couldn't believe someone was actually out there, looking at her. Then the woman had swung around, darted along the front of the house, and disappeared past the corner.

Kim had also swung about. She had run for the BMW parked down the block. *For godssakes, don't park in front of the house.* David's voice kept injecting itself into her thoughts, as if he were on the other side of the living room, issuing orders. He was always in control, managing all of his lives, she thought. She wondered which life she had fit into, or if she had really been part of any.

She took a last, long draw on the cigarette that was now no more than a butt, the heat licking at her fingertips, then squashed what was left into the saucer on the windowsill and studied the little flume of gray smoke that laced her fingers. She had been hurrying toward the house when she heard the gunshots. Three loud pops, like an engine backfiring, but different, more hollow and definite. She had heard gunshots before, last year on South Beach in Florida. She had seen the colored lights twirling over the bodies sprawled on the dance floor, the crowd shouting and pushing through the doors, and somehow she had managed to push with them and gotten outside. She remembered running down the street and weaving through the parking lot, frantic to find her car, finally getting behind the wheel and driving and not stopping until she was so far away no one would remember she had ever been there.

Last night, she had done the same, when she should have gone to him, gotten inside somehow, called 911. Maybe she could have helped him. David might be alive, and this thought was like a balloon expanding inside her head, a balloon filled with tears. When it exploded, and it would explode, she would never be able to stop crying. She pressed the tips of her fingers against her eyes. She must not give in. She had to think straight, fix in her mind everything she had done.

She had driven to her apartment, parked in the lot, and run—shoulders hunched around herself—through the lobby and up the stairs, which might have been a mistake. A neighbor could have seen her in the lot, heard her on the stairs, and checked the clock. Almost one o'clock. Enough time for her to have left David Mathews's house and driven home. She had spent the rest of the night huddled on the sofa, smoking, barely aware of the stuffiness and warmth of the apartment. She had felt colder and colder, as if her muscles and tendons and the blood in the blue veins that popped from her hands were turning into ice. At some point, she realized it was morning. Light glowed in the windows and ran like water around the living room. She had pushed herself to her feet, brewed a pot of coffee, and turned on the TV. Banners ran along the bottom of the screen. "Shooting at home of gubernatorial candidate, David Mathews. Male body found. No ID yet." She had turned it off.

Now she went over, flipped the TV back on and took up her perch on the sofa, cradling a mug of coffee in her hands. The heat warmed her palms. A woman announcer spoke over the scenes flashing across the screen, like scenes from a disjointed movie. ". . . positively identified the gunshot victim as David Mathews, the Republican candidate for governor. His body was found by his housekeeper at five o'clock this morning. Police estimate that Mathews was shot sometime around midnight."

A picture of the house appeared on the screen. The house and lawn and sidewalk marked off by yellow police tape, people milling about beyond the tape, cameras flashing. Then the front door opened, and two men in dark jackets wheeled a gurney down the sidewalk. "At this point, police say they have no suspects," the woman announcer said. A man's voice cut in: "We should point out the investigation has just gotten under way." The woman again: "Absolutely. We understand the victim's wife, Sydney Mathews, a prominent Denver socialite, was denied access to the house."

"Well, police always want to protect the scene, you know," the man said. "Only officials allowed inside. Police, medical examiner, lab technicians, people like that."

"The body was removed to the Denver morgue," the woman went on. "A viewing was held there, and Mrs. Mathews positively identified her husband." The woman was shaking her head. "David Mathews was a well-known figure, and his death is a significant loss to the community. The police will be under a lot of pressure to solve his murder."

The camera had focused on the opened door to the house, and for just a moment, a woman with blond hair appeared in the doorway. Kim gripped the mug that jumped in her hands. Hot coffee spilled onto her blue jeans and bit into her thighs. She got up and went to the TV. God! She had seen the woman before! Last night, coming out of David's house, standing under the porch light, running away. In an instant, the blonde was gone, melted into the shadows inside, and the camera had moved to the gurney being loaded into a white van with black letters, Denver City and County Coroner, across the side.

Kim stayed in front of the TV, waiting for another glimpse of the blond woman. David's killer in the house! It made no sense. No one had been allowed inside except for the police and people working with them. Unless the woman was someone the police wanted to talk to. But that didn't make sense either. Why would they interview her at the house? They would have taken her to police headquarters.

Which meant David's killer had a right to be at the house. She had to be some kind of official. Maybe a policewoman, a detective wearing civilian clothes.

Oh, this was good, almost funny in fact. The woman who killed David could be a detective. She could even be in charge of the investigation. Kim tried to swallow back the laughter that burned her throat like acid. If she were to start laughing, she wouldn't stop. Laughing, crying, screaming, she would lose herself in the hysteria she could sense crouching close, like a fanged monster ready to pounce and drag her under.

She refilled the mug, lit another cigarette and went back to the window. Morning traffic crawled along the street below, and the sun shone in the windows across the street. The sound of a horn came from a long distance. This was a new complication to consider, something she hadn't foreseen. If what she suspected was true, no one would believe her. She could go to the police, tell them that the woman she saw outside David's house last night was the same blond-haired woman, the same cheekbones and jawline, the same narrowed eyes, as the woman on TV, standing in the doorway, dressed in a dark blazer and tan slacks. A killer and, most likely, a detective. One and the same. By admitting she had seen the killer, she would be admitting that she was there last night, outside David's house. The police would look into her relationship with David, the on-again, off-again one-night stands that had gone on for six months, her stint as an escort in Denver, even though she had given that up shortly after she met David. It would never do, if their relationship became the subject of gossip, for anyone to think David Mathews had to resort to an escort service, even one with the assurances of quality and confidentiality as Morningtide, LLC. She would become the suspect—the former escort, the party girl from South Beach, the throwaway woman. They would never believe her.

But she had to tell someone. Someone had to know. She glanced over at the TV again, the sound so low she could barely make out the banter between the announcers. Again the gurney moved down the sidewalk in what seemed like an endless, revolving loop, and the blond-haired woman appeared in the doorway. For a moment, Kim thought about calling the TV reporters and telling them what she saw. An anonymous call with no hint of who she might be. She dismissed the idea. Why would they believe her?

She went into the bedroom, opened her laptop and typed in "David Mathews." A series of sites materialized, most linking to articles in the *Journal*. She clicked on the first. David's picture came up, standing on the top step at the capitol, all smiles and nods and victory fists thrown in the air, announcing his candidacy. The byline read: "Catherine McLeod, investigative reporter."

She had to think. Catherine McLeod had covered the campaign. She probably knew more about David than anyone else. But she couldn't call the newspaper from the apartment. She couldn't leave any traces. She glanced at her watch: almost ten thirty. Walmart was four blocks away. She found her bag, hurried across the room and stopped at the door. She had to compose herself. Nothing about her could seem unusual. There could be nothing that the clerks who helped her select a disposable cell phone or checked her out at the register might remember. Just another woman making a purchase.

4

The new offices of the *Denver Journal* occupied three floors in a sleek concrete building that rose against the skyscrapers of downtown Denver and overlooked Civic Center Park. A short walk from the capitol, library, art museum, history museum, dozens of restaurants and the shuttle that ran up and down Sixteenth Street. Catherine wheeled off a side street and onto the ramp that dropped like an amusement park ride into a fantastic underworld of dim, surrealistic light suffusing rows of parked cars. She slid into her slot. The sound of her door slamming bounced off the concrete walls. Musty chemical smells that accumulated with the dozens of vehicles that crawled up and down the ramp every day filled the garage. She hurried toward the swoosh and crank of the elevator in the far wall, conscious of her heels clicking on the concrete.

The elevator opened into the first floor lobby of gleaming tile floors and white walls that stretched toward a wall of windows. The morning crowd hurried past on the street outside. She jammed her badge into the slot next to the elevators across the lobby. The newspaper's business and legal offices spread over two upper floors, but the heart of the paper—the newsroom—was on the fifth floor beyond the small lobby where the stone-faced receptionist with tightly pulled back hair sat behind a desk and defied anyone to pass without permission. Six months ago, the paper had decamped across downtown from the old brick building it had occupied for fifty years. The shrinking financial statements, loss of classifieds and other ads, consolidation of departments and layoffs had all contributed to the move. Ironic, she thought, that as the paper got smaller, it had moved into a building appropriate for an expanding enterprise.

"Is it true? David Mathews murdered?" The receptionist wheeled her chair sideways and knocked a pen against the edge of the desk, like a conductor tapping the rostrum to bring the orchestra to attention.

"Looks like it," Catherine said, trying for a smile that said, "Sorry, no time to chat." She darted past the desk, inserted her badge into the security slot and hurried through the opening door into the newsroom. A wide corridor ran around the rows of glass-enclosed cubicles where reporters jammed phones into their necks and hunched over computer screens that glowed and jumped with black text. The sounds of ticking computer keys and subdued conversations buzzed like an electrical current. She knocked on the glass door with the sign that read Marjorie Fennerman, Managing Editor, before stepping into an office twice the size of the cubicles. Marjorie sat behind the desk, head tipped toward a phone with the speaker turned on. "Damn TV and bloggers." A man's voice, crackling and distant, erupted into the office. "They're ahead of us on this story, Marjorie. I don't like it. They're reporting that Mathews's wife identified his body. What the hell are your people doing?"

Behind Marjorie, pictures flashed across a small, muted TV, and Catherine caught a glimpse of the scene she had just left: David Mathews's house, the crowd of reporters and gawkers standing around, the gurney with the lumpy gray bag bumping out the door and down the sidewalk. Then Detective Ryan Beckman in the doorway.

"We're on it, B.J.," Marjorie said, and Catherine brought her attention back to the large woman with white, fleshy arms below the short sleeves of her red blouse, a mass of brown curls that radiated from her head and thick brown eyebrows that merged when she frowned. She had a desperate look about her, as if she might spring across the desk and pummel the phone. Bernard James Marshall had been the *Journal* publisher for a quarter of a century. With a scratch of a pen, he had let a dozen beat reporters, assistants and trainees go. He had closed departments, consolidated others. He could close down the newspaper. The atmosphere was always awkward and tense whenever B.J. inserted himself into the daily routine, as if he might be on the brink of stopping everything. "As soon as we have confirmation," Marjorie said, "we'll post the story on the website and in the blogs. I don't want to run prematurely with this, then find out the TV reporters got it wrong and some other guy was shot in Mathews's house. We have a reputation for checking facts and running accurate stories. We're not a bunch of self-appointed bloggers."

"Just get the damn story!"

"As I said, we're—" Marjorie stopped. The disconnect signal droned from the speaker. She pushed the off button and swiveled herself square to the desk. "You have the confirmation, I hope," she said.

Catherine told her that Jason had gone to police headquarters for a press briefing taking place in thirty minutes, and watched Marjorie study her wrist watch as if she could hurry the hands around. "From the way Sydney Mathews reacted at the house, I'm pretty sure she was convinced the dead man was her husband. The bloggers are going with that."

Marjorie continued to study the watch. "How the hell did the TV reporters know about the wife identifying the body? They've got to have somebody inside the coroner's office. It's going to be at least thirty or forty minutes before Jason can post the confirmation." She looked up. "I want a piece on your side, shock at campaign headquarters, reaction from party officials, that kind of thing. Scene at the house, anything else to flesh out the story." She gave a little wave of dismissal.

Catherine went back into the newsroom, ignoring the heads that swung toward her, the eyes that lasered into her, and the cacophony of questions that followed her down the corridor. "So what's the story?" "Mathews murdered?" "What happened?" She stopped outside her cubicle and looked back at what was a comical scene, really: reporters perched on the edge of chairs they had wheeled into the corridor, watching her with the look of a hungry pack of dogs. "It looks like Mathews was killed," she said, "but we're still waiting for the official ID." That seemed to satisfy them, because they began rolling back into the cubicles.

She took her own chair, turned on the computer and pulled her cell from her bag before stashing the bag in the bottom drawer. There was a new text from Nick that gave her a little jolt of pleasure and, for an instant, pushed away the somber reality that the man destined to be the next governor had been shot to death. "Afternoon flight. Dinner 2 nite? Gaetano's. 7:00 p.m."

She texted back one word: "Great." She would have something to look forward to all day, something relaxing and exciting at the same time, which was how her relationship with Nick had been from the beginning: solid, yet shifting and surprising, as if they were still taking each other's measure, not quite sure, but wanting to be, she thought. At least it was true on her part. She set the phone on the far side of the desk, out of sight. Gaetano's, 7 p.m. She didn't want any other texts that might mean a cancellation, a change in plans, the end of something that was just beginning.

She brought up the file with the articles on David Mathews that she had written over the last six months and began glancing through them, starting with the announcement of his candidacy last January. A bitter cold day on the steps of the state capitol—the people's house, where candidates traditionally made their announcements—snow piled on the ground and crusting the branches of the trees in Civic Center, and the freezing wind whipping her coat about her legs and working its way into her bones. She had waited with the TV and radio reporters, the bloggers, campaign volunteers, supporters and a few homeless men who had wandered over. Finally David Mathews had emerged through the double bronze doors and lifted both arms in a victory pose, as if he had already won the governorship. The crowd had gone wild.

"Thank you, everyone!" The man's voice had burst through the brisk air. "It's great to see all of you." He paused, as if to give the sincerity time to find its mark in the hopeful, upturned faces. "What do we want?" he shouted. A forest of red signs with white lettering grew from knots of supporters clustered in the front. The chanting began, encouraged by the sign holders who waved the signs overhead and pumped fists in the air. "Take back our state! Take back our state!"

Mathews had let the chant subside to a low, intermittent roar before he said, "The great state of Colorado has been in the hands of special interests long enough. Unions, federal regulators, oil and gas companies. I say enough! We must take it back. That's what I intend to do as the next governor of Colorado."

The crowd had shouted and screamed, Catherine remembered, a single, enormous animal crouching around her, energy focused on the handsome, silver-haired man standing on the top step, framed by the granite and bronze of the people's house. "Together!" he shouted. "Together! We will reclaim our heritage. We are Westerners. We are independent. We are self-sufficient. We will take care of our own business."

The animal roared and rocked to the words. "I'm a businessman," he went on. "I know how successful businesses work. I promise you that this state will be run like an efficient business. We will welcome new businesses in Colorado. Come to Colorado, we'll say. We understand what businesses need to profit and benefit the community. Count on me to provide the services and education our people need and expect. Can I count on you?"

The animal burst into cheers, then coalesced into another chant. "Count on us! Count on us!"

Catherine remembered writing furiously in her notepad, recording everything, even her own impressions. The event had been as organized and choreographed as a Broadway show at the Buell Theater a mile away. Plants in the crowd—all those signs and cheerleaders hadn't just shown up. David Mathews intended to go all the way to the governor's office upstairs from where he stood, waving his arms, smiling, glowing with the anticipation of success.

The story was half written in her head by the time Catherine had walked back to the Journal and settled in front of her computer. She filled in the background material she had gathered before the announcement. It was those background notes that she reviewed now: "Mathews is the president and CEO of Mathews Properties, formerly Mathews and Kane Properties, one of Denver's largest development firms. Founded in 2000, the firm has developed large properties throughout the Denver Metro area, including Landmark Homes, the Silverstone Condominiums, and the Orangewood shopping malls in Lakewood, Glendale and Leaning Tree. Last year, Broderick Kane had accused Mathews of fraud and demanded an investigation. The police turned the matter over to the district attorney's office, but Kane withdrew his complaint. The matter was settled amicably with Mathews purchasing his partner's interests and becoming the sole owner of the company. Sources close to the transaction said that Mathews paid close to five million dollars."

The notes had touched on other aspects of the man's life. How Mathews had moved to Denver in the late nineties from Chicago, leaving behind a decade-long career in real estate. "When you're a skier, you want to be close to the mountains," he said. "I can do business anywhere." How Mathews and his wife, Sydney, were active in social events and known for their philanthropic support of the arts in Denver.

Catherine read down the columns of text in the next articles. There had been no challenges to Mathews's candidacy from the party. At the convention in the spring, he had walked away with the nomination amid the party's glee at having found the perfect, silver-haired candidate, handsome, successful, admirable, with excellent name recognition. A few weeks later, he had chosen his running mate for lieutenant governor, a political hack the Republican party owed a favor to named Easton Sherer. David Mathews could have run with a salamander, and nobody would have cared. Even though Mathews was the only candidate, state law required a primary election. Mathews had set a record for the largest number of votes in a primary.

A message appeared on the screen: a new posting on the *Journal*'s website. Catherine clicked on the site. At the top was the byline of Jason Metcalf. "David Mathews, Republican candidate for governor, was found shot to death early this morning in his home in the Cherry Creek area. According to a Denver police spokesperson, Mathews sustained two gunshot wounds in the chest and one in the thigh. The chest wounds were fatal. His body was found at 5:00 a.m. on his living room floor by his housekeeper. Police are asking anyone who may have seen anything unusual in the vicinity last night to come forward."

Catherine opened a new window and began typing out her part of the story, recapitulating some of the background details, pasting other details from previous articles. Then she picked up the phone and called Mathews's campaign headquarters. The buzzing sound of a phone ringing on the ground floor of one of Mathews's buildings on Colorado Boulevard went on and on. No answer, not even voice mail. She called party headquarters. "Colorado Republican Party." A man had picked up after the first ring.

"Catherine McLeod of the *Journal*," she said.

"We have no comment, except that the death of an outstanding and talented man like Dave Mathews is a terrible calamity for the people of this state."

"And you are . . ."

"A spokesperson at party headquarters."

"What comes next?"

"How could we have any plans at this point?" There would be a statement later, he said, and hung up.

Catherine added the comments and sent the article to Marjorie. Nothing new, nothing substantial, but it was something to run alongside Jason's post.

She pulled her bag out of the drawer and got to her feet just as the phone rang. It would start now, she thought. All the people shocked and upset by the news, the sign wavers on the capitol steps last January, the volunteers who filled the campaign headquarters every time she had gone there, would start calling, wanting to talk about David Mathews's murder, hoping to tease out something behind the news that a reporter might know. She lifted the receiver. "Catherine McLeod," she said.

The line was quiet. For an instant, she thought no one was on the other end. Finally a woman's voice, little more than a whisper, floated toward her. Catherine had to press the phone tight against her ear and plug a finger into her other ear to block out the background noise.

"I know the killer."

"Who is this," Catherine said.

"It doesn't matter. I was there."

"Are we talking about David Mathews?"

There was no answer.

"You were at his house when he was killed?"

"I'm telling you I saw the killer."

"Have you gone to the police?" My God, a witness. Someone else had been at the house besides Mathews and the killer.

The voice on the other end dissolved into a shaky laughter that shifted toward hysteria, then went quiet. "They'll never believe me. Why do you think I'm calling a reporter? You've been writing about David. I figured I could trust you. Maybe I figured wrong."

"Wait a minute," Catherine said, hearing the urgency in her own voice, the fear that the woman would end the call. "Tell me what you saw."

"The killer coming out of David's house, right after I heard the gunshots." A tenseness, rippled with fear, in the woman's voice. "Standing there on the porch, under the light. I got a clear view of her face."

"Her? You believe the killer is a woman?" Sydney Mathews, Catherine was thinking. Whoever was on the line had seen Sydney Mathews come out of the house. "Why can't you go to the police?"

The laughter bubbled again, followed by the sound of breathing and the nearly imperceptible sound of fear, as if the woman had clamped a fist to her mouth and was trying to catch her breath around the edges. "They'll never believe me. They'll say I'm lying. They'll want to know what I was doing there. They'll suspect that I killed David. They'll arrest me . . ."

"They won't believe you? I don't understand," Catherine said again, but she was beginning to understand. Sydney Mathews was well-known in the community; she would have powerful friends.

"They'll never take my word against hers. She's one of them, don't you get it? She's a cop."

Catherine took a moment, struggling to make a space for this new idea to emerge around the scenario she had already mapped out. "You're telling me that you saw a policewoman coming out of Mathews's house?"

"She's the blonde I saw on TV when they were bringing out his body. She was in the doorway. She wasn't in any uniform. I figure she's one of the detectives."

Catherine realized she must have sat down, because the edge of the chair cut into her thighs. The rustle of activity, the clicking keys and the ringing phones, the bobbing heads in the cubicles faded into a background that blurred around the image of Detective Ryan Beckman, the blond woman she had seen in the doorway. The police would never believe it. An anonymous caller claiming to have seen a homicide detective at the scene of a murder! And yet, something in the caller's voice, something that ranged between terror and insistence, had the sound of truth. "Who are you?" she said. "I can't do anything unless I know your name."

"No names. I told you what I saw. You take it from here."

"Listen," Catherine began, but the line had gone dead. A hollow space had opened between her and whoever had been on the other end.

5

"She refuses to give her name? What does that tell us?" Marjorie sat sideways at the desk, eyes on the computer screen to her right. She continued typing as Catherine perched on a side chair. An anonymous caller in the newspaper business was about as valuable as a paper clip on the street. Nobody would stoop to pick it up. No-name calls came with every big story, breathless voices claiming they were part of the heist, witnessed the robbery, helped plan the murder, slept with the killer. It was the investigative reporter's job to sort through the fantastic claims, the inherent contradictions and decide whether the story deserved follow-up. Most did not, but by the time a reporter worked that out, fifteen or twenty minutes had been stolen from the real story and the actual leads.

"I called Jason. He's still at police headquarters," Catherine said. "He confirmed that Ryan Beckman is the lead detective on the case. She's been with the department three years. Before that, she spent eleven years with the Minneapolis PD. She's a good detective. Everybody on the force seems to like her okay. It probably helps that she's beautiful." She shrugged. "The caller could hardly go to the police and ID somebody like that." And yet, the voice on the line had been different from the usual anonymous calls. There had been the fear, tenacity and certainty ringing with truth. As implausible as the story might seem, Catherine could feel the truth of it in the pit of her stomach, like a physical object, sharp and real. *Listen to your life.* She could almost hear Dulcie Oldman's voice in her head. *Listen to your own sense of what is true and real.* So much of her Arapaho heritage to learn, Catherine thought. A whole different way of looking at the world.

She said, "The police would dismiss the caller as a crank."

"What makes you think she isn't?" Marjorie stabbed a key hard, swung around and locked eyes with Catherine.

"I heard the truth in her voice." It was all Catherine could do to keep from jumping up, circling the office and pounding the desk. "She called me because she has nowhere else to go. Look, Marjorie. If she saw Detective Beckman at Mathews's house, it's possible the detective also saw her. She's scared. She knows her life could be in danger. We're her only hope."

Marjorie had a face like granite. Hardly the flicker of a shadow in her expression. Beneath the thick eyebrows her eyes were deep and motionless, perfect camouflage to whatever thoughts moved inside her head. It was a long moment before she stretched out an arm, picked up the phone and said, "Tell Jason I want to see him the minute he gets in."

She turned back to Catherine and drummed her fingers on the edge of the desk. "The story sounds preposterous. There could be a dozen reasons someone wants to implicate a police detective. How about this scenario? Detective Beckman arrested the caller for prostitution, the caller saw the detective on TV and decided it was payback time. Here's another: The caller is a police officer, pounding the sidewalks, and along comes a beautiful woman from another city who gets promoted without paying her dues in Denver and rockets into the homicide squad. Maybe the caller wants to take her down. Or let's say, two women, both in love with David Mathews—quite an attractive guy from his pictures—and one decides to take revenge on her rival."

Catherine was on her feet, patrolling the carpet, new possibilities jumping in her mind. "You're saying that Detective Beckman and Mathews might have been having an affair?" She stopped moving, as if her feet had stumbled into wet concrete. "My God," she said. "Sydney Mathews could be the caller!" That possibility led back, like a rope uncurling itself, to Catherine's initial suspicion that Sydney Mathews might be involved in her husband's murder. But the voice on the phone was unfamiliar, and Catherine had interviewed Sydney, spoken personally with her. Still, Sydney could have disguised her voice.

"Suppose Mathews's wife killed him and is trying to throw suspicion onto Detective Beckman," she said.

"Suspicion on Detective Beckman?" Jason must have walked through the door behind her, but she hadn't heard him. She spun as he nudged the door shut with his boot. Then he plopped down on the side chair beneath the wall of plaques with his name in black, bold type and framed newspaper photos of his grinning face. "What're you talking about? What's up?"

"Tell us about Detective Beckman," Marjorie said.

"Like what? Is she a murderer?" He let out a loud guffaw. "Come on."

Catherine dropped onto her own chair. "I got a call from a woman who said she saw Detective Beckman on Mathews's porch right after he was shot."

"Let me guess. A caller who refused to give her name." Jason gave a massive shrug that sent his shoulder muscles rippling through the fabric of his blue shirt. "You know how many so-called witnesses contact the police department every day? Too many, I can tell you. A case like Mathews, they've probably already collected a dozen useless tips. Your caller probably called them, and they dismissed her as a crackpot, so she called here. Hopes to send us chasing our tails over some crazy fantasy."

"What kind of detective is she?" Marjorie said.

"Moot question, from what I hear. Beckman had taken a few days off and was in Breckenridge when Mathews was shot. She got called in to handle the investigation . . ." Catherine started to interrupt, and he lifted one hand. "Okay. Okay. Breckenridge is only a couple hours away. From what I hear, she's got a pretty good clearance rate, okay reputation. Professional, far as I know. Plus, she's a babe, in case you didn't notice." There was something lazy and settled in the way he gazed around the office out of half-closed eyes. "Isn't an officer at headquarters who wouldn't like to get to know her better, you know what I mean. But she keeps to herself. Doesn't mix business and pleasure, looking out for her career. The guys respect that."

"Was she having an affair with Mathews?"

"Mathews?" Jason's mouth hung open a moment. "You tell me," he said, stabbing a finger at Catherine.

"I don't know," Catherine said. This was the big gap she had never been able to close in David Mathews's life. The rumors that trickled around him like water, then dried up and disappeared the moment she tried to track them. Mathews, a ladies' man, and yet, until recently, Sydney Mathews had stayed by his side. Campaign stops, formal dinners, speeches, shaking hands and munching on hamburgers in a dozen rural communities, and Sydney right beside him, smiling, patting him on the back. She had stood on the top step of the capitol last January, flakes of snow blowing around her, a smile frozen on her face. But it wasn't Sydney who had found her husband's body; she hadn't been home last night. It was possible she had spent the night at their home in Evergreen, the hideout, Mathews had called it in an interview a few weeks ago. "When I need to get away from the madness, I go there," he'd said. Catherine could still see the fleeting, wistful look in his expression. "Recharge my batteries, you know what I mean?" She had nodded, and scratched the words in her notepad: even candidates need to get away.

"I assume Detective Beckman has a private life," Jason said, getting to his feet. "That's how she keeps it: private."

"What if we were to tell the police about the call?" Marjorie had a way of probing that was nothing more than looking for confirmation on decisions she had already made.

"It would go to Internal Affairs. They'd look at it, because they have to, and determine if there was any plausibility."

"How hard would they look?" Catherine said.

"Like I told you." Jason patted a few strands of hair over the bald place on top of his head. "Detective Beckman has a clean record. They'd look at the anonymous complaint, talk to her for two minutes, lose the complaint in a filing cabinet."

"We can't go to the police." Catherine glanced over at Marjorie who sat immobile, hands tipied under her chin. Finally she gave a little nod and Catherine turned back to Jason, wanting to make sure the police reporter who liked to shoot the bull with his off duty officer pals understood the risks: "If there's the slightest possibility the caller has told the truth," she said, "we can't alert Detective Beckman. Look at it from her point of view. If she is guilty, she could have seen the witness outside the house. If she learns that she has been ID'd, she'll use every resource she can muster to find the witness. If Detective Beckman has killed once, she'll kill again."

Catherine sank back onto the chair. "The caller figured that out," she said, looking past Jason to Marjorie, still leaning onto her tipied hands. The caller's words rang in her mind. *I know the killer.* "I heard the terror in her voice" she said. "Raw, naked terror."

Jason puffed out his cheeks and blew a stream of air. "What does she expect from us? We're not in charge of the investigation. We're not the police."

"She expects us to run down the truth," Catherine said.

"Right! Without any help from her. Leave me out of this," Jason said, lifting his voice an octave. "Go after the bad detective killer, if that's the way you want to waste your time."

Catherine dug her fingernails into her palms. She stayed quiet a couple of seconds before she trusted herself to say, "It's not a scam, Jason. You would know if you had heard her voice."

"Any other thoughts?" Marjorie said, focusing her gaze on the police reporter.

"I'd say let it go. If she's as scared as Catherine says, she'll probably call back. Try to get her name. Then we can go to the police. Let them sort it out. It's their investigation, and I sure don't want any part of withholding information or impeding an investigation. No name, forget it. We're up the old creek without the old paddle."

"So," Marjorie said, drawing out the long, soft sound. "We wait and hope she calls back."

"We could wait until she's dead," Catherine said. "She's assuming we'll investigate her story. We would be waiting each other out. In the meantime, Detective Beckman could be looking for the witness. And if she finds her . . ."

"Okay. Okay." Marjorie threw both hands into the air, as if someone had just pulled a gun. "How do you imagine you can find this anonymous caller?"

"She could be a neighbor," Catherine said. "Out walking her dog." The caller hadn't mentioned a dog, she was thinking. "She could have been on her way to Mathews's house. Maybe she's a campaign worker, a friend."

"A friend!" Jason let out a little snicker.

"I have to find out if she just happened to be outside or if she was on her way to visit David Mathews."

"Okay," Marjorie said. "Take some time and see what you can run down. A couple of days, no more. Gubernatorial candidate murdered! It's the biggest story of the year. There will be a lot of sidebars and fillers. Who's going to take his place? How will the party regroup? What happens to the campaign and all those volunteers who expected a nice, cushy state job after their man got elected? You have enough to follow up on without getting sidetracked on what could be somebody's sick idea of a joke."

"We done here?" Jason was at the door, gripping the knob.

"Nothing we've said leaves this room," Marjorie said.

"Yeah. Yeah." Jason flung the door back and stepped into the newsroom. "I got it," he called over one shoulder.

"One more thing," Catherine said.

Marjorie emitted a nearly inaudible groan. She had already swung back to the computer, both hands poised over the keyboard. She gave Catherine a sideways glance. "I'm not sure I want to know."

"I have to find out if there was anything between Detective Beckman and Mathews. Any reason for her to be at his house at midnight. If I can tie them together, it would give more credence to the caller's story, even if I'm unable to find her."

"Find her," Marjorie said.

6

"No one saw anything." Sergeant Earl Crowley, egg-shaped gourmand and all around pain in the butt, crossed his arms over his chest and shot Ryan a look of incredulity and annoyance. From his perch on the edge of the desk, Martin tossed her a quick here-we-go-again look. The sergeant blocked the entrance to the cubicle that served as her office. Past his broad shoulders and thick head, she could see other detectives sauntering in and out of other cubicles. A low undertow of voices sucked at the air. At the far end of the detectives' area, the blurred mid-morning sun filtered through a bank of tinted windows. Thirteenth Street ran below, and every once in a while, howling sirens and squealing brakes broke through the thick, concrete-block walls. "Three gunshots at midnight in a neighborhood where even the Jaguars don't backfire, and nobody went to a window or opened a door and looked outside to see what in blazes was going on?"

"That's what the neighbors are saying." Martin pushed himself off the edge of the desk and moved behind Ryan. Always looking out for her, covering her back, she thought. As far as partners went, Martin Martinez, strung as taut as piano wire with roped veins in a thin neck that rose out of the collar of his white shirt, was every detective's dream. "First thing the neighbors knew anything was wrong was when Mathews's housekeeper, woman named Edith Burrows, started pounding on their door at 5:00 a.m. They called 911."

"Names?"

"Lee and Carol Kramer," Ryan said. "They don't want to be involved." She felt nervous and unsteady. It was an effort to keep her voice from cracking. She had investigated dozens of homicides, peered at mangled and bloody bodies, seen with her own eyes what people did to one another. She had never expected to see David's body, to see what *she* had done. The morning had been surreal, moving through the house, investigating the crime scene, staying out of the way of the lab techs, all on automatic. Her official self in charge, but that other self, the one that had pulled the trigger, kept threatening to erupt, take over, push away the thin veneer of control and competence. She had never meant to pull the trigger, but the other self had come out of nowhere. Then the loud concussion of gunshots, and David falling, falling. She blinked hard, trying to banish the image.

She realized Crowley was watching her. "You okay?" he said.

"I was looking forward to a few days off, Sergeant. You woke me up and ordered me back to work. Why would I be okay?" Ryan gave a shrug that she hoped would pass for normal. "Kramer's the CEO of Maxwell Energy. His wife's on two or three nonprofit boards."

Crowley shook his head, as if he had seen and heard everything, and this new information only confirmed that fact. "Social types that don't want to sully their reputations with any connection to a murder. I'm surprised they bothered to pick up the phone." He dipped his head, still focusing on Ryan through half-mast eyes. "Tell me you have something more than what we handed that pack of media hounds. Gubernatorial candidate shot to death in his home! That's it? That's all we have? The murder's all over the national news. We'll have TV talking heads from New York and Washington descending by this afternoon. They'll come looking for raw meat, and we better throw them some. I don't want this department looking like a bunch of hick amateurs stumbling over our shadows."

"It wasn't a burglary," Ryan said, still trying to corral the thoughts that bucked and raced around her head. In all the careful planning, the request for three vacation days that she'd put in last week, the untraceable Sig she had managed to slip out of the evidence room—it was still in her bag inside the lower desk drawer—she had never imagined she would be placed in charge of any investigation. She had never thought there would be an investigation, and there wouldn't have been, if David had only listened. Still she had taken every step to protect herself, in case anything went wrong, she guessed. Set up the perfect alibi; registered at a condominium complex in Breckenridge. Then she had driven back to Denver and gone to David's house at midnight when no one would be around. She knew the neighborhood. Shut down by ten o'clock, as if there were a curfew on fancy houses and expensive cars.

And yet, someone else had been there. The dark figure of a woman standing on the sidewalk. The woman had seen her, and this fact, Ryan realized, had unnerved her, set her off balance.

"We figure Mathews opened the door and let in his killer," Martin said. "It was someone he knew."

The sergeant gave a loud guffaw. "That only leaves about five thousand people, give or take a few."

"Shot at close range. Two fatal shots to the chest, one in his thigh."

"Could be a professional." Crowley looked up out of the corners of his eyes, as if he were remembering some previous case. "Someone could have arranged for a hit man to get close to Matthews and show up at his house."

This was too close, Ryan thought. The muscles tightened in her chest; God, she could be having a heart attack. She was a skilled shooter; first in her police academy class. "It wasn't an assassination," she said.

Martin nodded, backing her up again. "A pro would have dropped the weapon, and it would be untraceable. He wouldn't bother to pick up the casings. From the bullets the techs dug out of the wall, we know he used a 9mm. I doubt a professional would have risked nosy neighbors hearing the gunshots and showing up at Mathews's house. Lots of better chances to get at somebody like him. Dark garages, parking lots where a hit man could move in fast and clear out. Even if people were around, nobody'd see anything."

"All right. Let's look at another possibility," Crowley said. "Three shots, two deadly, one in the thigh. An act of emotion, spur of the moment. After firing the first shots, the killer realized what happened and flinched."

"Lab techs didn't find any suspicious fingerprints or hairs," Martin said. "The killer didn't leave anything behind. Cool and unemotional, I'd say."

"Maybe not," Ryan said. Both men turned toward her. "Maybe you're on to something, Sergeant. Whoever shot Matthews could have faltered on the third shot." This was dangerous, she was thinking. She had faltered on the third shot. The image flashed again in her mind—David, stumbling backward. She turned to Martin. "How did you read the grieving widow?"

"Distraught, probably in shock."

"What are you saying?" Crowley shifted his gaze between Martin and Ryan. "You think Sydney Matthews shot her husband?"

"She wasn't at home last night." Ryan pushed on, feeling herself on firmer ground. The idea had hit her when she heard Sydney Matthews screaming out in the front like a animal with a leg caught in a steel trap. She had looked out the window as the uniform led the woman to the patrol car at the curb. She had crumbled inside the backseat, still screaming, out of control and helpless, in a way. The perfect suspect. It was only a matter of making the evidence conform to the premise. "Mathews had a reputation for chasing skirts. We've got the computer from the house. It's possible he e-mailed his lovers." Martin had gone to the district judge this morning and gotten a warrant to search the house and seize anything that might shed light on the murder, including the computer. David was scrupulous about never e-mailing her, and she assumed he treated his other women the same. *Never leave a record*, he'd said. *Never leave anything behind that somebody might use against you.* Still, she intended to check the computer and make certain there was no mention of her before the techs looked at it.

She hurried on: "Maybe Mathews's wife got fed up with sharing him." Ryan could almost sympathize with the woman. She had felt the same way. "Could go to motive," she said.

"Sydney Mathews says she spent last night at the Evergreen house," Martin said, jumping on board. Ryan could see the logic catching fire in his eyes. The spouse or partner was always an initial suspect, always the person who had to be eliminated before the investigation could move forward. It would be up to her, Ryan was thinking, to make certain Sydney Mathews wasn't eliminated, and Martin would back her up.

"The question is, Why was she in Evergreen?" Ryan said. "Quarrel? Separation? Does the woman own a gun?"

"We can find out," Martin said.

Crowley took a moment before he said, "Where is she now?"

"Back in Evergreen," Martin said. "She's number one on our interview list."

Crowley nodded. "Don't get locked into a theory. Stubbornness has derailed more than one investigation. I suspect Mathews had his share of enemies. Nobody gets to run for governor without stepping on toes and ruffling feathers. What about his company? I remember his partner coming in and wanting to file a fraud complaint a year or so ago." He nodded at Ryan. "We sent him to the DA's office. But you had taken the initial complaint, if my memory's still working, and the DA's investigator kept you in the loop. Called on you a few times since you had experience with fraud cases back in Minneapolis."

"The whole matter was a misunderstanding," Ryan said. "The partner withdrew the complaint." She had met David Mathews then, tall and silver haired, smiling, blue eyes twinkling, and so handsome every head turned to follow him through a restaurant or hotel lobby. She could picture him coming across his office, hand outstretched, when she had gone with the DA's investigator to interview him. How tanned he had looked in the middle of winter, but David was always tanned, she learned later. Sailing on Lake Dillon in the summer, skiing Vail and Aspen in the winter. "Good of you to look into this matter," he had said, as if he welcomed the investigation. He shook their hands, holding on to her hand a moment too long, she had thought. The feel of his palm next to hers had sent a chill down her spine. She remembered pulling her hand free. She was a police detective, a professional, and he could be a criminal. There was no room for any personal connection. As far as anyone knew, she had maintained her professional demeanor and composure during the investigation that had barely gotten under way when David Mathews and his partner, Broderick Kane, appeared on TV together, stating that the misunderstanding had been cleared up, and the complaint withdrawn. Kane had accepted Mathews's offer to buy him out, and the name of the firm had been changed from Mathews and Kane Properties to Mathews Properties. Despite the agreement, a reporter at the *Journal,* named Catherine McLeod, had kept probing, asking questions about the quick, private settlement, but after a while, even she had moved on to other stories.

When the news had faded from the TV and newspapers, Ryan had taken a chance and called David Mathews. He had taken her call, which didn't surprise her. She had seen the way he looked at her the day she had gone to his office with the other investigator, even deferred to her, bestowing on her that little lopsided smile of his. He would love to meet her for a drink, he had told her. He suggested a quiet bar in Highland, a neighborhood place that had been around forever. No one he knew was likely to be there.

Ryan tried to concentrate on the conversation: Crowley saying they should interview Broderick Kane as well as the campaign staff, and Martin assuring him they were also on the list of interviewees. "We'll need assistance," Ryan said. "At least two officers to recanvass the neighborhood. Lean on the neighbors about what they may have seen." This was not something she could do, she was thinking. What if the woman on the sidewalk were a neighbor? She could picture Detectives Beckman and Martinez knocking on a door, asking if anybody had seen anything, and the neighbor looking hard at her and saying, "Yes, I saw you coming out of the house seconds after I heard the gunshots." She wondered if Martin would stand by her then. She clasped her hands to hold them still. It was bad enough the stupid TV cameraman had caught her this morning, she had made the mistake of showing herself in the doorway. There couldn't be any more mistakes. She had to stay strong and confident. No one would suspect the lead detective, no matter how many times the TV images played in living rooms.

"You can have all the officers you need," Crowley said. "Get this wrapped up as neat as possible."

Martin drove, pushing the Ford sedan over sixty-five miles per hour, changing lanes and passing the semis that hauled themselves up the steady grade on I-70 into the mountains. Usually Ryan drove, but she was glad to let Martin take the wheel. She was still too unsteady to drive, and exhausted. So many unexpected twists in the last twelve hours with almost nothing going the way she had planned. They had picked up coffee before getting on the highway, and Ryan sipped at the creamy, hot liquid and watched the pines and boulders crawling down the mountainsides. The sky was a perfect blue, interrupted by white clouds drifting past the sun. One moment they were in shadows as deep as night, and the next, in blinding sunshine. As they came around a curve, Ryan could see the high peaks ahead etched in snow. The air conditioner hummed over the sound of the tires. She shivered in the coolness.

Martin glanced over. "Want me to turn down the air?"

"I'm all right," she said. They were slowing down. The horn of a semi blasted behind them and other vehicles shot past. Her bag was on the floor next to her feet, and as Martin maneuvered over to the right exit lane, she could feel the weight of the gun against her ankle. He followed the ramp to a stop sign and turned right. A spiderweb of black roads glowed on the dashboard GPS screen. Martin came to a Y, turned right and followed a road that narrowed through a forest of junipers and lodgepole pines as it wound up the mountainside. The sun glistened in the tops of the trees, but deep, velvety shadows lay over the road.

"Some neighborhood." Martin tapped an index finger on the steering wheel. "Looks like Mathews didn't like company."

As they came around a long loop, the forest pulled back. Through the opening ahead, Ryan spotted the two-story house, with logs and stucco, long porches and balconies. The windows across the front reflected great balls of sunshine. Pines and boulders had been artfully placed in the wild grasses that covered the yard. Parked at random angles on the grass were four SUVs. "Looks like Sydney has company," Ryan said.

7

Through the beveled glass door that loomed over the stone-paved porch, Ryan could see the dark, blurred figures moving about on the far side of an entry large enough for a hotel. She held her bag close, conscious of the weight tugging at the leather. Martin pushed the bronze bell a second time. The chiming inside went on for a while before a slim, angular man in dark slacks and tan shirt started across the entry. His footsteps pounded out a syncopated rhythm that sent tiny vibrations onto the porch. The door swung open. "Yes? What is it?"

"Denver police." Ryan showed the badge she had dragged out of her bag. Martin was also holding up his badge. "We'd like to speak to Sydney Mathews."

"You've got to be kidding!" The man had straw-colored hair brushed away from a forehead that jutted over narrowed, gray eyes. "My sister's in mourning. Her husband has been shot to death. Have you no decency? No compassion? She spoke with police officers this morning. Anything else can wait until she's had a chance to pull herself together."

"Your name?" Martin said.

"My name, as if it has any relevance whatsoever, is Wendell Lane. I suggest you call for an appointment later in the week."

"I'm afraid the investigation of David Mathews's murder can't wait," Ryan said. "There are a few things we'd like Mrs. Mathews to clear up. I'm sure she's eager to have the killer arrested."

Wendell Lane gripped the bronze doorknob. "This is harassment, pure and simple." He stared out into the rock and vehicle strewn yard, and Ryan could almost see the options clashing in his expression. Slam the door, or let them in. Either way, they were going to interview Sydney Mathews sooner or later. Finally, the man seemed to reach the same conclusion. His shoulders sank, and he stepped back, motioning them into the entry with his head. "Five minutes," he said. "Anything you want to ask my sister after five minutes will have to wait." He threw out an arm directing them into the formal living room on the left, an expanse of gleaming antique chests and tables and thick-cushioned, taupe-colored sofas. Blue velvet draperies had been pulled to the sides of the windows allowing the sun to stream across a section of polished wood floor.

Living room for formal occasions only. David's voice was as clear as if he had materialized beside her. Ryan remembered how he had waved toward the living room, his voice echoing around the entry. He had brought her to Evergreen only that one night. Sydney had gone to New York to shop, he'd said. They would be alone. He had showed her his study on the other side of the entry, then guided her through the great room that ran across the rear of the house, the kitchen, an expanse of cherry cabinets, steel and granite, the music room and theater with raised, leather seats, the projection room with a screen against the far wall. Then up the stairs that wound above the entry and along the corridors that led to five or six bedrooms—she hadn't bothered to count. On into the master bedroom suite with its own living room, kitchen and bathroom, and closets bigger than her apartment. That night, she had felt as if it were all hers. David, and the house, and the exhilarating atmosphere of his life. Sydney didn't exist. Nothing else had existed.

Ryan realized that Sydney Mathews's brother had left her and Martin standing in the living room. There was a shuffling noise of people breaking up, hushed tones of farewells and a hiss of movement across the entry. Out of the corner of her eye, Ryan caught sight of Sydney Mathews encircled by supporters patting her shoulders, pulling her in for hugs, and Wendell Lane flinging open the door and ushering the visitors out.

"I'm going to want to look around the study," Ryan said, leaning close to Martin. "We need to know if Mathews kept a computer here."

"Where do you think the study is?"

Ryan had to stop herself from nodding in the direction of the double doors across the entry. How would Detective Ryan Beckman know where the study was located in a home she had never seen before? "We'll find out. Just keep the widow out of the way while I have a look around."

Martin nodded as Sydney Mathews walked into the living room, Wendell Lane at her side. "I suppose I should thank you," she said. "At least you cleared out the crowd just when I was on the verge of throwing them out. Why does everyone think the survivor—God, what a terrible word—needs to hear a lot of platitudes and saccharine comments from people she hardly knows and doesn't, frankly, give a damn about?" She drew in a long breath, ran her gaze around the room and across the furniture, as if she were assuring herself that everything was in place. "We might as well sit down. You could have offered them a seat," she said, glancing at her brother.

Ryan perched at the edge of a sofa and dropped her bag at her feet. The gun made a soft thump on the Oriental carpet. Something about Sydney Mathews was off-key, a sour note. This wasn't the widow who had thrown herself at the officers this morning, screaming and shouting. This woman was self-contained, rational and angry. Ryan had seen reactions like this before from the family members of murder victims. The shock and grief were set aside and, in their place, a focused intent on revenge. Sydney Mathews wanted nothing except to see her husband's killer identified and brought to justice. She was dangerous.

"What is it you want?" Sydney dropped onto the thick armrest of a side chair and focused a steady gaze across the inlaid wood coffee table. Drops of sunlight sparkled on the surface and shone in the glass vase of fresh flowers that, Ryan realized, explained the faint funereal smells suffusing the living room.

"Why weren't you at the house with your husband last night?" Ryan said.

"What kind of question is that?" Wendell Lane stood behind the chair, hovering over his sister.

"Just answer the question, Mrs. Mathews." Martin remained standing. He was thumbing through the pages of the small notebook he always kept in his jacket pocket. He would not sit down, Ryan knew. Both officers could not be at the disadvantage of being seated in any situation.

"You don't have to answer," Wendell said.

Sydney's nostrils flared; she opened and closed her mouth before she said, "This is also my home. Why wouldn't I be here?"

"We understand Mr. Mathews spent most of his time in the Denver house," Ryan said. It was true, but she hoped Martin would think she was guessing. "How would you characterize your relationship with your husband? Was it usual for you to live apart? Were you separated? Had you quarreled?"

"I find your questions outrageous," Wendell said. He placed a hand on Sydney's shoulder. "You don't have to answer anything."

"Oh, for godssakes." Sydney brushed her brother's hand away. "Who are we kidding? Everybody in Denver has heard the rumors. Did my husband chase other women? Yes. It was part of his makeup. He was handsome, rich, powerful and weak. Frankly, any number of tramps threw themselves at him. But when his little affairs ended, he always came back to me. And I forgave him because I loved him and he needed me."

"Don't say any more," Wendell said.

"Mr. Lane," Martin said. "You'll have to wait in another room."

"What?"

"We're interviewing Mrs. Mathews. You have to leave."

Wendell Lane took a long moment before he started across the room, slow, jerky movements as if he were trying to latch onto a reason to turn back. "Call me, if you need me," he said, throwing a glance at his sister before he went out into the entry.

Sydney said, "We had an understanding, David and I. He had a certain amount of freedom, shall we say, and in return, I was Mrs. David Mathews. I was the only one who could help him get what he wanted more than anything else in the world—recognition, applause, adoration. The governor presiding at the capitol, living in the governor's mansion, driving around in a chauffeured sedan. That was his dream since he was a little boy, a poor, stupid boy from most assuredly not the right Chicago neighborhood. David wanted to be somebody. I was the ticket to fulfilling his dream, and he came close, very close." Her voice cracked, and she looked away for a moment. "I was behind him all the way to the governor's mansion, the dutiful, proud, uncompromised wife. As long as none of his affairs embarrassed me publicly, I had agreed to stay with him." She gave a nervous gasp of a laugh and hurried on: "He didn't keep his promise. The rumors started running rampant. By the time a reporter asked about David's unfaithfulness, I knew he was no longer being discreet. So two weeks ago, we separated. Naturally, I hoped we could work things out, but—" Her voice cracked and vibrated. "There wasn't time."

Ryan had to grip the edge of the cushion to keep from sliding to the floor. Lies, all of it lies. Everything David had led her to believe. How he and Sydney would stay together only until the election was over. How the marriage was nothing but a sham. Then, two weeks ago, he had told her he and Sydney had reconciled. Reconciled! She wanted to throw her head back and laugh out loud. Two weeks ago, he and Sydney had separated. The reconciliation he claimed was nothing more than campaign spin, as if Ryan were the public and he was a faithful husband. All the religious conservatives who might have a hard time voting for an adulterer could, in good conscience, pull the lever for David Mathews.

Lies, lies, lies. My God, she had believed him when he said he was going back to Sydney, but that was only the excuse he had used to break things off with *her.* She felt as if her heart might stop beating. The picture was clear, as if a curtain had been pulled away from a window. She saw everything now. There was someone else in David's life. The woman on the sidewalk. Ryan swallowed hard and held on to the cushion. The room twirled in slow motion at the periphery of her vision.

Ryan tried to concentrate on what Sydney was saying. Something about the money Daddy had left her allowing David to buy a partnership in the company, the Lane family name and reputation opening the right doors. "You'll learn the truth sooner or later," Sydney said, shifting about and glancing around the room. "You might as well find out now. It's background information, wouldn't you agree? Yes," she said, answering her own question and facing Ryan again. "My husband was a flawed man. Ambitious and greedy and susceptible to flattery from any woman stupid enough to believe she could replace me. Any number of people might have wanted him dead. I want his killer drawn and quartered, do you understand? I want his killer tracked down like the animal she is."

"She?" Martin said. "You suspect a woman killed your husband?"

Ryan felt sick and disoriented. She was grateful to Martin for asking the question and giving her a moment to collect herself. Before the woman on the sidewalk could ever identify her, she had to close the case with solid evidence that could not be overlooked or swept aside. Airtight evidence any jury would find compelling without a reasonable doubt. She lifted her bag into her lap and pressed her fingers against the hard metal of the gun inside.

"I suggest you start with his whores."

"Names?"

"What makes you think I was privy to any of the sordid details?"

"Anyone who might have the information?"

"I'm sure you'll check with his campaign staff," Sydney said. Ryan could feel the woman's resolve—it was like a physical object in the room. A woman intent on having her husband's killer brought to justice. "The groupies that gave up their own lives to get David elected. They really thought he'd take them along to the capitol. Nice jobs with big paychecks. They didn't know him. Did I mention that my husband was a user? He used me, I admit, but the difference is that I allowed it. I fell in love with David Mathews when I was just out of college, a debutante in a white dress with the choice of dozens of wealthy, respectable suitors from the right families." She tossed her head back and emitted a tiny, strained laugh. "And I had to fall for David. Funny, when you think of it. At least I knew he was a man on the way to the top. He would never drop me, unlike those poor saps working in his campaign, because he couldn't."

"Did you keep a gun in the house?" Martin said.

The woman closed her eyes a moment, as if she were trying to readjust to a new and unexpected scenario. "David bought a gun some time ago. Said I should have it for protection when he wasn't here. I told him to get rid of it. I didn't want it around."

This was good, Ryan was thinking. They could take this to the district judge to get a search warrant for the house: the grieving widow had access to a gun.

"Did your husband have a study here?" Ryan heard the sound of her own voice, disembodied and distant.

"On the other side of the entry," Sydney said, tossing her head backward.

Ryan got to her feet and fitted the strap of her bag over her shoulder. "Do you mind if I take a quick look?"

"Why is that necessary?"

"This is an investigation," Martin said. "We might find something that leads to the killer or to other avenues for us to look into, you never know. I'm sure you are eager to have us find your husband's killer."

"Take a look if you must." Sydney shrugged and got to her feet.

"We can finish up here," Martin said, stepping in front of Sydney before she could head into the entry.

Ryan walked past them, passed Wendell Lane in the entry and let herself through the double carved wooden doors. *The home office,* David had said, opening the doors a few inches so that Ryan had only the briefest glimpse of the dark wood desk, the computer and printer, the gilded leather books lining the shelves on the far wall. *Nice, quiet place to get some work done, but I have no intention of working tonight.*

She had to hurry. She had sensed the uneasiness in the way Sydney had jumped to her feet, the reluctance to allow anyone into David's study. Wendell Lane would surely sense it. Martin might hold both of them for a couple of minutes, if she was lucky. She found the handkerchief in her bag, stepped behind the desk and pulled out the middle drawer, using the soft cloth on the handle. An assortment of paper clips, Post-it notes, a stapler and a box of rubber bands. She shut the drawer and opened the top drawer on the left. Too shallow to slip the gun underneath the ream of stationary. She could hear Martin's voice, a low drone, punctuated by the impatient voice of Wendell Lane. Then she sensed the slightest change in the atmosphere, the motion of bodies. They were coming into the study.

Ryan had the middle drawer open. Papers and folders stuffed inside. Nothing looked organized or in place. She wrapped the handkerchief around the gun in her bag and slid it out. Then she set it in the back of the drawer and pushed the papers on top. She jammed the handkerchief back into her bag.

"What the hell are you doing?" Wendell stood in the doorway.

Behind him, peering around his arm, was Sydney Mathews. She elbowed past her brother and marched across the study. "You have no right to look inside David's desk," she said.

Ryan started to say this was a murder investigation, but Sydney Mathews put up one hand. "What are you looking for? Something to incriminate me? Is that it? You think I killed my husband because he was unfaithful? You're crazy! You have no right to rummage in my husband's private papers."

"You're mistaken," Ryan said. "I haven't touched anything in this desk. I've merely confirmed you have a computer here. We'll want to take a look at it."

"Get a search warrant," Sydney said.

8

“Looks like they’ve closed.” Martin peered through the narrow rectangular window that abutted the door. Plastered to the door itself was a brown plastic plaque with stenciled white letters: Mathews Campaign Headquarters. Doors to the other offices along the corridor were also closed.

“I hear somebody moving about inside,” Ryan said, pounding on the door. The sign jumped and vibrated. Out of the corner of her eye, she saw Martin flip open a wallet and press his badge against the window.

The door swung open, and a big man with bushy hair and glasses, dressed in blue tee shirt and khakis, waved them into an outer office. Computers, printers and opened cartons were strewn about the floor. Sheets of papers towered beside a shredding machine in the corner. Side chairs and desks were almost lost under cardboard boxes and piles of folders. The noise of a ringing phone burst from the debris on a desk.

"I'm Don Cannon, David's campaign manager," the big man said, ignoring the phone and throwing a glance about the office. "You can see, we're packing up. Packing it in. All our hopes and plans flown out the window. The state's the big loser, you know. David Mathews would've been the best governor in our history. Wondered when you'd be showing up." He hadn't drawn a breath.

Ryan said she was Detective Beckman. "Detective Martinez," she said, tilting her head toward Martin. "We're investigating Mr. Mathews's homicide. Anything you can tell us that might help find his killer? Did he have any known enemies, anyone angry enough to want him dead?"

"You must be joking." Cannon gave a raspy laugh. "Everybody loved David. He didn't know what an enemy was."

"Somebody shot him to death," Martin said. He held a ballpoint over the notepad cupped in his hand. "Recent altercations? Traffic disputes? Anything happen that might set somebody off?"

Cannon was shaking his head. "David would've told me. We discussed everything."

Ryan felt her breath knot in her throat. David, who took such stringent precautions. No e-mails, no phone calls, except on the disposable cells that he changed every week, no meetings in public. She had slunk around, hiding in hotel rooms until his campaign staff had cleared out, leaving by the stairs so she wouldn't run into anyone. And he had discussed everything with Don Cannon?

She made herself push on through the list of routine questions: "Did Mr. Mathews seem despondent recently? Upset or nervous?"

"No, nothing like that," Cannon said. "Recent polls showed David ahead by thirty points. I mean, that's phenomenal. David was ecstatic."

Ryan had to look away. The polls seemed real, more real than she was. She half expected them to start dancing in front of her eyes. Was that all David had cared about, the polls? Had their breakup meant nothing, not even the slightest disturbance to his equilibrium? The truth of it coiled inside her like a poisonous snake that might strike and kill her. She'd had the right to protect herself. It was clear now. David had deserved to die, a man incapable of understanding the suffering he had inflicted, strolling through a charmed life, thirty points ahead.

"What about the rumors of Mr. Mathews's infidelity?" Martin said. Ryan felt a wave of relief that he had asked the question; she needed a moment to trust her own voice again. She crossed her arms and dug her hands into her sides to quiet the tremors. They had discussed *everything*, David and Don Cannon? Even a breakup that had meant nothing to David?

Cannon hesitated. He pushed up the glasses that had slid down his nose and fixed them in place with an index finger. Then he drew in a long breath that expanded the blue tee shirt, as if to steel himself for whatever turn the conversation might take. "If there were any indiscretions," he said after a moment, "and I'm not saying there were, they were in the past."

"We've spoken with Mrs. Mathews," Martin said. "She doesn't deny her husband was unfaithful. We understand they were separated."

Cannon shrugged. "Only temporary. Sure, Sydney flew off the handle once in a while, but they always reconciled."

"Flew off the handle?" Ryan said. Oh, this was helpful; she had to remember this: a jealous wife who flew into rages.

Cannon hesitated, as if it had struck him that he shouldn't have started down this road. "Only once that I saw. Came in here one day and gave David hell. They got into a big shouting match, but I figured it would all blow over."

"We need names of the women he had affairs with," Martin said.

"Can't help you there." Cannon pulled a face as if he were disappointed. "Maybe David took risks, and I'm not saying he did, but he was very discreet. He was a focused man, focused on his business and his political ambitions. He wouldn't have let anything get in the way."

"And yet he and his wife were living apart." Martin kept going, and Ryan had to stop herself from saying, I think Mr. Cannon has answered our questions. "If he was planning a reconciliation," Martin said, "maybe a jealous mistress . . ."

Cannon waved one hand between them. "Let me clear something up. David loved his wife. Any dalliances he might have had were passing flirtations. Hardly serious enough to drive somebody to commit murder."

"What about the campaign staff?" Ryan said, desperate to steer the conversation in another direction. Dalliances? Flirtations? She was thinking she had been no more than an object that David could attach to his belt, a wallet or eyeglasses case that he could toss aside when he chose. Cutting her loose had been an automatic response, nothing that required thought.

"The campaign staff?" Cannon blinked behind the lenses of his glasses. "Everybody here worked their butts off because they believed in David one hundred percent, no holds barred, no reservations. We were devastated when we got the news this morning. We started packing up, but I had to let people go home. Everybody was upset. Crying. Sobbing."

"What about you?" Ryan said. "You feel the same way?"

"Yeah," Cannon said. "I'm not the sobbing type. That's why David put me in charge. But did I feel the loss, the pain? Like I was the one that took the bullets. He was my friend, my boss. I would have walked through fire for him."

"His running mate feel the same?" Martin asked.

"You mean blustery Easton Sherer? He's been on vacation in Spain for two weeks. Figured nothing he could do would make any difference. David was the whole show. Frankly, it wouldn't surprise me if Easton pulled up stakes and stayed over there. He's got plenty of money. Only reason he agreed to run was so he could bask in David's sunshine for a while."

"Oh, sorry to interrupt." The door had opened, and a man still in his twenties, with the wiry, knotted physique of a cyclist and short-cropped sandy hair stepped into the office. There was a dejected look about him—the slumped shoulders, the lost, random way his hands moved about. He finally grabbed the side of the door, slammed it shut and turned toward Cannon. "Should I come back?"

Ryan could hear her heart pounding. She recognized the man—the staffer who had seen her and David last June in Aspen. What had she been thinking, coming here? She should have asked Martin to handle the interview. He could have taken a uniform along. God, she had to get herself together. Everything depended on it.

"Detectives Beckman and Martinez." She realized Cannon was making the introductions. "The campaign's scheduler, Jeremy Whitman. The man who kept David on time; made sure he accepted invitations that would pay off in new voters, you know, give the fence-sitters a firsthand impression of how great David was." He looked at the young man. "They're here about David," he said. "I told them we were pretty beside ourselves this morning, so I sent everybody home. I wasn't expecting you back."

"Christ, have you arrested the killer?" The young man's voice rose on clanging notes of hope.

"We're still investigating," Martin said.

"Oh." Whitman looked from Martin to Ryan, and Ryan felt his gaze focusing in on her. He rubbed a hand over his eyes—blue eyes peering at her past long fingers and short, chewed nails. Then he dropped his hand and went on staring. She tried to suck in a breath, but the air clogged in her nostrils.

Martin had launched into a rerun of the questions: Anything you can tell us? Altercations? Anybody who might want Mathews dead? Any past romances you might know about? Any names?

Jeremy hadn't taken his eyes off her; his arms now rigid at his sides. Finally he stepped backward and looked over at Cannon, as if he were trying to guess what Cannon had already told them.

"How about it?" Martin prodded.

"No," Jeremy said, settling his gaze on Martin. "I don't know anybody who'd want to harm David. I never knew anything about his personal life. I'm afraid I can't help you," he said, making a deliberate effort not to look at Ryan.

And now she was certain that he had recognized her. He could connect her to David, raise a lot of unsettling questions, get her pulled from the investigation, and turn the investigation down a path she could never allow it to take. At the moment, at least, he had chosen to remain silent. Witnesses were like that at times, shutting up inside just as the questions got uncomfortable, afraid to say anything that might draw them more into the case.

"I came back for my jacket," Jeremy said, shouldering past them.

"We may want to talk to you again," Martin said. "Where can we reach you?"

"He's got a loft in the old Hudson warehouse," Cannon said. "Any other staffers you want to talk to, you can reach through me. Everybody in this campaign is available whenever you say. We want David's murder solved."

Jeremy had pulled a tan Windbreaker from under a carton. He hung the Windbreaker over a shoulder and made his way back across the office. "Yeah," he said, tossing a quick glance over one shoulder. "Anytime you want to talk."

Then he was gone, slamming the door behind him, a slim, slump-shouldered figure moving across the rectangular window next to the door.

Martin pulled a white sheet of paper out of his inside jacket pocket. "We have a search warrant for the computers, phones, fax machines. Also campaign records, personnel, finance—that sort of thing." He nodded toward the equipment and cartons. "Lab techs are on the way to photograph the location of any evidence we find. They'll take the items to the lab."

Cannon nodded, as if Martin had only confirmed what he'd already figured out.

"Whitman knows something, you ask me," Martin said. He rapped the steering wheel with his thumb and squinted into the brightness drifting past the lowered visor. The air conditioner labored over the heat that had built up in the car. Ryan sat ramrod straight in the passenger seat. They had spent a couple hours collecting file folders, boxing up computers, fax machines and telephones. After the tech guys had loaded everything into the van outside, Ryan had tossed Martin the car keys. She was the better driver, they both knew, faster reflexes, the ability to multitask, but now she was too shaky, too distracted to negotiate the late afternoon traffic.

"What makes you think so?" she managed, wondering if Martin had noticed Jeremy staring at her.

"Come on, Beckman." He tossed her a look and gave her a smile that flashed a row of perfect, white teeth in the dark complexion of his face. There were streaks of white in his Marine-cut black hair. "Don't tell me you can't feel when somebody's holding out."

"Okay," she said. "Let's say he's holding out. What could he know? He's stuck behind a computer all day, a real geek. I doubt he'd register a threat to bomb the place."

"He would have seen any threats against Mathews on the Internet. We'll know more after the techs look at the computers. You hungry?"

Ryan shook her head. The thought of food made her want to retch. Everything depended on finding the murder weapon in the desk drawer. She hadn't expected to be the lead investigator. What a lucky break that was the way it had turned out. She willed the nerves in her stomach to stop jumping around and reminded herself she was in control. She had to make the most of it, steer the investigation toward the grieving widow, the first person any detective worth his salt would look hard at. All she had to do was get a search warrant on the Evergreen house, which wouldn't be a problem. Sydney had admitted that David owned a gun. The warrant would specify the computer, gun, any documents—letters, financial records—that might shed light on the investigation. With all the national attention and pressure to solve David's murder, the judge would affix his signature to any warrant she and Martin wanted. She would make certain someone else found the murder weapon, and the case would be closed.

"You need to eat." Martin swung the car onto the pavement of a fast food restaurant and headed into the drive-through lane. "Hamburger? Chicken sandwich?"

"Oh, God, no," she said. The thought of food sent her stomach into new spasms.

Martin gave her a sideways glance, then shouted his own order into the outdoor intercom—double cheeseburger, double order of fries, coffee—then she leaned over and said she would have a Coke. "One large Coke," he shouted.

As soon as they picked up the order, Martin stripped the wrapping off the hamburger and took a big bite. Guiding the car with one hand, he drove across the pavement and out into the traffic moving north. "I say we need to talk to Jeremy Whitman again."

"He's in shock." Ryan sipped at the Coke. The combination of sweetness and ice knocked back the acid rising in her throat. She could feel her head clearing. Jeremy had been frightened when he saw her—a police detective involved with the victim! He hadn't known what to say, how much to divulge. No one else had seen Ryan and David together. David had assured her of that. It would be Whitman's word against hers. But he knew that she also recognized him; she had seen it in his expression. He would think things over, maybe talk to Cannon—God, had he already returned to the office? Chances were he hadn't. Oh, she knew the type: methodical, careful, anything but impulsive. The type who lived in his head, and that's where he would work out whether he should tell the police about Aspen, and that could take a few hours.

"You can't make anything out of the way he acted," she went on. But she had made everything out of it, she was thinking. Jeremy Whitman had become an unforeseen problem that she had to solve.

Martin chewed for a moment, then dug a hand into the white paper bag on the console, helped himself to a bunch of fries and chewed some more. "So we wait until tomorrow," he said finally, "and we go have another heart-to-heart with Jeremy Whitman."

9

The neighborhood was as still as a photograph. Giant, contemporary houses with the moneyed look of stucco, decks and oversized windows arranged under elms and oaks, like a movie set with the feel of vacancy about it. The occupants had decamped for the day to the downtown steel and glass skyscraper offices that rose against the sky in the distance. Catherine had taken the chance someone might be at home, a woman in between social committee meetings or a tennis match at the country club a few blocks away. Someone who might have seen something unusual last night and remembered a tiny fact that could help her find this morning's caller.

Catherine slowed past Mathews's house, which looked a little out of place, more extreme in its glass and steel architecture, more prominent, just like Mathews himself, she thought. Always wanting to stand out from the crowd. The yellow police tape stretched across the front yard and the bouquets of flowers, photographs of a smiling Mathews and condolence cards piled along the sidewalk where the reporters and gawkers had milled about were the only signs that something unusual had happened there. The official vehicles gone, the crowds vanished. She parked in front of the next-door neighbor's house, found the small notebook inside her bag. It had taken about two minutes to find the names on the Internet: Carol and Lee Kramer. She glanced through the notes she had made. Lee Kramer had called 911 at 5:06 a.m. Reported body in house next door.

The bronze front door of the gray stucco house was about twelve feet high, inserted with strips of artfully arranged glass that gave Catherine a fragmented view of the black-and-white tiled entry. She rang the bell and waited for someone to emerge from the depths of the interior. There were no footsteps, no faint tremors of movement. Only the lingering muted echo of the gonglike bell inside.

She was about to start back down the sidewalk when the door opened and a short, gray-haired woman with pink cheeks and a prominent, purplish nose peered out. "Yes?" she said. Beyond the woman, at the edge of the entry, a dark-haired, middle-aged woman stood hugging herself, her face creased with curiosity and anxiety.

Catherine introduced herself, said she was with the *Journal* and would like to speak with Mr. or Mrs. Kramer.

"They're not at home." The woman in the doorway enunciated the words as if there were an invisible list of phrases that she was accustomed to using, and this was the most familiar.

"Where can I find them?" Catherine said, hoping the door wouldn't slam in her face. The dark-haired woman had moved forward and was now only a few feet from the door.

"I'm not at liberty to divulge that type of information," the first woman said.

The other woman stepped closer. "This about Mr. Mathews?"

"Edith, I don't think this is a good idea." The woman in the doorway glanced over her shoulder, then started to push the door shut.

"No, wait." Edith muscled her way into the doorway. "What do you know about his murder?" she said, craning forward. She had dark eyes with gray pupils that looked cloudy and unfocused.

In an instant, Catherine understood who she was. "You're his housekeeper. You found his body," she said. "How terrible that must have been for you."

Edith opened the door. "You can come in for a minute."

"I can't take the responsibility," the first woman said. She had a worried, nervous look about her. Her hands twitched at her sides.

"Stop worrying, Mary. I'll take the responsibility." Edith motioned Catherine inside and into a great room that extended into a kitchen at the rear of the house. Catherine could sense the nervousness in the gray-haired woman hovering behind them.

"Mr. Mathews was always good to me," Edith said. She positioned herself in front of a table and dabbed a tissue under her nose. She was probably in her fifties, fit and attractive, despite the redness that rimmed her eyes and the tousled look of her hair, as if she had been raking it with her fingers. "Whoever killed him deserves the death penalty. What do you know?"

"Mrs. Kramer will be here any minute," Mary said. She had moved to the window and was peering outside. "She won't be happy you let in a reporter."

"He shouldn't have died like that. He was a good man. He took care of people like us." Edith nodded toward the woman at the window. "We don't have much. We're not educated and smart like he was. He was always generous. Gave me nice bonuses at Christmas. Gave you a little extra, too," she said, directing the comment toward Mary. "He didn't forget where he came from, people just like us. He would've been a great governor 'cause he would've remembered the little people." She blew her nose, blinked several times and looked straight at Catherine. "Those detectives, they're chasing their tails, asking stupid questions. What did I see? Who came to visit Mr. Mathews last night? How would I know? I was home in my own bed with my husband. You ask me, they need to look hard at people that hated Mr. Mathews and didn't want him to be governor. I guess they got their own way, 'cause he's not gonna be governor now. Please tell me what you know." She looked as if she might burst into tears, and Catherine suspected she had been crying since this morning and had probably turned to her friend, the woman who worked next door.

Catherine took a moment, considering how much to divulge. She decided to take a chance. "We believe there may have been a witness," she said.

"What?" Edith's head snapped backward. She stared at Catherine out of wide, round eyes. "Somebody saw Mr. Mathews get shot?"

"We don't know for certain," Catherine said. "We're looking into the possibility. What about the neighbors? Does anyone walk a dog at night? Anyone ever come home late at night?"

Mary let out a strangled laugh. "Not in this neighborhood."

"Perhaps you can tell me if Mr. Mathews was accustomed to visitors late at night."

"You gotta leave now." Mary took a step toward Catherine. "Mrs. Kramer's meeting ended thirty minutes ago. She'll come straight home. I'll lose my job if she finds a reporter here. The Kramers don't want nothing to do with this."

Edith swung away and stared out into the entry. Her expression hardened, as if her muscles had turned to stone. She looked back at

Catherine. "You're just like the detectives. Asking stupid questions to ruin the reputation of a fine, upstanding man. I won't be party to it."

"That's not my intention," Catherine said, trying for a conciliatory tone that would let the woman know she only wanted Mathews's killer brought to justice. "Someone may have been outside when Mathews was killed. There were rumors he was sometimes unfaithful. If that's true, some woman may have been on the way to the house."

"She killed him."

"Who?" Catherine said. She was thinking of what the caller had said: if the police find out I was there, they'll think I killed him.

"Whoever came last night." Edith's shoulders crumbled, and she dipped her head into her hands and started sobbing. "One of his women," she said, the words muffled and tear filled. "I don't know who they were. I've never seen them. They'd still be there in the mornings when I got to work, but they'd leave real fast. Duck out the door under their scarves so I wouldn't see their faces."

"I told you, you should've just told the detectives," Mary said. She held out her arm and stared at her watch, as if it were ticking off the last minutes of her life. "Let them interview his mistresses."

"How could I do that?" Edith shouted. "How could I betray him like that? Nobody would see his good side, the kind of man he really was. People would just see a cheater. I couldn't do that." She swiveled toward Catherine. "You can't print this. It's what you call privileged information, off the record or something."

"You want Mr. Mathews's killer caught, don't you?" Catherine said, still the conciliatory voice. "It's possible one of the women killed him. Or maybe one of the women he was involved with saw the killer. Is there anything else you remember, anything you know that could help me locate these women?"

"Oh, God," Mary said. She was doing a nervous jig in front of the window. "She's home. Go out the back door." She lunged for Catherine and started pulling her toward the kitchen. "We've got to get her out of here," she said, pleading with Edith.

"What's going on?" Carol Kramer stood in the entry. She slammed the front door behind her and came into the great room. "I see we have another visit from the press," she said, approaching Catherine. She looked crisp and businesslike, unlike the wrinkled, disconcerted woman this morning. "We've already told you everything we know." Turning to her housekeeper, she said, "You had no right to let her in."

"I let her inside," Edith said. "I swear to you, Mrs. Kramer, I didn't say anything that might embarrass you or Mr. Kramer."

"I stopped by on the chance you may have remembered something else from last night," Catherine said. "Someone walking on the sidewalk, a strange car in the neighborhood? We're trying to investigate rumors of a possible witness and determine if they have any credibility."

For a moment, the woman kept her lips together in a thin, tight line. Then she said, "My husband and I did our civic duty by calling the police when Edith arrived at our house. We did not hear any disturbances from the Mathews's house, and we don't know anything. We barely knew David and Sydney Mathews, although . . ." she hesitated. "I'm very sorry for Sydney. She seems to be a perfectly nice woman. But we can't be involved with this sordid business. We don't deserve to be drawn into a murder investigation for being good citizens."

"It may be unavoidable," Catherine said. "Your 911 call is part of the official record, available to the public."

"Oh, I get it." Carol Kramer threw up both hands, tossed her head back and laughed at the ceiling. "How foolish of me. We're in negotiations, do I have it right? You'll keep our names out of the paper if I remember seeing something or someone last night. Well, what shall I tell you? What will make you go away and be quiet."

Catherine could feel her muscles tense. She had interviewed sources like Carol Kramer before, arrogant, self-centered, rich and powerful. It wouldn't surprise her if the Kramers were friends with the *Journal*'s publisher, who could call Marjorie and demand that Catherine be fired. Her ex-husband had come from a family like the Kramers, and she had spent six years watching them use their power, connections and money to ruin reputations and people and casually walk away afterward and dine by candlelight at the club, violins playing softly in the corner.

"There is no deal," she said.

Carol Kramer lifted one eyebrow in surprise. They were used to getting their own way, women like her. Dealing the cards, making the rules. Catherine knew that when the article appeared in the *Journal* naming Carol and Lee Kramer as the neighbors who had reported the gunshots, she would get a call to Marjorie's office. "I'm investigating rumors connected to Mathews's murder, and I intend to continue my investigation. I'm sorry you can't help."

"I've seen something," Edith said, stepping closer.

"Stay out of this." Carol Kramer swung an arm at the older woman, as if she had wanted to push her back, make her disappear.

"I don't work for you," Edith said.

"You'll never work for anybody in this town if you don't shut up."

"What did Mr. Mathews ever do to you?" Edith said. Out of the corner of her eye, Catherine could see Mary folding into herself, becoming smaller. There was an air of expectancy in the way she cocked her head to the right, as if she heard best out of that ear and didn't want to miss what may come next. The electrical current flowing between Edith and Carol Kramer was so strong that Catherine wouldn't have been surprised it if had started crackling. An image floated in her mind: Carol Kramer, scarf draped over her head, making a hasty retreat from David Mathews's bedroom.

"You impertinent woman!" Carol Kramer said. "Leave this house immediately, and take your reporter friend with you."

Edith didn't move. "Sometimes when I got to work in the mornings, I seen a black BMW parked down the street a ways, on the other side. I knew it didn't belong there."

"This is ridiculous." Carol Kramer was digging into the bag slung over one arm. She extracted a cell phone and flipped it open. "Either you both leave now, or I'll call security and have you thrown out."

Catherine pivoted about, walked through the room and across the entry. She let herself out through the glass-striped door and kept going until she was in the street next to her convertible. She waited as Edith hurried down the sidewalk, chest heaving, arms swinging. "Can I give you a lift," she said.

The woman shook her head. "I got my car in back. What I told you about the BMW's not going to hurt Mr. Mathews's reputation, will it? You won't put any of it into the newspaper?"

"I can't promise that," Catherine said. "I don't know if it's important. But I will promise that, whatever happens, I will write about David Mathews's kind, generous side."

10

Catherine drove south on Colorado Boulevard, the voice of Diana Krall floating over the hum of the engine. The bumper-to-bumper rush hour traffic ground to a jerky stop at a red light. Odors of exhaust and dry, hot dust wafted across the convertible. She liked driving with the top down, the elusive sense of freedom that came with the wind in her hair. In the distance, the mountains glowed gold and magenta, as if they were lit from within. Clouds billowed across the sky, and a jet out of DIA laid a long, straight contrail. The traffic started forward, and she made it all the way to the intersection before she had to stomp on the brake again, keeping an eye on the rearview mirror to make sure the red SUV managed to stop behind her.

She couldn't get the voice on the phone out of her head. The anonymous caller, the witness on the sidewalk in front of Mathews's house, had heard the gunshots, seen a woman walk out of the house and hesitate for an instant in the light over the front door. That woman was Detective Beckman. A crank call? It was always possible, and yet Catherine had heard the cold, abject fear in the caller's voice. Every instinct she had honed as a reporter over the last ten years told her the caller was telling the truth.

And there was the black BMW that Mathews's housekeeper had occasionally seen parked in the neighborhood when she'd arrived for work in the mornings. A scenario was starting to come together, the story line playing itself out. The woman with the BMW could have been on her way to Mathews's house for a prearranged midnight rendezvous when she heard the gunshots and saw the murderer. She had retreated, not wanting to get involved. Then she had seen Detective Beckman on TV and realized who it was she had seen. Still, she might have remained uninvolved, except for the fear that the murderer had seen her and that, sooner or later, a police detective could discover her identity. Then she would become the suspect, maybe even be charged with murder, especially when the detective found out that she often visited Mathews in the middle of the night and might have a motive to kill him. So she had called the *Journal* in a desperate attempt to save herself.

The traffic inched forward. Six more blocks, another couple of red-light stops, and Catherine swung into the parking strip abutting a multi-storied blond brick building. Three men in light-colored slacks and pastel shirts, jackets slung over their shoulders, came through the double-glass front doors and broke into different directions as they headed into the lot. One thing was certain, Catherine was thinking. Detective Beckman had to find a way to charge someone else with the murder and close the case.

She left the convertible in a spot that one of the men had just vacated and hurried across the hot asphalt. The air was still in the afternoon heat. Bits of paper and clumps of grass lay limp and dry alongside the curb that marked the boundary between the lot and the sidewalk.

Campaign headquarters could be closed by now, she was thinking. Permanently closed, with the candidate dead. She had intended to get here earlier this afternoon, but the day had collapsed in on itself. Everything demanded more time than she had expected: reviewing six months of articles on David Mathews, writing an article for the *Journal*'s website and another for tomorrow's paper, both rehashing old stuff. David Mathews, business entrepreneur, president of Mathews Properties, Republican candidate for governor, selected at the state convention by acclimation—no prospective candidates had come close to the votes he gathered. He had sailed through the primaries and into the weeks before the general election with strong support from the party and the public. Everyone loved David Mathews.

And someone had to know the identity of the woman in the BMW.

Catherine let herself into a narrow entry that spilled down a corridor on the right and up a flight of stairs on the left. Attorneys, insurance and real estate firms occupied offices behind the closed doors. Cold blasts of air blew out of the ceiling vents. Campaign headquarters took up the far end of the second floor. Catherine passed two doors that she knew led into a back office where volunteers sat at telephones and called and cajoled donors. She rapped on the next door and peered through the long window that flanked it. The office looked as if a hurricane had blown through. Upended, empty cardboard boxes, crumbled pieces of paper, plastic containers strewn over the floor and across the desks. Drawers hung open, chairs pushed haphazardly around the stacks of newspapers and magazines that littered the green carpeting. Hung at an angle on the far wall was a campaign poster with large, black type—Take Back Our State—above a smiling David Mathews. The honest blue eyes, gleaming silver hair, and frank, open smile, all meant to convey the message: trust me.

There was no one in sight, and yet Catherine could sense the faintest movements somewhere beyond the doors that opened off the room. She knocked again, louder this time. The sound reverberated along the corridor. A tall man with bushy gray hair and thick eyebrows shadowing his eyes, dressed in a blue tee shirt and khaki slacks, came through one of the doors. He stared at the window, locked eyes with Catherine, then looked away. She could see the hesitation melt into acceptance in the way he ran a hand across his mouth. Finally he moved sideways. The door juddered open.

"No comment." Don Cannon, the campaign manager, held the door ajar.

"No comment?" Catherine stepped past him into the room. The stuffy smell of discarded things and futility filled the air. She had visited campaign headquarters on numerous occasions, looking for a quote, an explanation, the behind-the-scenes story that might reveal the real candidate. Usually she got to see Cannon, while other reporters were directed to Larry Elders, official press liaison. She suspected that her coverage of Mathews's business troubles had relegated her to a higher status, as if Cannon wanted to make sure she didn't stumble onto the truth.

"Your candidate was murdered," she said, "and you have no comment?"

Cannon closed the door, pulled a chair over and dropped down. "This isn't a good time." He waved a fleshy hand at the furniture that most likely awaited a moving van. "Cops were here this afternoon, asking a lot of inane questions. Armed with a search warrant. Pretty much cleared the place out."

"Detective Beckman?"

"And Martinez. Who do I think pulled the trigger? Who wanted David dead? Had he received any threats? Suspicious telephone calls, e-mails? Any altercations? Enemies? He was a politician; what do they think?" He jabbed a finger at the notebook Catherine had pulled from her bag. "That's off the record, by the way."

Catherine tapped her pen against the notepad. "Was David expecting anyone last night?"

"You sound like the cops. How would I know?"

"You were close to him. You managed his campaign. You were on the way to the capitol with him as chief of staff or some other appointed position, right? He confided in you."

Cannon didn't say anything, and Catherine went on: "It's possible someone besides the killer was at the house."

"What are you talking about? The cops didn't say anything about somebody else being there."

"I'm conducting my own investigation," Catherine said. "Did you send one of the women from the campaign over to the house to drop off documents or speak with Mathews about something important? Anyone at all?"

"Oh, man!" Cannon leaned back and ran a hand across his forehead, as if he could wipe away the implications. "Was David having an affair with someone on the campaign staff? No, he was not."

"Let me put it another way," Catherine said. "Do you know who might have gone to his house last night? Which one of his affairs?"

Cannon was quiet a long moment, sucking air through his nostrils. "What makes you think anybody else was there?"

"It's something I stumbled onto," she said. "It may or may not be true."

"So this person who may or may not have been there might have seen something?"

"That's what I'm trying to check out. Anybody around here drive a black BMW?"

"You kidding me?" Cannon gave a howl of laughter. "David was generous, but not that generous."

"What about the volunteers?"

Cannon took a minute. His gaze roamed across the cartons and chairs and debris, as if somewhere in the leftovers of the campaign, the image of a black BMW with a face behind the wheel might materialize. "Not that I know," he said. He pitched himself forward and laced his fingers between his knees. "I'm not saying anything on the record." Catherine nodded, and he went on. "David was a powerfully attractive man. Men like that get a lot of women. Maybe it's not what they want, but the temptations are great, you understand? All I know is what I heard. Rumors, the same ones you've heard. Not that I cared what he did in his private life, but the problem is, candidates don't have private lives. He and Sydney were the ideal couple, beautiful and rich. Everybody wanted to be around them. Hell, they wanted to *be* them. The image we projected in the campaign was of the successful, brilliant man and his loving wife. It goes without saying, the image conveyed faithfulness. We'd lose the conservative votes if there was any sign the rumors were true. Get my meaning?"

"Did you ever confront him?"

Cannon nodded. "Soon as one of the volunteers started asking about the rumors, I knew I had to have it out with him. He was about to blow the whole campaign, put an incompetent nobody in the governor's office. At first, he denied the rumors. Vicious lies spread by his political enemies, he said. Slapped my back. Told me not to worry so much. Go get a beer, relax. I'd been working too hard. That was David. He had a way of deflecting any unpleasantness, anything he wanted to ignore. I sat down in front of his desk and told him I wasn't leaving until he told me the truth. That was last June, after a staffer came in, all long-faced like his hero had just been toppled, said he'd seen David in an Aspen bar with a babe who wasn't his wife. From the way David was pawing her, the woman was more than a friend."

"What did David say?"

"He admitted everything," Cannon said. "Just like David, always knowing when to bluff or punch it out and when to retreat. Retreat, marshal his forces and get right back into the game. He'd gotten involved with somebody, he said. Wasn't proud of it. Wasn't who he was. The woman had pursued him, made herself available any time or place. She had been discreet, he had to give her that. He was besotted with her at first. For David, everything was about the adventure, the conquest of something new. But it was over, he assured me. He apologized profusely that a staffer had happened to see them together. Said he'd told the staffer himself there wasn't anything to what he'd seen. Just an old flame he'd happened to run into in Aspen. They'd had dinner and a couple glasses of wine. He had probably gotten more familiar with her than he should have. They had parted outside the bar, and he didn't plan to see her again. He asked me to tell the staffer the same thing, smooth things over, you know?"

"This staffer, whoever he was, bought the story?"

Cannon lifted both arms. "The truth? I think David went up a few notches in his estimation. You know, a big enough man to admit his mistake, take the blame, and start over. Everybody loved David. They wanted him to be the man they thought he was."

"The woman in Aspen? Who was she?"

"David never told me her name. I guess the affair went on for a while because Sydney eventually found out. Came in one day and started a big argument with David. Then she moved to the house in Evergreen. It was the last thing we needed weeks before the election—David and Sydney separated. David had promised he would end the affair and set everything right with his wife."

"When was this?" Catherine said. She felt a sharp pinprick of memory. Lawrence, her ex, making extravagant promises, buying extravagant gifts, but nothing ever changed. She had finally realized that he couldn't help himself, that something was missing in his makeup, a cog that might have kept him moving along a normal route. She had divorced him, and she wondered when Sydney Mathews might have done the same. Not until after the election, most likely. Maybe not until David had served his term in office. First Lady was a tantalizing position, worth steeling yourself against the pain and humiliation. Maybe Sydney Mathews would never have divorced her husband.

She scribbled on the notepad, circles and triangles and lines that she drove into the paper, trying to marshal her thoughts. Detective Beckman could be the woman in Aspen, angry at the breakup, hysterical, even out of her mind. She could have gone to Mathews's house, confronted him, begged him to reconsider and, finally, pulled out a gun and shot him. The thought made Catherine feel a little weak, almost sick that someone so out of control and dangerous, a murderer, was in charge of the investigation.

"Did you tell the police about the woman in Aspen?" she said.

"They asked about his affairs and dalliances. I kept the answers vague. Told them that whatever may have happened in the past was over. I didn't have any names, so what else could I say? I don't want them dragging up a lot of unsavory stuff that will harm David's reputation. He deserves better than that."

"You gave them the name of the campaign worker?"

"Jeremy Whitman? He walked in while we were talking. The cops fired the same questions at him. He didn't mention Aspen. Besides, I had confirmed David's story, told him that the woman was an old flame he'd happened to run into and it didn't mean anything. I could see he wanted to protect David. He loved the man. But he was real nervous, kept glancing over at me like he hoped he was doing the right thing for David. No sense in tarnishing David's reputation because he'd had a drink with an old friend."

"Where can I find Jeremy?" Catherine said. My God, if the woman in Aspen was Detective Beckman, then Jeremy Whitman must have made the connection, which explained his nervousness. No wonder he didn't say anything; he was trying to hide what he knew. He was in as much danger as the woman on the phone this morning.

"You're not going to write about this," Cannon said. "Everything I've told you is off the record."

"Whitman could help solve David's murder."

Cannon went quiet again. Finally he said, "Loft in LoDo. The old Hudson warehouse."

"Thanks." Catherine got to her feet and started for the door. She swung back. "As far as you know, did David ever meet Detective Beckman?"

Cannon pushed himself to his feet and ran the palm of his hand across his forehead again. He looked worn, spent, as if he might fold like an accordion, the wind sucked out of him. "I think she might've helped on the investigation into the stupid fraud charges his partner tried to bring. That ugly business was settled. No charges were ever brought. Yeah, to think of it, Beckman was working with the DA's investigator. If I remember right, she had some experience with fraud cases. She helped bring the whole thing to a close." He walked over and stared down at a pile of cartons. "Now she's investigating David's murder. Ironic, isn't it?"

11

Catherine plunged into the stream of vehicles flowing through LoDo on the edge of downtown, the warehouse district at one time, with blocks of nineteenth-century brick buildings boasting ramps from the streets and double-bay doors that had accommodated horse-drawn wagons and trucks. She remembered coming to LoDo with Dad when she was a kid. He would check on the cabinets he'd ordered for a building he was constructing, and she always hung on to his hand, a little scared of the buzz and whine of machines, the smells of oil and electricity and the golden dimness of the dust-filled air. Now the warehouses and factories were art galleries and restaurants and high-ceiling condos with crowds spilling onto the sidewalks. Many of the names from that other time remained stenciled on the brick walls.

She pulled into the curb behind an SUV that was pulling out and hurried a half block toward the six-storied corner building with HUDSON splashed in black letters above the windows on the top floor. Groups of people swirled around her, tourists in shorts and tee shirts and locals with dress shirts plastered to their backs, briefcases swinging, cell phones stuck in their ears. A high-pitched energy ran through the shouts of laughter and hum of voices. She had turned forty this year, and the failures and compromises dogged at her steps. A failed marriage, a couple of affairs that had worn themselves out, leaving her without solid footing, a proper place to fit into. She wanted to laugh at herself hurrying through LoDo like everyone else. Catherine McLeod, investigative reporter, on a story about a man who was shot to death. And last year, she had shot a man to death. The thought never left her mind. It was always in the background somewhere, emerging at the least expected moments, clanging in the nightmares.

But something else had happened last year. She had learned she was part Arapaho, and something inside her had begun to pry itself open. She had met Dulcie Oldman at the Indian Center and begun connecting with a part of herself that, like the old buildings rising around her, used to be something else before they were changed.

The Hudson building stood at the far end of the block, a triangle of redbrick walls jutting toward the street corner. Catherine followed the bricks around to the large glass-framed door with bronze hinges and a bronze knob shaped like an anvil. Inside was a lobby with white marble floors and hundred-year-old exposed beams running across the high ceiling. The walls were a muted gunmetal gray. On the right, a set of elevators, and straight ahead a gray-haired man in a dark suit watching her from behind a mahogany counter.

"I'm here to see Jeremy Whitman," she said, walking over, heels clacking on the marble.

He gave her a matter-of-fact look, leaned over a computer and tapped a few keys. "Haven't seen him come in. He expecting you?"

"Catherine McLeod, from the *Journal*." She tried for a tone that said whether she was expected made no difference. She dragged the small leather envelope out of her bag and extracted a business card.

"He's not responding," the man said.

Catherine turned over the card and scribbled her cell number. Then she wrote, *Call me ASAP. Very important.* "Please give him this as soon as he comes in," she said, pushing the card toward the gray suit.

The sun had dropped behind the mountains, and streaks of violet, orange and magenta flared in the sky as Catherine drove over the Fifteenth Street viaduct. Ahead the hilly mesas of Highland lifted themselves out of the riverbanks. It was still daylight, but dusk was coming on fast, and there was an orange cast to the air. Denver had started at the confluence of the Platte River and Cherry Creek, she knew, mobs of gold-seekers and adventurers a hundred and fifty years ago overrunning the land that had belonged to her own people. Frank McLeod had been a great storyteller; she had loved listening to the stories he'd heard from his father and grandfather. How settlers, crowded in log cabins and bungalows, mired in the mud and offal of the river bottoms, had looked out across the river to the high lands and dreamed of moving up. The Irish had gone to Highland first, then the Italians and the Jews and, finally, the Hispanics, each group making its own community, remnants of which still existed. She loved that about the old neighborhood, known as North Denver, even though it was northwest of downtown. Pastrami, Italian sausages and cheeses over here, kosher salami, bagels and rugulach there, fresh tortillas and chilis a few blocks away, and clusters of cafés and bakeries, galleries and theaters and an old Carnegie Library.

By the time Catherine parked in the driveway off the alley behind her bungalow, it was almost dark, and long shadows lay over the alley and the yard. Nick was probably already at the restaurant; he was always early. She let herself inside and walked through the house. Rex was waiting in the backyard, head bobbing and tail flapping. She patted his head, rubbed his ears, then filled his dish with his favorite dog food and gave him fresh water. Five minutes later, she had brushed her hair, touched up her lipstick and was retracing her route toward the river and Gaetano's at the edge of Highland.

Nick sat at a corner table in the far room behind the bar. The place was packed, every table taken, people stacked around the hostess podium. There was an air of celebration, glasses clinking and waiters darting about. Aromas of spicy tomato sauce, sausages, warm bread and strong wine drifted toward Catherine as she made her way past the smiling faces of the Smaldone brothers and their associates looking out from the framed photos on the walls. Gaetano's was another remnant from the past, a place with its own history and right to belong. The Smaldones, Denver's own version of the underworld, once owned the restaurant, running bootleg booze during Prohibition, and illicit gambling for decades later from corner tables. One of Frank's stories was how the kids in the neighborhood liked to shoot basketballs into the hoop outside the restaurant. Anytime a police car pulled up, the kids fired the balls at the wall itself to warn the men inside. Later, somebody would come out and give them a couple of quarters.

Nick was on his feet as she approached. He reached out and tugged her toward him. She could feel his heart thudding next to hers, the power in his arms and the warmth of him flooding over her, as if she had arrived in a place toward which she had been heading for a long time. She kissed him back hard.

"I've missed you." He led her to the chair across the table corner. He had black hair, flecked with gray that made it look silvery under the ceiling lights, and a strong face with sculptured features, not handsome, exactly, but confident and engaged. He had grown up a few blocks away;

he was as much a part of the neighborhood as Gaetano's, and that sense of belonging somewhere, she supposed, was one of the things that had drawn her to him.

"How was L.A.?" she said, settling in the chair. A half glass of red wine twinkled in front of him. He liked Merlot.

"Hot, windy and trying." He motioned to a waiter. At the next table, a small child banged on a plate, then tossed the spoon onto the floor and started howling. "A week at the L.A. jail interrogating gang members who would've stuck us with a shiv if they could have." The mother had pushed her chair back and was about to get up, when the waiter swooped in and handed the child another spoon. The howling subsided into loud, smacking sobs.

"Sorry to start without you," Nick said when the waiter turned to their table. "What would you like?"

"The same." Catherine nodded toward his glass. She had started drinking Merlot since she'd met Nick Bustamante.

"Bring us a bottle," Nick said, looking up out of the corner of his eyes. Then he leaned forward and set his hand over hers. He had a way of looking at her, Catherine thought, as if he were trying to glimpse something below the surface that swam just out of view. He was looking at her like that now. "I would have preferred to be here with you. Rough day?" he said.

"It's not every day a gubernatorial candidate is murdered." She allowed her hand to rest in his. The murder moved itself again to the front of her thoughts. The caller's voice was still in her head. She pressed her fingers against his a moment and tried to ignore the fact that Nick Bustamante worked every day with Detective Beckman. "If you'd been in town," she said finally, "it might have been your case."

"The whole department's on it," Nick said, "from the chief to the guys on the street. The cable channels have set up in front of headquarters. They'll be broadcasting live tonight. Reporters all over the place. I saw Metcalf in the lobby."

Catherine slipped her hand free, sat back and waited while the waiter poured a glass of Merlot and set the bottle on the table. She ordered ravioli and salad, and Nick said he would have his usual. The waiter nodded and smiled. Spaghetti with sausage. After the waiter walked off, she said, "Is something about to break?" Beckman could have arrested someone—anyone—to keep suspicion away from herself.

"It won't be long." Nick shrugged. "High-profile murder, probably only a few primary suspects. It's a matter of zeroing in, determining who wanted the candidate out of the way. Starting with the widow." He took a sip of wine and seemed to reconsider. "You're not working, are you?"

"No," she said, and yet, she was working, she knew, all of her instincts on alert. Nick could say something that might link Beckman to David Mathews, drop a hint, an innocent word.

"It's simply a matter of eliminating everyone close to the victim," Nick continued, "working your way outward."

The waiter brought the pasta and salad and made a great flourish of grating veils of parmesan over the plates. "What's your opinion of Beckman?" Catherine said when the waiter disappeared.

"Catherine . . ." He picked up his fork and held it over the pasta a moment. "You know I can't talk about police business."

"I'm just wondering how competent she is. Like you said, this is a high-profile case. The whole country's watching."

"She's competent. Learned the ropes in Minneapolis. Denver gets the benefit of what she knows. The case is in good hands, in case the *Journal* is wondering." He wrapped the spaghetti around his fork—the way his mother had taught him to eat spaghetti, he'd once explained—and took a bite. Then he sliced into the sausage.

"Do you work closely with her?" Catherine sampled her ravioli. The taste of tomato sauce and melted cheeses was sharp on her tongue.

"What's this about?" Nick said, wrapping another forkful of spaghetti.

"I'm wondering if she's capable of solving Mathews's murder."

"She's not working alone. Martinez is on the case with her." He took another bite, then patted his napkin at his mouth and sat back, looking at her as if he hoped to peer below the surface.

Catherine lifted her glass and took a deep drink of wine. She had pushed too far, she was thinking. And what had she hoped for? That Nick Bustamante might tell her that Detective Beckman could be capable of murdering a man she was involved with? "So what kind of fishing trip are you on?" he said. "I work closely with a lot of women. It's part of my job. I just spent eight days in L.A. working with a detective on the L.A. force. I don't sleep with my colleagues, if that's what you're thinking."

Catherine finished the wine, set down her glass and waited while Nick refilled it. Things had gone off track. She was a reporter, for godssakes, used to asking questions that elicited information. How had she given Nick the idea that this was personal, that she was jealous of his colleagues? She sipped at the wine, aware of the muted warmth spreading inside her, willing it to move faster. The undertow of conversations at the other tables pulled at the silence that had descended between them.

"Are we breaking up?" Nick was smiling. Only half joking, she thought.

"No. No," she said. "This isn't about us. I'm curious, that's all. What would happen if an officer were accused of some crime?"

"What the hell are you talking about? What do you know?"

"I don't *know* anything," Catherine said. "Reporters hear things sometimes."

Nick worked at his spaghetti for a long moment, then sat back and regarded her. "My dad used to talk about the rogue cops in Denver back in the early sixties. A whole burglary ring of cops. The joke was that if a burglar broke into your house, you should get his badge number. Every other cop in Denver, including my dad, was furious and ashamed. The good cops were the ones that brought the bad ones down. They cleaned up the place. We've had a professional department for fifty years. What are you saying? You know something about Beckman or Martinez or somebody else?"

"I didn't say that." They'll consider the source, Metcalf said this morning. An anonymous source, and they'll drop the accusation into a well. Even worse, she knew, was that Beckman would know for certain there was a witness.

"But you're on a fishing expedition," Nick said.

Catherine sliced a piece of ravioli, then pushed the pasta away and took another drink of wine. She wasn't hungry, and this was all wrong. She'd already said too much, alerted Nick. He might go back to headquarters and mention something to Detective Beckman, put her on alert. The last thing Catherine had wanted. She wasn't sure what she had been hoping for: a little inside information, a hint Beckman may have been investigated for something else? Even a minor infraction of the rules would show that the woman broke rules, stepped over lines. And yet, she and Nick had an agreement: she would not use anything he told her about his job, and he would do the same. She had been the one stepping over a line.

She heard the muffled coughing of her cell and dug into her bag. Not a number she recognized. The man's voice sounded young and tentative. "This is Jeremy Whitman." Behind his voice was the clanking noise of a bar. "You wanted to talk to me?"

"Yes," she said. "Where can I meet you?"

"I'm at Old Sally's."

"How will I know you"

"I'll be waiting at the front door."

"I'm sorry, Nick." Catherine snapped the phone shut and got to her feet. "It's someone I've been trying to get ahold of. I have to talk to him," she said. Then she swung about and started back through the restaurant, conscious of the dark, perplexed gaze drilling into her back.

12

The man standing under the neon sign that blinked "Old Sally's" was medium height, with a wiry, cyclist's build, light-colored hair plastered back from his face and a drawn, unsteady look about him. Little groups of people moved along the sidewalk, but he was watching the cars that crawled down the street, as if he expected Catherine to jump out of one. She hurried past the three girls tottering along in five-inch heels and short skirts and came up beside him. "Jeremy?" she said. He jumped back at least two inches and started to stumble. She thought he might fall. Regaining his balance, he blinked at her.

"You the reporter?" Catherine read his lips. Music pulsed out of the bar, pounding rhythms mixed with laughter and shouts that spilled onto the sidewalk.

"Catherine McLeod," she shouted. "I know a quiet place. Do you mind walking?"

He hesitated. The annoyance and grief in his expression finally gave way to a squint of curiosity. "Let's go," he said.

Catherine started back the way she had come, the young man beside her, Top-Siders scuffing the sidewalk. Out of the corner of her eye, she could see the deliberate way he walked, arms at his sides, shoulders straight ahead, like a drunk driver desperate not to break any traffic rules. "This about David?" he said when they escaped the bubble of noise. "The worst thing ever happened in my life. I can't believe it." He had choked up; his voice dropping a half octave. "Keep telling myself it can't be true. He was a great man. A great man," he said again, head bobbing in affirmation.

"You might have some information that could help find his killer," Catherine said. They had passed her parked car and were stopped for the red light where Sixteenth Street butted into Wazee. A block away, the massive gray stone façade and tiled roof of the Union Depot loomed under the streetlights. In another time, another world, Catherine thought, hundreds of train passengers had traipsed along these same sidewalks every day to the nearby hotels and restaurants. On the corner was the Tattered Cover bookstore, and beyond, the tall buildings that ringed the edges of LoDo, bright yellow lights gleaming in black windows. Traffic shunted past, spitting out exhaust fumes and dust. The air was cool, a sweater evening. She wished she had thought to bring a wrap.

The walk light flashed, and Catherine hurried across the street, Jeremy still in tow. He seemed to have lapsed into himself, consumed with his own thoughts. They made their way up the steps and through the heavy wooden doors into the Tattered Cover, past the knots of people browsing books stacked on tables and arranged on shelves of movable bookcases, the vividly colored book covers jumping out under the ceiling lights. The patina on the old floor boards took on a metallic cast.

Catherine motioned Jeremy into the coffee shop. "What can I get you?" she said.

"Nothing for me." He sank onto a chair at the only vacant table. The coffee shop was quiet; the other customers intent on the books propped in front of their coffee cups. At least their table stood apart, out of earshot. "The day's been too weird. I'm sticking with booze tonight," he said. At the counter, she ordered black coffee, carried it over and sat down across from him.

"What did you mean, I might know something?" A worried note sounded in his tone. Tiny red veins mapped the whites of his eyes.

Catherine took a sip of coffee, then took her cell out of her bag. She touched one of the icons and held up the phone between them. The TV news from this morning started replaying in miniature: The gurney, the bulky form of David Mathews's body in a gray, plastic bag, the coroner's officers at both ends, and the barely audible monotone of the newscaster announcing that a body had been removed from the gubernatorial candidate's home. Then, the briefest glimpse in the opened door of a beautiful woman with stylish blond hair and a dark blazer and khaki slacks. She might have been one of the newscasters, Catherine thought.

"I already saw it," Jeremy said. He seemed slightly offended, lifting a hand to shield his eyes. Then he shifted about, and she followed his gaze toward the nearest table where a gray-haired man in a professor's sweater with leather elbow patches bent over a thick book with a cover of swirling comets and stars.

Catherine replayed the newscast, and this time, she stopped on the image of Detective Beckman. "Do you recognize the woman in the door?" she said.

The young man took a moment before slowly turning back. He squinted at the image. "One of the investigators," he said. "Otherwise, why would she be in the house?"

"She's the homicide detective in charge, Detective Beckman." Catherine could feel her heart accelerating. "Anything familiar about her?"

"Why would there be?" Jeremy looked away.

"I spoke with Don Cannon this morning," Catherine said. "He told me you had spotted Mathews in Aspen with a woman a few months ago. Could the woman have been Detective Beckman?"

Jeremy stayed quiet, staring out into the bookstore, hands clasped on the table. Finally he looked back at the tiny image of Detective Beckman. "When I saw the news this morning, I recognized her. I knew I'd seen her before. But that's crazy. Why would David have anything to do with a homicide detective?" The weight of the implications seemed to crash over him, like a falling wall. He sat back, not taking his eyes from the image. "It's so bizarre. I keep telling myself it can't be true." He was murmuring at the screen. "A police detective involved in murder?"

"We don't have any evidence," she said. God, what was she doing? Jeremy Whitman would show up at campaign headquarters tomorrow and tell Cannon everything. How long before Detective Beckman learned Whitman identified her? "All I have so far," she hurried on, "is a possible link between Beckman and Mathews. If you saw them together in Aspen, it would be enough to have her removed from the investigation."

"David told me she was an old girlfriend." Jeremy waved away the cell, and Catherine tucked it back inside her bag. Dejection clung to him like sweat; she could almost smell it. "I loved that man," he said. "I believed him. He happened to run into her, that was all, and they'd had a drink. You're saying it was a lie? There was something going on between them?"

"I don't know," Catherine said.

"Oh, come off it!" Jeremy shouted. The gray-haired professor at the next table lifted his eyes from the book and glanced over. Catherine could feel the annoyed stares from the other tables. "Don't come around telling me I have important information, show me a photo, then tell me you don't know anything. Jesus, I loved the man." He shot a look around; then, lowering his voice, he said, "I loved him, and he lied. He was chasing around, like his enemies wanted the public to believe. I thought they were lying, trying to ruin a decent man. I told myself, David and Sydney Mathews were the perfect couple with the perfect marriage. I wanted to be just like him. Rich, successful, beautiful wife, great houses, everybody eating out of my hand. He would've been the best governor Colorado ever had, and now you tell me it was all a lie?"

"Was anyone else from the campaign in Aspen at the time? Anyone else who might have seen them?"

Jeremy drew his lips into a tight line a moment. "Just fricking me," he said finally. "I was the lucky one that got to catch David in his lies. God, I need a drink." There was a helplessness in the way he looked around.

Catherine pushed the coffee cup toward him. She hadn't touched it. "Try a little coffee," she said. Sometimes, she had discovered, caffeine had a way of soothing the need for a drink.

Jeremy stared at the cup a moment, then took a long sip. He set the cup down hard, as if he feared missing the table. A tiny puddle of brown liquid started to spread. "We'd gone to Grand Junction," Jeremy said, "David and I and a couple of staffers. David spoke at a chamber of commerce luncheon. He had driven himself. David liked to drive alone. He said it gave him time to collect his thoughts. After the luncheon, he told me he was going back to Denver. The other staffers stayed in Grand Junction to check up on things at the campaign office for the Western Slope. I'd taken the weekend off. I had my gear in the back of my Subaru, and I headed to the Maroon Bells outside Aspen. Spent two days climbing and camping. Like David, I needed some time to get my head clear."

"So Mathews knew that no one on the trip would know whether he did, in fact, drive back to Denver."

Jeremy nodded. "Looks that way." He sipped at the coffee again. "Caffeine's not doing it for me," he said. "I need a drink. Can we get this over with?"

"Tell me what happened."

"Nothing happened," he said. "After I got off the mountain, I wandered around town, checking out the bars. I wandered into the Hotel Jerome 'cause I'd heard it had a great old bar. David was sitting at a table in the corner with a babe, you know? All I could think was what's he doing here with her? He saw me, got up and came over. He took my arm, I remember, and steered me out of the bar and into the lobby where I couldn't see the babe. 'It's not what you think,' he said, and he gave me some bullshit about happening to run into her and having a drink for old time's sake. I said I'd understood he was going back to Denver. 'Well, that was the plan.' David could finesse anything. God, he was the best. Nobody could rattle him or throw him off his pitch. That's why he was so great on the campaign trail. Farmers out on the plains, ranchers in the mountains, professors, students, soccer moms, there wasn't a question they could throw where he didn't have the perfect answer. It was like he'd been expecting that question all along."

"You believed what he told you?"

"Everybody believed David Mathews." Jeremy waited a long moment before he went on. "I wanted to believe him. I hated the doubt, but I couldn't shake it. If any of the rumors proved true, it would ruin the whole campaign. Colorado voters like their politicians to be square shooters, and if they aren't, they don't want to know about it."

"So you talked to Cannon?"

"I ran it by him. He told me to forget it. Don't go making something out of nothing. Next day, he pulled me into his office and gave me the same story David had given me. The woman was an old girlfriend he had happened to run into. They had a few drinks and that was it. So I should forget about it. We had a campaign to run. I was glad to have Cannon telling tell me what to do, you know? Made it easier to put it aside, not think about it anymore."

"Listen, Jeremy," Catherine said. She started to suggest that they go to police headquarters right away, then thought better of it. He was half-drunk. She didn't want to give Internal Affairs any reason to discount his story. "I want you to come with me to police headquarters first thing tomorrow," she said. "I'll get an appointment with Internal Affairs. You can tell them what you saw in Aspen and what David told you."

"I don't think so." He pushed the coffee cup away and managed to stand up, knocking the chair back a little, wobbling on his feet. "My word against a police detective's? Who they gonna believe? If she had anything to do with David getting murdered, I'm hanging below the radar. Let somebody else link them together."

Catherine stood up. "There might be someone else. Someone who saw her outside David's house seconds after he was shot. You would be corroborating each other's story. You'll make a stronger case together. Internal Affairs will have to intervene, take her off the case, investigate her involvement with David. Are you with me?"

"Who is it?"

"Give me a day or two," Catherine said. A day or two to run down an anonymous caller? It could be impossible. She hurried on: "I'll go with you to Internal Affairs first thing in the morning. But you could be right about staying under the radar. Beckman might want to interview you, and when she does, she could recognize you from Aspen. I know she saw you this afternoon. She could have recognized you then. She'll know you can tie her to Mathews. Is there somewhere you could go for a couple days until I locate the other person?"

He seemed to consider this, a sober look about him now. "My dad's got a fishing cabin up in North Park."

"Good; go there after we talk to Internal Affairs," Catherine said. The North Park area in the northwestern part of the state was nowhere, a vast expanse of wilderness surrounded by mountains, home to bears and mountain lions and brown trout.

"Right now I need a couple drinks."

They walked back through the store, across the street and down the sidewalk toward the thumping noise at the end of the next block. Catherine left him at her car along the curb. He had already gone inside the bar when she drove past. Fifteen minutes later, she parked in front of a block of condos that overlooked downtown from the other side of the Platte. A small porch butted against the front door at the middle condo. In a corner was a ceramic planter with a few petunias poking around the dried daisies. The door opened before she could press the bell, and she was aware of Nick Bustamante, black hair and dark, shadowy face, and white shirt, taking hold of her hand and leading her inside.

"You surprise me, Catherine McLeod," he whispered in her ear. "Every time I see you, I wonder if I'll ever see you again."

"I'm sorry I had to leave so abruptly." She pulled back a little. Pinpricks of light shone in his dark eyes. "It was an important interview I couldn't miss."

"Always the reporter," he said. "I guess I'll get used to it."

13

Computers tell a story. Names, events, motivations, recriminations, revenge, love, hate, whole memoirs, autobiographies, even novels, captured in e-mails sent and received and websites visited. Ryan bent close to the monitor and tapped the keys. She had told the techs to leave David's computer on her desk. They would examine it later. Any evidence relating to the murder would have to be validated by the experts, not by a detective who happened to locate sent e-mail messages. The guts, invisible wires and connections, those were left to experts. But first she had to know if there was anything about her on the computer. That fool staffer could have e-mailed David about seeing her and David in Aspen, or maybe David had e-mailed him, making excuses, claiming their meeting was nothing more than an accident. What was the name? Jeremy Whitman, the only person, besides the woman on the sidewalk, who could connect her to David Mathews.

She surfed through David's e-mail inbox, three hundred and some notes, most about the campaign. Nothing personal. Even the messages from Whitman confirmed speaking engagements and appearances, interviews with the press. A couple dozen routine messages had gone to employees at Mathews Properties. David had taken a leave of absence from the company after the caucus in the spring, but it looked as if he hadn't backed away entirely. Somebody named Martin Johnson was supposedly running the company, but the e-mails told another story. Johnson was a puppet, and David had pulled the strings.

No mention of her name.

Ryan searched the deleted e-mails. Hundreds more, a cascading avalanche of letters, notes, congratulations, advice, questions. David had forwarded whole batches, along with stock replies, to campaign headquarters where some volunteer must have sent the replies. It would have been beneath David to reach down and touch the common folks who had reached up to him and would have put him in the governor's office. Another story began to emerge, one she hadn't expected. The imperious David Mathews strolling through people's lives, strolling through hers, brushing off any residue, never connecting. What a fool she had been, believing him, believing in him, accepting everything he said as the truth, just like the people who had e-mailed him. *We're behind you one hundred percent! I've mailed in my contribution to your campaign. I'm praying the Lord will let you be elected. We need you.* How easily David had shunted them to a volunteer at campaign headquarters. She wondered if he had even bothered to read the messages.

A user, Sydney had called her husband. David Mathews used people to get what he wanted. He had used her, Ryan thought. She'd had experience working financial frauds in Minneapolis, and she had suggested to the sergeant that she could help the DA's investigation into Broderick Kane's allegations against David. She had advised the DA against pursuing the matter. Allegations, the whole complaint was nothing but allegations. One accounting firm contradicting another. Not worthy of the taxpayers' money. She had wanted to get close to David, that was all. She had met with Broderick Kane and suggested he settle the matter. And by then, David's wife had stepped forward with the money to buy out Kane. Case settled amicably.

David had used her.

A sickening tightness took hold of her stomach. This was the man she had killed! And now her own life could be sucked into the sewer. She couldn't let that happen. David had been adamant about never e-mailing each other, never leaving a record, and she had adhered to his rules, believing he wanted to protect her and her career from any unpleasant publicity that could leak out should some snoopy campaign staffer or volunteer come across any e-mails between her and David. Now his concern was like a sick joke. David Mathews's only concern was for himself. Still, she had to be sure that David had kept the rules. She skimmed through the last messages, her muscles stiff with the possibility of finding herself.

"When you gonna knock off?" Ryan flinched. The voice was like a bullet out of nowhere, zinging past her ear. She had assumed she was alone in the detectives' area, fluorescent ceiling lights blazing over vacant cubicles, the faint sounds of nighttime Denver drifting past the windows.

"You said you were going home." Ryan swiveled around and faced her partner who was leaning against the wall, gripping a foam cup in one hand and a brown paper bag in the other. The odor of stale coffee invaded the cubicle.

"I figured you'd still be here, working the case." He swung the bag over onto the desk. "Brought you a sandwich. You haven't eaten, right?"

She said that was right and thanked him, trying to swallow back the acid rising in her throat. The thought of food and sleep, anything normal, seemed impossible, something for other people. Normal people. She could scarcely believe such ordinary things were ever part of her life. Still, she was grateful for the way Martin looked after her. Even if a thin thread linking her to David Mathews should turn up, Martin would fight with the last bit of his strength to protect her.

"Forensics report just came in on the murder weapon. The lab techs dug two bullets out of the wall, and the autopsy turned up the third 9mm." He worked at his coffee a moment, then gave a half nod toward the computer. "Find anything?"

"I'm afraid not." They had recovered the bullets, she was thinking. As soon as they found the Sig in the Evergreen house, the case would be closed.

"The techs might pull something Mathews tried to delete," Martin said. "Scary when you think about it. Nothing ever truly deleted. Follows you around like a bad odor." Ryan flinched; she felt as if he had hurled a rock at her. What he said only confirmed why she'd had to check the computer first. She had to be prepared.

"Why not call it a day and let the techs take over tomorrow? You're taking this way too personally."

"It's an important case, Martin." God, what had he meant by that? "What about the officers who canvassed the neighbors? Anybody remember anything?" The shadowy image of the woman on the sidewalk flared in front of her again, as if the woman were still watching her. A neighbor out walking her dog? Ryan hadn't noticed a dog, but that didn't mean there hadn't been one nosing in the bushes. Someone who needed to get away from the house for a while, needed a breath of fresh air, a cooling off time? Any number of scenarios could send a woman fleeing her home. God knows, she had investigated enough domestic abuse cases to compile a list of scenarios as long as her arm, but usually the police were called because the woman hadn't fled.

Martin was shaking his head. "They talked to every neighbor within three blocks. Nada."

Ryan glimpsed the hesitation in Martin's manner, as if he had stumbled onto something he hadn't realized was there. "What?" she said.

"The next door neighbors, the Kramers. They made the 911 call when the housekeeper showed up, ranting about her boss being dead. They say they've told us everything they know. Any further contact will be nothing but harassment and intimation by persons in authority, or some such legal gobbledygook. They've lawyered up. We want to talk to them again, we gotta call the lawyer."

"Why would they do that if they don't have anything to hide?" Ryan said. Carol Kramer, the woman on the sidewalk? Which meant that this morning, when Ryan had talked to her, the woman could have recognized her and was too frightened to say anything. Ryan turned away and clapped a hand over the smile she could feel pulling at her lips. Ironic. She had more power as a murderer than as a police detective; but combined, she was invincible.

"I think we should talk to them again with their lawyer," Martin said. "If they do know anything, the lawyer can advise them about withholding information and impeding a homicide investigation."

It was the last thing Ryan wanted. Give Carol Kramer a chance to point at her in front of a lawyer and say, "You're the one. I saw you." She tapped an index finger on the edge of the desk. "He's a CEO and she's a socialite," she said. "They're the kind who want to stay as far away from criminal matters as possible. Arranging a meeting with their lawyer could look like harassment, especially when we're on a fishing expedition. There's no reason to believe they're withholding information. They said they didn't hear anything until the housekeeper pounded on their door. Then they called 911. I think we should back off. We have other people to look at. How about the records of Mathews's phone calls? Do we have them yet?"

Martin rolled his eyes. "Look, I was planning to knock it off for the day, and you should do the same. We can check it out first thing in the morning."

"I want to look at them now," Ryan said.

"How long have you been on duty? Fourteen, fifteen hours? Come on, Ryan, enough for one day. What is it with you?"

Ryan kept her eyes on his, not saying anything. After a long moment, Martin finished off the coffee and tossed the cup into the wastebasket. Shrugging, he backed out of the cubicle and headed for the corridor, and she went back to surfing through David's deleted e-mails. Here was something new. On a four-day-old e-mail, in the "from" line was the name: Kim. Ryan had never seen the name before. There was no message in the e-mail itself, blank, as if Kim, whoever she was, had started to write something, thought better of it, and inadvertently tapped the send key. Ryan highlighted the name, and the e-mail address came up: Kim@goodtimes.com.

Good-times Kim. Who the hell was she? Where did she fit into the story? There was no one else, David had assured her for months. No other woman in his life, except Sydney, but he and Sydney had an agreement. As soon as the election was over, she would file for a divorce. *We'll be together. Just you and me, babe, like you want.* Then two weeks ago, everything had changed. The earth had erupted, tectonic plates shifting, casting her down into a black, surreal world she didn't recognize, a world without David. He and Sydney had come to another agreement, one that didn't include Ryan Beckman, and he was truly sorry things hadn't gone the way they both had wanted. Oh, he was as disappointed as she was, he wanted her to know that. But it was for the best.

He and Sydney putting their marriage back together, going to the governor's mansion together. Sydney would be a great First Lady, a real asset to his career. In four years, the U.S. Senate seat would open up, and Washington would be the natural step for a popular governor. A governor without any scandals dogging him.

She had descended into a black well, the sides pulled around her, going through the motions: gang fight in Park Hill, random beating of a tourist in LoDo, the files moving across her desk like an assembly line and she, the robot pushing them along, knowing an essential part of herself had been destroyed. She had called David on his throwaway cell. It was how they had contacted each other—on the cells he replaced every couple of weeks. No trace left behind, no records.

He hadn't answered her calls. She had left messages, begging to see him. If she could only talk to him in person, she could make him understand how wrong this was. They could work everything out. Even if he didn't leave Sydney, what difference would it make? They could go on in the same way. She wasn't proud; she would do anything, as long as David was in her life. Now she understood why he hadn't returned her calls. It had nothing to do with Sydney. He had met good-times Kim. The woman on her way to David's house in the middle of the night, the dark figure on the sidewalk.

Ryan could feel the chill running like water down her spine. Whoever was on the sidewalk could identify her, but the woman would be frightened, not wanting to get involved in a homicide committed by a police officer. First thing tomorrow, she and Martin would have to get a search warrant to present to the Internet provider. By afternoon, the techs would place Kim's name and home address on her desk.

Ryan shut down the computer. She had to play her cards carefully. Charge the most likely suspect, Sydney Matthews, and close the case. Gambling that Good-times Kim would want to stay uninvolved, and with the case closed, Kim could slink into the shadows out of which she had come.

"Good news and bad news," Martin bellowed behind her. He strode into the cubicle and plopped the thin stack of papers onto her desk. "Good news, we got the phone records for the last three months. Bad news, you're going to want to go through them right now." He drew up a chair and sat down beside her.

"We have to close this case. You heard the sergeant. The *New York Times*, *Los Angeles Times*, AP, CNN, Fox News, ABC and NBC and CBS—they all expect results. What are we doing? Gubernatorial candidate shot to death, and they make us look like we're sitting around playing video games." She lifted the first batch of sheets, records from the landlines at David's home in Denver, and glanced down the list of names and numbers. "We won't have any peace until we solve this thing." Her eyes stopped on the calls to J. Whitman from almost three weeks ago. Hardly important. Whitman worked for the campaign. The chance that they had discussed Aspen was slim; Aspen had happened last June. She thumbed through the other pages. August. July. June. A total of twelve calls to Whitman. What had they talked about then? David cajoling and pleading with Whitman to keep his mouth shut, promising him what? A position in the governor's office? And the more he had promised, the more certain Whitman would be that what he had seen with his own eyes was the truth.

"You find something interesting?" Martin was scouring the records from the landline in Evergreen.

"Calls to campaign workers," Ryan said. "Nothing unusual."

"What about this?" Martin slipped a sheet toward her. "Check it out. Five calls to the Denver house the night of the murder." He knuckled the sheet. "The widow didn't say anything about talking to her husband."

Ryan went back to the first page of the Denver records. God, she had missed the most obvious calls, she'd been so worried about finding calls to Whitman or Good-times Kim. "Looks like he called her back three times," she said. "They had a real conversation going on."

"Or an argument."

"We can add this to the request for a search warrant on the Evergreen house." She could feel the pieces tumbling together, like marbles rolling into predestined holes. This was what she needed, another reason for officers to tear apart the house where Sydney Mathews had been living.

There was only one other problem she had to solve.

14

Ryan drove the black, unmarked sedan out of the police garage, around the edge of downtown and north through Park Hill and beyond. The deeper she plunged into the neighborhood, the seedier it became, bare-dirt yards that wrapped around bungalows with boarded windows and stripped siding. Spindly, half-dead trees hung in the dim overhead street-lights. A pale orange glow of the lights reflected in the black sky; thunder clouds eclipsed the moon. The streets were alive with people on the sidewalks, traffic slowing, pulling over, speeding up. An undercurrent of noise tied one block to the next: rap music thumping full volume, dogs barking, people shouting, arguing. She spotted the house she was looking for. Parked at the end of the driveway was a souped-up truck with chrome fittings and four-foot-high wheels. Light streamed out of the house, illuminating the dark faces of the men standing around watching her.

She slammed out of the sedan and walked over, recognizing most of the grinning, smirking faces. "Hey, trick, you come to party?" somebody shouted. Crips members, arrested at various times on drug violations, assaults, burglaries. She had arrested some herself. They had probably all done time.

"Where's Devon?" she said.

"Ain't no Devon here." A thin, slope-shouldered man elbowed past the others, the self-appointed spokesman, she guessed. Still in his twenties, with a white scar running down the right side of his face. "Ain't that correct?" He tossed his head about and shot glances at the others. "We ain't never heard of no Devon. You should go back to your own side of town before something real bad happens. Don't want nothing bad happening to a gorgeous trick like you."

Ryan flipped open her wallet and shoved the badge close to the guy's face. "We can make this easy or hard. I press this button." She pulled her blazer aside and set her thumb on top of the radio on her belt. "In two seconds, this block will be swarming with cops and you'll all be taking a ride. Anybody here without priors?" She shook her head and snorted a laugh. It was a gamble that they wouldn't call her bluff. Nobody knew she was here. She'd told Martin she was going home, and he had believed her, nodding and commiserating about how she'd been called away from a well-deserved vacation. Murderers could be so inconsiderate, he'd said, laughing at his own stupid joke. She was alone here. No backups, no squad cars ready to ride in and rescue her.

You could never back down. She had learned that in basic training when that big SOB sergeant had kept pushing and pushing, hoping to break her, reduce her to tears and wash her out of the police academy. She'd spent weeks lifting in the gym and working with the tae kwon do master, and she'd flipped that SOB so hard he'd had to be helped to his feet. When the enemy is tough, you have to be tougher.

"I tol' you she was a cop." The voice came from one of the dark faces by the porch.

"You've got one second," Ryan said, keeping her eyes on the skinny guy in front of her, her thumb on the button.

He flipped a hitchhiking thumb toward the house. "Devon's inside."

Ryan shouldered past and headed straight for the group in front of the house, forcing them to move aside. She took the steps, crossed the concrete porch and let herself through a lopsided door with the screen punched out, ragged at the edges, hanging off a broken hinge. The living room, if you could call it that, was filled with rancid smelling mattresses, cardboard cartons, broken sofas and chairs and litter of all kinds, tee shirts and towels and faded artificial flowers stuck in foam blocks, baseball caps and a deflated football. The remnants of what looked like a playground set was over in one corner, the plastic seat cracked, the chain rusty.

"Devon? You here? I need to talk to you."

No sound apart from the ghostly whisperings of the pieces of cardboard and paper stepped on. "Try the back bedroom." The voice startled her, coming from behind. She whirled around. The slope-shouldered homeboy was right behind her. He'd opened the rattling screened door without making a sound. She felt her heart go into overdrive. Never go into a risky situation unless your partner has your back! Lesson number one at the academy, and here she was, caught in the middle of a junk room, the door outside barred by a gangbanger a head taller than she was. Stupid. God, she had to do better than this. She should have found another way to meet Devon Waters, but the image of Jeremy Whitman, the geeky campaign staffer, the only person who could tie her to David Mathews, had crowded her vision, consumed her thoughts.

"Go get Devon," she said, forcing herself to meet the homeboy's eyes and ignore the way his lips turned up into a part smile, part smirk. He'd called her bluff. There weren't any squad cars covering her, nobody else had come; nobody else cared what happened to her.

She saw the hesitation flicker in his eyes, the half smile freeze on his lips. "Could get funky," he said. "His lady's not gonna like the interruption." Shrugging his shoulders as if he were shaking out a charley horse, he started down the hallway not bothering to walk around the piles of clothing and broken toys that snapped under his boots. He banged a fist on a closed door. "Hey, Devon. You got company."

"Tell 'em to stick it." There was the sound of booze and some kind of narcotics in the muffled voice.

Ryan walked down the hall, jammed herself between the man and the door and gripped the knob. She threw the door open onto a room packed with more debris, piles of dirty, worn clothes, chairs pushed together, a narrow bed nearly lost under tossed blankets and pillows. Devon sat against the headboard, a blanket pulled up to his waist, a girl with dyed blond hair beside him, both swallowing the smoke from the reefers between their fingers. Clouds of marijuana smoke rolled around the room.

"Get out," Ryan said to the girl who might or might not be a juvenile. It was hard to tell, with the hollowed face and the black raccoon heroin eyes.

The girl let out a little whimper, like a lost puppy. It was pitiful the way she glanced up at Devon who had pulled his back straight against the headboard, shoulders at the top of the girl's blond head.

"Do it," he said, not bothering to look at her. He waited until she had slid off the bed, skinny arms and legs and knobby spine, cutoff jeans and a cropped Rockies tee shirt that exposed her belly button. She moved like a cat, slinking around the dirty clothes that littered the floor, almost jumping for the door. Smoke curled out of the fist she had made over the joint.

"What right you got comin' around?" Devon said. "I ain't done nothing."

Ryan kicked the door shut behind her. "How you been?" she said. "Haven't seen you for a while. What? A good two months now since we talked about that gang shooting over on Lincoln Street. Terrill Monroe and Lee Balsam. Remember them? Cutting into your territory, right, so they had to be stopped."

He reached around to a small table and snuffed out the joint on a chipped saucer. "You said we had a deal. Nobody needed to know what went down there."

"You remember the condition, Devon. I said I might be needing your help some time."

"You want me dead? That why you come around now? They see you come in here . . ." He threw his head in the direction of the front of the house. "I'm a walking dead man. I'm gonna be in the Dumpster tomorrow."

"You tell 'em I'm looking into random assaults on the mall and up and down LoDo. Got the citizens and tourists real upset, thinking about black gangs roaming around assaulting folks just because they happen to be white. That's got businesses real upset, too. People might get reluctant to go to restaurants downtown. Now that's a shame. Anything you might know about that?"

"I never heard nothing. Maybe they come out of Aurora. You think about that?"

"I'm thinking it could be you and your buddies outside," Ryan said. "Just like you and your buddies took care of the problems on Lincoln Street." Sweat had started to bubble on his forehead, and Ryan pushed on. "Detective Bustamante, you know who I'm talking about? He went to L.A. to talk to your homeboys. He's on to what went down, Devon. That should give you the shakes. He thinks somebody gave the order to take out Monroe and Balsam, and he thinks you and your boys know who it is and you've been covering up." She was bluffing, guessing at all of it. "Things are going to hell for you soon as he gets to the bottom of it. Conspiracy charges, accessories to homicide, impeding a lawful investigation," she said, pulling her fingers one at a time. "You guys have been running wild. You think you're unstoppable. I can have you all pulled in tonight, see who wants to save his dirty soul by giving up everybody else. All I have to do is call Bustamante, give him some names, tell him what you told me last time we talked." She waited a moment, giving the threat time to work its way past the sweat-bathed forehead. "Or you can do me a favor and maybe I won't help Bustamante with his investigation."

Devon lifted his eyes and stared at her. White flecks of light shone in his black pupils. "I told you before, don't come around. I'm not snitching."

"Come off it, Devon," she said. "You've already snitched out your buddies. You want to take your chances with Bustamante down at headquarters? He's gonna be real unhappy to learn he went all the way to L.A. for information he could have gotten from you, right here under his nose."

"What do you want?" He shifted about, gathering the blanket and pulling it closer, and she realized he was naked.

"A gun. .38 or bigger. Pistol, revolver, I don't care, as long as it's loaded and untraceable."

"Go somewhere else." He held a wad of blanket at his waist. "Go talk to some fool that don't know that soon's the cops get their claws in you, you're a dead man."

"Bustamante's real disappointed. I saw him after he got back. Ten days in L.A. and nothing definite to show for it? You can see how eager he'll be to get some solid information. He pulls you in, your buddies are gonna think you're talking, even if you keep your mouth shut. Guy that gave the order will probably give another order, only your name will be on it."

"I get you a gun, you give me your word you don't come around again?"

"Now, Devon, why would I ever do that? I'll give you my word that every time I come around, there will be something in it for you. I like fair, and that's fair."

He was looking at her with slit eyes, hatred shooting out like laser beams. "I need a week," he said.

"You have an hour."

"You're smoking, Beckman. What planet you live on?"

"One hour. I'll be waiting at the Tiger Diner. You know the place? I'll be inside trying to choke down the swill they call coffee. The black sedan out in front will be parked at the side where there aren't any lights. I'm going to make it real easy for you. The passenger window will be rolled down. You show up at exactly—" She glanced at her watch. "At exactly eleven-forty and drop the package onto the seat. You don't drive to the diner. You walk up the alley where you won't be seen. You leave the same way. Got it?"

"It's gonna cost you a grand. It better be on the seat."

"No. No. No." Ryan folded her arms and shook her head. She felt as if she were a teacher with a particularly dim student. "Let's go over it again. You bring the package, and in return, you won't be arrested for the gang shooting or any of the assaults on the mall or in LoDo your boys have been up to. Look at it like a stay-out-of-the-way-of-Bustamante ticket. I'm buying you time to clean up your acts, get your stories straight, work out your alibis so if Bustamante ever does come calling . . ."

"You just said you'd call him off."

"Wrong again. What I said was I wouldn't sic him on you."

Devon didn't say anything, his bare chest rising and falling. He was like a trapped animal, shifting about, as if he wanted to jump off the bed and run out of the room. "Bitch," he said under his breath.

"I'm your best friend," she said. "I'm the only thing between you and Detective Bustamante."

"What difference does it make whether it's you or Bustamante talking to me. I'm a dead man."

"Fifty-six minutes now," Ryan said. She swung about, pulled open the door and walked back through the house, looking straight ahead past the gang members stationed around the trash in the front room, the wiry, black-eyed blonde. There were others out on the porch. She went down the steps and looked back: "I'm putting the word out on the street that you're all snitches," she said.

She took her time walking across the dirt yard and sliding into the black sedan. She could feel their eyes drilling into her back. The adrenaline rush pounded through her. She felt high, weightless. It was all she could do not to throw her head back and laugh.

15

Ryan took the far corner booth where she had a clear view of the parking lot in front of the diner and the nighttime traffic streaming past. The lot was empty except for a semi parked at the corner and a brown sedan with cardboard stuck in a rear window. The trucker worked on a plate of fried eggs and bacon and sipped on coffee at the counter. In the booth near the door, a young couple sat with their arms stretched around hamburger baskets and soda glasses, hands clasped together in the middle of the table. Teenagers, with a weary, hangdog look, worn jeans and tee shirts and straggly hair, and a deadness of experience about them.

She felt invisible, a hidden camera watching life unfold in the diner, parsing the stories. Behind the counter was a big-stomached woman with thin gray hair tucked back in the kind of hair net Ryan remembered her mother wearing when she went off to work at the bakery. The trucker just off I-70 on a cross-country run with a load of lettuce or chickens or tires or lumber or who knew what. The teenage couple, broke and desperate, on their last dime, the type that might rob a bank tomorrow, if they didn't rob the diner tonight. The idea of squad cars, sirens and firing lights converging on the parking lot and Detective Ryan Beckman on the premises gave her a sharp twinge, as if she'd been jabbed by the point of a knife. She forced herself to look away, as if she might transfer the idea by watching the couple, and sipped at her coffee. A stale, bitter taste coated her tongue. She had pulled on the sweatshirt she kept in the office for undercover work, tied her hair into a roll at the base of her neck, and bunched the hoodie around her neck. The woman behind the counter had hardly glanced her way when Ryan ordered coffee, black. She had carried the full mug over to the booth. She was nobody.

She glanced at her watch. Five more minutes and the package should be on the passenger seat. She had left the car in the shadows next to the building. No one driving past would notice a man darting out of the alley and dropping a package across the rim of a car door. Devon would deliver. He had no choice. He'd spilled his guts to her after the killings—a conscientious snitch, Devon. Asked for a meeting in an alley, strung out, needing a fix bad. She'd given him fifty bucks and he'd laid out the whole scenario with names, dates, places. Who gave the orders, who carried them out. She had told him to sit tight, keep his mouth shut. She had no intention of passing on the information from her snitch to Detective Bustamante. Let him chase himself around. Devon wouldn't last a day on the streets if word got out he was pulled in for interrogation, and Devon was worth more to her alive than dead.

She left some bills on the table and walked past the couple still clasping hands, past the thick, curved back and stubbly neck of the trucker. Outside she hurried around to the sedan. She could see the package on the seat as she got behind the wheel—bulky, wrapped in newspaper. It might have been five pounds of sausage. She fingered the hard rounded edges of the barrel, then drove down the alley, out onto the dark, empty side street, and headed for the tall buildings with lights blinking against the midnight sky.

Jeremy Whitman's building stretched over a corner in LoDo. Glass-door entry under a canopy, flare of lights. Traffic was almost nonexistent, and only a few stragglers still out on the sidewalks. Most of the bars would be closed soon; the restaurants had stopped serving an hour ago. The dead time of night, she thought. She slowed past the entry and glanced past the glass door. A uniformed security guard sat behind the counter across the entry. She rounded the corner and turned up the alley in back of the building, peering over the steering wheel for a door she might be able to unlock. The door was there, wedged between a Dumpster and what she took for a mound of trash, until the trash moved and she realized a homeless person had bedded down for the night. It didn't matter. A building like this, with security at the front, would be wired throughout. She might open the door without waking the homeless person, but the siren would wake the entire building.

She circled around toward the front door again, weighing her options, none of which looked good. She could hardly march into the entry, flash her badge and tell the guard she wanted to see Jeremy Whitman. Not only would the guard know who had come looking for Jeremy, she would be caught on the security cameras that probably covered the entry. There were other security cameras in LoDo, she knew. The HALO, High Activity Location Observation, video cameras the department had placed around the neighborhood after the outbreak of random assaults. She had to be careful and park beyond the range of the cameras.

She could phone Jeremy and ask him to come outside. Tell him that she and Detective Martinez wanted to speak with him. Jeremy wasn't likely to agree to see her alone, not after he had recognized her this afternoon. She had to believe he wasn't stupid. And what if he weren't alone? Some wide-eyed, David Mathews volunteer up in the loft—male or female; it could be either with Jeremy, she suspected—mourning the death of the almighty leader, trying to comfort each other. Jeremy would tell the volunteer who he was going to meet, which wasn't acceptable.

She pulled the hoodie up over her head and low on her forehead as she circled through LoDo, playing out the scenarios in her mind. Jeremy Whitman lived in a castle, an old brick building with concrete floors and two-foot-thick brick walls with Hudson splashed across the south wall, as impenetrable as if a mote of alligators circled outside. There was no way to get inside without being caught on some camera, no way to make it look like a home invasion gone bad where Jeremy Whitman happened upon the invader and ended up dead. She had to lure him outside the mote.

She was on the outskirts of LoDo. Somehow she had wandered into Five Points, Denver's historic black neighborhood with jazz clubs and barbeque joints, the whole neighborhood undergoing rejuvenation now, Victorian homes looking new and stately. She pulled into the deserted parking lot of a strip mall, her headlights running like fire across a row of black windows. For a second, words came to life: "Pizza, Nails, Insurance, Used Books."

The cell phone she dug out of her bag felt cheap and lightweight, a piece of innocuous plastic not made to last any longer than necessary, which was perfect. A trick she had learned from David, and hadn't David mastered all the tricks? Pay cash for a cheap throwaway cell at some store where you never shop and no one has ever seen you before. Use the cell for calls you don't want traced. After a week stomp the cell into pieces and ditch the pieces in a Dumpster. She tapped in the home number for Jeremy Whitman that she'd gotten at campaign headquarters and watched the small screen blink and fade out in the light from the dashboard.

"Jeremy here." The name was slurred and faint against the bar noise in the background. Undercurrents of conversations, clinking glasses, a ringing phone.

Ryan hesitated. She had assumed he was at home, safely tucked away in the castle loft. But he was still at a bar. She shut the phone, aware of the adrenaline pumping through her. She pulled the hoodie low over her forehead, then jammed her foot on the accelerator, wheeled out of the lot and headed for the castle. The cell started ringing. God, Jeremy was calling back. She fumbled with the buttons and managed to shut it off. She would have to get rid of the cell tonight. Jeremy could be starting home now. She could picture him hurrying along the sidewalk, crossing the street at the corner, dodging under the canopy into the entry. Smiling and waving at the guard, stepping into the elevator. And she was blocks away. She pushed the accelerator to fifty, sixty, squealing around the corners, then forced herself to slow down. There couldn't be any record of her being pulled over. How would she answer the questions? What were you doing in the neighborhood when one of Mathews's staffers was shot?

She kept the sedan at the speed limit through LoDo. The bars had let out, and groups of people were wandering about, weaving across the middle of the streets, calling to one another through the traffic. She looked hard for the tall, slim, muscle-knotted man with blond hair who had stared at her this afternoon and looked away, a mixture of recognition and fear blossoming on his pink face. He was nowhere.

Ryan parked two blocks away from the Hudson building. The video cameras, she knew, stopped at the next block. She pulled back the layers of newspaper on the package until the .38 Ruger, black and shiny, new looking, was exposed and slipped it inside the pocket of her sweatshirt. For an instant, she stepped back in time. She was a rookie cop in Minneapolis, walking the streets and once in a while drawing a surveillance, the kind of assignment that had allowed her to prove herself and had gotten her promoted.

She got out and, staying close to the buildings, hunched inside herself, she made her way toward the Hudson building. Even when the cameras picked her up, she would be nothing more than a dark shadow moving against brick walls. She had a clear view of the glass front door, the overhead lights flaring across the sidewalk, from the doorway she ducked into. After only a few moments, she saw Jeremy Whitman lurching down the sidewalk toward her. He was alone. Every few steps, he pressed his shoulder against the wall for a moment before pushing off. He was drunk, and that made things easier. She waited until he was at the doorway, then she stepped out. "Hello, Jeremy," she said, keeping her shoulders hunched, turned in on herself, away from the cameras.

He did a series of rapid eye blinks, as if he were trying to conceal the fact that he recognized her. The smell of alcohol poured off him like the odor of a wet cat. He took a couple of steps backward, then tried to lurch past, but she took hold of his arm and held him in place. The hard knots of his muscles meant nothing; he was drunk. She could topple him with one shove. She smiled at the idea, and that seemed to unnerve him even more. He rammed his arm toward her, as if he could push his way through a crowd. "Get away from me," he said.

"I want to talk to you." Ryan stayed in front of him, still hunched forward. His eyes darted about, as if he expected someone to materialize out of the brick walls and whisk him away. "We have a great deal in common. We both loved David Mathews."

He swallowed hard, his Adam's apple bobbing like a cork. He licked at his lips, gathering courage, she guessed, before he said, "You were at his house when he was killed."

She could feel herself still smiling. "That is ridiculous." He had surmised more than she anticipated. Somehow he had placed her at the house. The image of the dark figure on the sidewalk floated before her. Jeremy Whitman on his way to David's house last night? Oh, this was perfect. She had thought there were two people who might link her to David, but there was only one, the scared, drunk guy in front of her reeking of alcohol and fear. Tonight she would solve both problems.

"I want to find David's killer as much as you do," she said, the good cop, cajoling him toward a place of safety from which he was unlikely to bolt down the street screaming. "I wouldn't want to be removed from the investigation because you happened to see us together."

"You killed him." He seemed almost sober.

"We need to straighten things out." She nudged him toward the car. She knew exactly where she would take him; she hadn't known before, but now it was as clear as a map on her GPS. Out to Lakewood, along an old creek bed where a new light-rail was under construction, with piles of dirt and bulldozers and tractors, where a body might not be noticed for days. "We'll go to headquarters, and you can tell the officers on duty everything you know about me. I'm anxious to get this behind me. I want to worry about finding David's killer, so let's clear the air. What do you say?"

"You must think I'm stupid," he said. "I'm not going anywhere with you."

"Get in the car." She removed the gun slowly and pressed it against his side.

"You gonna kill me, like you killed David?" He seemed to settle into the sidewalk, as if his boots had gotten stuck in cement. "You'll never get away with it. I'm not the only one who knows."

Ryan pushed the nozzle harder into his side. "What are you talking about?"

"Somebody saw you last night. A witness was outside. She heard the gunshots and saw you leave David's house. You gonna kill her, too? You gonna keep killing until nobody's left?"

"Where did you hear this?" Another campaign staffer, she was thinking, on her way to see David last night. To sleep with David! Did he not have any pride? Any sense of decorum? Any sense of risk? "Who told you?"

"It doesn't matter. The truth will come out. The newspaper knows about the witness."

"You're lying!" Ryan was aware of her hand shaking. It was impossible, and yet it made sense. The shadowy figure out on the sidewalk had been too afraid to go to the police. She might be dismissed as a crank, and the detective she had accused would know who she was. So she had gone to the *Journal*. But the *Journal* couldn't prove any connection between her and David, until Jeremy Whitman had lumbered into the picture. Jeremy, who could also connect her to David. She tightened her grip on the gun, her finger quivered on the trigger.

Jeremy made a move as if he intended to walk away, and Ryan jammed the gun into his flesh, close to his heart. "You're not gonna shoot me," he said. "There would be witnesses." There was no one around, she was thinking. The sidewalks had emptied, there was no traffic. "Somebody looking out the window," he went on, the cockiness about him making her hate him. She could feel the hatred erupting inside, the way it had with David, grinning and wagging a finger at her, saying, "You're not going to shoot me."

She pulled the trigger and watched Jeremy stagger backward, the shock of it registering on his face, just as it had registered on David's. She leaned over his body, warmth emanating from his chest and face, his eyes wide and frozen, and managed to extract the wallet from the back pocket of his jeans. The area was deserted, the old brick buildings silent, lights glinting in the windows here and there. She walked back to the sedan, hovering close to the buildings, and made sure no one was around before she got behind the wheel and drove away.

16

The shivering had started before she reached her apartment. On the Dumpster dump, stomping on the cell phone and tossing the pieces in different Dumpsters in different alleys, watching over her shoulder for the moving shadow of some homeless guy huddled in a cardboard box who might get curious and go looking for what she left behind, or a patrol cop checking alleys in LoDo.

Shivering as she drove across town to the Golden Triangle and the one-bedroom apartment in the 1920s building with the steel and glass art deco façade. Shivering so hard in the elevator, she had trouble pressing the button for the sixth floor, the number jumping in front of her eyes. It had taken three tries before she managed to jam the key into her lock. Thirty minutes in the hot shower, shivering, dropping onto the floor, gripping her legs to her chest, pulling in on herself with the water pounding her back. Now, trussed up in the worn blue terrycloth robe that had followed her through twenty years, Ryan lay on top of the bed, curled into a fetal position, images playing in her head and projecting themselves on the walls and ceiling, dancing about with the slats of light that worked past the blinds. She couldn't escape. She would drown in the images.

This was not the way it was supposed to be, everything so twisted and messed up. They were supposed to be together, she and David. Not right away, she had accepted that, but soon after he had settled into the governor's job. There would be the early months in office when the press would scrutinize everything he said and did, every policy he proposed. But that would also be the honeymoon period when everyone wanted the new governor to succeed. No matter what the reporters wrote, the people would give him the benefit of the doubt.

That reporter—who wrote the articles she had seen in the newspaper? Catherine McLeod?— had been a pain in the neck. Digging into the fraud charges brought by the idiot old man who had been David's partner. Even after the charges were dropped and the matter settled, McLeod had kept showing up, asking questions, delving into public records. David had finally made a call to the publisher with a pointed but gentle reminder—David was a master at throwing a steel punch inside a velvet glove—that the fraud issue was over, settled. After all, David and the publisher served on civic boards together. They were the same kind of people, as David had put it. Ryan remembered wincing at that, as if he had thrown a steel and velvet punch at her, a reminder she was not one of them.

McLeod had kept on during the campaign, probing beneath the smooth surface that David and his staff created. And now this! She could feel the pressure of her knees tight against her chest. Somehow McLeod had learned about the woman on the sidewalk. She must have told Whitman. How else could he have known? She had probably insisted that Whitman go to Internal Affairs and spill everything about Aspen, and that would have been the beginning of the end. Pulled off the investigation, asked a lot of questions about her relationship to David Mathews. She would have become a suspect. Some bright investigator might have gone to the evidence room, found her name on the sign-in sheet the day before she left on vacation. Maybe even discovered that a gun was missing. Oh, that would have taken some work, but it could have happened. The missing gun could have been identified as the murder weapon.

Then Catherine McLeod would have played her trump card—the witness. The image of the dark figure on the sidewalk burst past the other images: David stumbling backward, the blond-haired staffer crumbling against the brick wall, the same stunned look in their eyes. Like a projection on the wall across from the bed was the slim figure on the sidewalk, swaying a little as if she were caught in the wind or summoning the energy to run. Whoever she was, she had contacted McLeod. But here was the thing: McLeod couldn't do anything.

Ryan loosened her grip around her legs and watched them stretch down the bed, as if they belonged to someone else, the feet wrinkled and gray in the slatted light. She let her arms fall along her sides, willing herself to relax. McLeod could do nothing. She had counted on Whitman to tell Internal Affairs about Aspen. But Jeremy Whitman would not be talking to anyone, which meant that, more than likely, whoever had been on the sidewalk would refuse to stick her neck out.

Except, the bitch had already contacted Catherine McLeod, and McLeod was the kind of reporter who couldn't let things go.

Ryan pushed herself off the bed, went over to the dresser and stared at herself in the mirror. Her hair was still wet, plastered to her head. Her face had a scrubbed, skeleton look, eyes dark and opaque. She couldn't see into them. Her work wasn't done yet. She had known all along, she realized, and it was the knowledge that had brought on the terrible shivering. Jeremy Whitman was only part of the problem. She would have to find the witness and silence her before Catherine McLeod could convince her to go to the police. And then, of course, she would have to deal with Catherine McLeod.

The morning was cool, the first hints of autumn in the air, but Catherine could feel the warmth of the sun on her shoulders and the backs of her legs as she jogged along the sidewalk with Rex pulling ahead on the leash. She'd had a few glasses of wine last night, and a dull ache buzzed in her head. Highland was a hilly neighborhood, built on bluffs, and she had felt the strain in her calf muscles as she and Rex ran up a steep hill a few blocks from home. They hit an easy stride across the top, running past deep front lawns and trimmed bushes that abutted the brick bungalows, the sun wavering ahead. She tried for a run with the dog every day, either in the mornings or the evenings, whatever worked out. Yesterday nothing had worked out. She'd left for the office after hearing about Mathews, and she'd gone to Nick's last night.

They rounded the corner and started downhill. Rex knew the route by heart; it was as if he were leading her, ears flattened, nose pointed, intent on his job. He'd been dancing around the kitchen by the time she got home last night. Early morning, really, almost 3:00 a.m. She hadn't meant to fall asleep at Nick's. Somewhere in the blackness, she had become dimly aware of noises, a ringing phone, rushing water, padding footsteps. She had sensed the movements and displacement of air and bolted awake, disoriented for a moment, the familiar surroundings of her own bedroom nowhere in sight. Nick had leaned over and she had felt his lips brush her forehead. "Sorry to wake you," he'd said. He was dressed in dark slacks and a light-colored shirt with the sleeves rolled partway up. "Have to go to work."

"What time is it?" Catherine had pushed herself up on one elbow and squinted at the clock on the bedside table. 2:17 a.m. Panic had rushed through her. She'd had every intention of going home before midnight and getting some sleep. She had wanted to be at her best this morning when she met Jeremy. There was always the chance he would decide against going to Internal Affairs. After all, he'd been half-drunk last night, and how well she knew that things had a way of looking different in the sober morning. She would need her wits about her if he had changed his mind. She had swung her legs off the bed and begun gathering her clothes strung over the floor. "Rex is waiting," she said.

"If I weren't so secure in our relationship"—Nick had walked into the bathroom and was combing his hair in front of the mirror—"I'd be wondering, who's Rex?"

She had dressed hurriedly, pulling on her blouse and skirt, stepping into her high-heeled sandals and running her fingers through her hair. She must have asked Nick about the phone call because he told her some guy had been mugged in LoDo, robbed and shot to death.

"Another random gang attack?" she'd said. The *Journal* had covered the attacks, that is, whenever Jason Metcalf had been able to pry new information out of the police. Random gang attacks wasn't a story anybody in Denver wanted plastered on the front pages, certainly not the restaurants, galleries and theaters that depended on people coming downtown. Nick had worked the investigations from the beginning, but the attacks weren't something they talked about. His work and her work were incompatible in some ways. Best left at the front door.

"I really can't speculate," he said, the smallest edge in his voice that suggested he was aware he was talking to a reporter. Had just slept with a reporter who—he had to know—was halfway in love with him. Still there was always that line that dropped between them at the most unexpected moments.

He had walked her outside, across the small concrete porch and down the sidewalk to her convertible. The neighborhood was still, except for the intermittent clicking noise of a cricket. The daisies and petunias that she and Nick had planted last May had a washed out, green cast in the moonlight. Before he closed her door, he'd leaned over and said, "I'll call you tomorrow."

She had driven through the empty streets of Highland, turned into the alley behind her house and parked next to the garage. Shadows filled the rows of backyards on either side of hers. The houses were dark, except for a couple of lights glowing in the windows next door and the light she had left on in her kitchen, which threw an eerie illumination across her yard. In the kitchen window, she could see Rex jumping about. His barking was muffled, but she recognized the tone—a mixture of scolding and relief.

The minute she unlocked the door and pushed it open, Rex had come bounding outside. She closed the door and watched him from the window. This affair with Nick Bustamante really wasn't fair to Rex. Leaving him alone so many evenings, missing his walks. She wondered if it was fair to anyone.

As soon as Rex had scratched at the door, she let him in. Then she had poured a glass of red wine. She had meant to put the bottle away—it was always better when the wine bottles were pushed far back in the cabinet, easier to tell herself she no longer needed a drink when she couldn't see the bottles. But the bottle was still on the counter, shimmering in the light. She carried her glass down the shadowy hall into her bedroom. By the time she had finished the wine and gone back to the kitchen to refill her glass, Rex was snoring on his bed in the corner of her bedroom.

She could always count on jogging to push the dull, fuzzy headache into some peripheral part of her brain where it wasn't as noticeable. It was working this morning. Rex took the corner a half block from home and broke into a run. She unhooked the leash and jogged after him, not taking her eyes away as he raced up the little grassy hill in front of her house. It was a moment before she realized that a black sedan had pulled close to the curb and was slowing down. Nick was behind the wheel. He had the passenger window rolled down before she ran over. She leaned into the window, jogging in place. "What is it?" she said, still keeping an eye on Rex who must have seen the car before she did because he came bounding toward her.

"We have the ID on the mugging victim," he said. "I thought you might like to know."

"Who is he?" The sense of dread was like a weight pressing down on her. It was unlike Nick to want to inform her about any investigation he was on.

"One of Mathews's staffers," he said. "Name of Jeremy Whitman."

Catherine pressed her hand over her mouth and looked away. She was aware of Rex crowding her legs, and she reached down and grabbed his collar. The leather felt rough against her palms. She grabbed the leash, giving herself a moment, a jumble of thoughts racing through her head. Jeremy would have alerted Internal Affairs this morning, and by afternoon, Detective Beckman would have been pulled off the investigation. Now Jeremy was dead.

"Are you okay?" Nick got out of the car and came around to her. He set a hand on her shoulder.

"I just needed a minute," she said.

"You knew him?"

She tried to swallow, but it was as if she had a mouth full of sand. "I've seen him at campaign events. I met him for the first time yesterday," she said. "What happened?"

"Mugged," Nick said. "Robbed. Wallet's missing. Probably tried to put up a fight and was shot."

Catherine had to look away again. There was nothing to say. If she told Nick Bustamante about Mathews and Beckman in Aspen and the witness on the telephone, he would have to take the information to police headquarters. And what would that accomplish? Nothing. Stories from a dead man and an anonymous caller? But Detective Beckman would know someone besides Jeremy Whitman knew about her.

"I've got to get to the newsroom," Catherine said. She was aware that Nick intended to kiss her, but he had only brushed her cheek with his lips before she started running up the sidewalk behind Rex.

17

The Evergreen house, an oasis hidden in the pines, and the pines singing in the wind. Quietly sumptuous, not loud and clamoring for attention like some houses where Ryan had gone on domestic disturbances, but filled with quiet antiques and art she had seen in magazines, flipping the pages, wondering if anyone actually lived like that! All tastefully furnished with Sydney's money, she had assumed when David brought her here. She had even asked if that was the case as she sunk into the deep, soft mattress with the silky sheets, candlelight flickering over the damask walls, worry nipping at her that he might not want to risk losing such luxury. David had given her the kind of smile meant to evaporate her concerns. "I can buy and sell Sydney," he said, crawling in beside her and taking her in his arms.

Now Sydney Mathews stood at the front door, barefoot, looking as if she had slept in the black tee shirt and knit slacks static plastered to her legs. She ran her fingers through her hair and shifted her gaze from

Ryan to Martin and out to the Jefferson County sheriff's officers below the porch steps. "I've told you all I know," she said. The smallest quiver of uncertainty split her voice, as if she knew the fate about to overtake her, and also knew there was nothing she could do. For an instant, Ryan almost pitied the woman.

"Contact my lawyer," Sydney said.

"We have a search warrant for the house and premises." Ryan held out the warrant signed by a Jefferson County district judge this morning after she and Martin had produced the phone records showing numerous calls between the two houses in the hours before David was murdered. The warrant specified computers, phones, financial records and a possible gun. They had also informed the judge about the couple's public argument at campaign headquarters and separation. A slim thread of evidence to connect Sydney to the murder, Ryan knew, and she had held her breath as the judge rubbed his chin and studied the warrant. Finally he had picked up a pen and scratched his name.

"Search the house?" Sydney let out an angry scoff. "That's ridiculous! I'm getting my brother." She leaned into the house and yelled: "Wendell! Wendell! I need you!"

"What is it?" Ryan could see the man galloping down the stairway that ascended along the entry wall. He wore a navy blue exercise outfit, casual and rumpled with white stripes running down the sides of the pant legs.

"They say they have a search warrant," Sydney wailed, as if the idea was inconceivable, something that occurred in the public housing projects and other places she never went. She leaned against her brother who slipped an arm around her shoulders to hold her up, Ryan thought, because otherwise, the woman looked as if she might crumble onto the polished wood floor.

"Take your search warrant and shove it," Wendell said. "We're calling our lawyer." He grabbed the door and started to shut it, but Martin had already shouldered himself inside.

"Call all the lawyers you want," Ryan said. She was aware of the scratch of tires behind her, the slamming of car doors. Searching a house this big would take at least six detectives. Sergeant Crowley would be here in a few minutes. "We're searching the house and grounds," she said. "Two detectives will take the outside." She tossed her head back toward the Jeffco officers standing below the porch. "The other detectives will take the upstairs. My partner and I will search the main floor. You and Mr. Lane will wait in the corner of the great room under an officer's guard."

"This is preposterous." Wendell shifted from one tennis shoe to the other, a man accustomed to being in control, Ryan thought, giving orders, not taking them, out of his comfort zone now.

Martin kept his shoulder against the door. "Let's go," he said.

Out of the corner of her eye, Ryan saw two detectives peel off and start moving around the boulders and pines in front of the house, kicking at piles of leaves and pine needles. The other detectives came up the steps—burly sport coats pushing past the couple, ignoring Sydney Mathews with her wide, affronted eyes and her fist jammed against her mouth, ignoring her brother with the angry red rash rising on his neck above the collar of his shirt. Wendell was trying to sooth his sister, speaking softly, as if Ryan and Martin and the other detectives couldn't hear, pulling his cell phone out of the clip on his belt, saying he would call the lawyer, she wasn't to worry. One of the Jeffco officers ushered them toward the back of the house.

The other two detectives started up the wide staircase in the entry just as Sergeant Crowley and four lab techs came through the door. "We're just getting started," Ryan told the sergeant. "I thought I would take the rooms at the back of the house. Martin will concentrate on the living room and office." She nodded toward the rooms on either side.

Crowley wore a satisfied look on his fleshy face, and Ryan knew the sergeant would take the entire house, walking around, assisting in the search, making sure everything was done by the book. With a high-profile case like this, there couldn't be any mistakes. One of the lab techs pulled a camera out of the bag on his shoulder as the other techs followed Martin into the living room.

Ryan headed into the great room where a bank of windows framed views of the high mountain peaks, crevices laced with snow. Clouds shot through with sunlight drifted across the sky. Just beyond the windows clumps of yellow and purple mums rose out of a bed of rocks and scraggly bushes. Sydney and Wendell were huddled on a small sofa in the far corner, the uniform standing beside them.

Ryan pulled on a pair of plastic gloves, lifted the cushions of the larger sofa onto the floor, and began checking for unusual bumps or hard places. She ran her fingers along the inside edge of the sofa. Nothing, but what had she expected to find in this poor, deluded woman's house? Believing her husband's lies, agreeing to take him back. God, it was pathetic.

She left the cushions on the floor and moved on to the tables and credenzas, yanking out drawers, rifling through the collections of papers, notebooks, scissors, rubber bands, feeling a little electric charge moving through her. There was something almost unbearably exciting about trashing the place in front of David's wife. She was barely aware of the soft whisperings on the other side of the room: "It'll be all right. Routine in a murder investigation. Landon's on the way." Landon being the lawyer, Ryan knew.

She walked over to the bookcase that occupied an entire wall and began pulling the books from the shelves, taking pleasure in it, memories crowding around her: *You mean you haven't read Gibbons? What about Shakespeare? Don't tell me you haven't read* Hamlet! *What about Jane Austen? I would think you had devoured her, all those women desperate for men?*

"I'm afraid I haven't had the time, David," she had told him. They had stood in front of the shelves, and he had removed one book, then another, holding the gilded leather covers as if they were real gold, thumbing the pages so gently they might have been breakable, amusement and a sense of superiority floating off him like aftershave. She had wanted to pick up a book and smash his face. She had come off a pig farm in North Dakota, the kind of life that exceeded David Mathews's powers of imagination, given the name of the boy she should have been—a boy who would have grown up to run the farm. She had a two-year associate's degree in the local community college. Oh, my God, how proud she had been of that associate's degree, until she found out how little it meant to people like David with a degree from the University of Illinois. She had learned about herself that evening in front of the bookcase. She was smarter than David Mathews in the ways that counted. She could handle herself; she knew how to get what she wanted. He would leave his wife for her, that was a certainty. She had that kind of power.

He had set the books back on the shelves. "If Sydney notices anything out of place, she'll wonder what I was doing," he'd said. "She knows I like to show the books to friends." He had bestowed another one of those smiles. "And lovers." Then he had hurried on—she could almost feel him beside her now, tidying up the shelves, hear the familiar tone of his voice—*We have the whole night. Sydney won't return from New York until tomorrow afternoon. The whole night, just for us.*

Ryan had wanted more than one night, and she had told him so. "We belong together," she'd told him a dozen times, and he had agreed, lying on the big silky mattress with the silky sheet tucked around his waist. He would have agreed to anything then, she realized now. She removed a stack of books, flipped through the pages of one and threw it on the floor. Then the next, and the next, looking for nothing. Except, perhaps, a letter from Good-times Kim. She decided to be more vigilant, actually look inside the books, instead of going through the motions. Such a letter might exist.

"For godssakes, be careful," Sydney said. "They're very valuable. They've been in the family for years."

Wendell started whispering again, something about not expecting Ryan to care about such things. She slammed another book hard on top of the stacks growing at her feet. The book slid off and clunked onto the floor. Sydney groaned.

The piles of books stood almost two feet deep when Ryan moved on to another credenza across the room. She turned the drawers upside down and shook out letters and papers, wondering when Martin would finish in the living room and move on to the study. She went down on one knee, lifted each letter and examined the address. Most were from Chicago, some dated years ago, probably from Sydney's family and friends.

"Those are private," Sydney said.

Ryan opened one of the letters. The painstaking script was the kind she hadn't seen in years, not since the elementary school posters of beautiful handwriting plastered on the walls. The letter was signed "Your loving Mother." Ryan glanced through the scrolled words.

"How dare you," Sydney shouted. "You have no business reading my private correspondence."

Ryan went back to pawing through the other letters from Sydney's mother. So Sydney had married David Mathews against her mother's wishes. Even in the last letter, she had urged her daughter to leave David. "He has never been one of us" she had written.

Ryan left the letters tumbled over the floor and headed into the kitchen. Out of the corner of her eye, she saw Martin stride across the entry. Her heart started hammering. My God, was it possible he would neglect to search the desk drawers? Then another possibility worked its way into her thoughts. What if Sydney or her odious brother had found the gun, realized it had been planted, and disposed of it?

Sunlight flared through the wide windows that overlooked the L-shaped kitchen counters and dark cherry cabinets and shiny steel appliances. "We hardly use the kitchen," David had said. "We eat out, or take in." He was talking about himself and Sydney, giving her a little glimpse into their private, domestic life, and Ryan had wanted to throw up. "Don't tell me about her," she had said. "She doesn't matter. We're all that matters." They'd eaten Chinese out of the cartons at the granite-topped counter dividing the kitchen. She had picked up dinner on her way to Evergreen.

Now she started yanking open the drawers, rummaging through them, dumping them on the floor. The bastard! And all the time he was making love to her—promising, promising—he had been planning to reconcile with Sydney. Her family money had bound them together.

"I hope you intend to clean this up." Wendell shouted from the great room.

Ryan walked back into the room and faced the man. "Where were you the night he was murdered?"

"Talk to my lawyer."

"Hey, Ryan." It was Martin shouting from the front of the house. Ryan pulled out a drawer and let it drop onto the floor before she started for the entry. She could hear the detectives moving about upstairs. Martin stood in front of the desk in the study, two of the techs beside him. His hideout, David had called the study. The only place he could get away from Sydney, he'd said, and she had believed him. She had wanted to believe him.

"Look what we have here." Martin held the middle desk drawer open while one of the techs trained a camera on the Sig Sauer 226. "Nine millimeter," he said. "Same as the murder weapon. If it is the murder weapon, that woman is stupid to leave it around." He shook his head in the direction of the great room. "Or just cocky."

There was the swoosh of the front door opening, the hard clack of footsteps in the entry. "Sydney?" It was a man's voice.

Ryan watched Sydney Mathews rush past the door and throw herself into the arms of a bulky, gray-haired man in a dark suit creased across the crotch. The officer moved next to Sydney, her brother a couple of steps behind. "Thank God you're here, Landon." Sydney sounded as if she might burst into tears. "They've torn up my house. God knows what they're doing outside, probably digging up the grounds."

Wendell moved in closer, placed a hand on his sister's shoulder and pulled her out of the lawyer's arms. "What right do they have to do this?" he said. "My sister is mourning the horrible murder of her husband. This is unconscionable."

"You have a signed warrant?" Landon the lawyer strolled into the study, and Ryan slipped the warrant out of her blazer pocket. Before she could hand it to the man, Sergeant Crowley materialized between them. He took the warrant and handed it to the lawyer who took his time perusing the document, studying the judge's signature. "I want a list of everything you remove from the house," he said, dropping the warrant on the desk.

Martin held up the gun he had just placed inside a plastic bag. "Could be the murder weapon in a desk drawer," he said.

"You can't possibly believe that!" the lawyer said. "My client is entitled to own a weapon. You have no evidence the gun was used to kill her husband."

"Landon, the gun's not mine." Sydney gripped the lawyer's arm, her face a white mask, blue eyes bulging and bloodred lips stretched in a grimace of shock. "I've never seen that gun before."

The other detectives pounded down the stairs and shouldered their way into the study past Sydney and the two men. "Clear on the second floor," the first detective said, his voice low.

"The gun could have been David's." The lawyer reached around and patted Sydney's hand. "Don't worry. It means nothing. Ballistic tests will prove the gun was not used . . ." He stopped and drew his lips into a tight line.

"This is an outrage," Wendell said, turning toward Crowley. "You have no right to persecute my sister. Take what you've found and get out of here."

"It's not that simple," Crowley said. He held the gaze of the lawyer, still steadying Sydney Mathews. "We have reason to believe Sydney Mathews went to the house in Denver two nights ago, argued with her husband, and shot him to death. I'm confident ballistics will show that she used this weapon."

"So you have a gun," the lawyer said. "You have no proof this weapon was used to murder David. You're making an outrageous supposition." The lawyer half turned toward the woman gripping his arm. She had the faraway look in her eyes that Ryan had seen in the eyes of other suspects, as if they were floating away from reality, looking for someplace to hide.

"Try not to worry." The lawyer slipped an arm around Sydney's shoulders. "This will all be cleared up. They have nothing."

Ryan watched them taking photos of the study, placing a plastic bag over the computer, sealing it, initialing the bag. There wasn't yet probable cause to arrest Sydney Mathews for the murder of her husband, but there would be soon. A sense of euphoria swept over her. She was the leader of the parade.

18

"Police are calling Whitman's death a mugging." Jason Metcalf perched on the corner of his desk, dangling one foot, tapping out an intermittent rhythm on the floor with the other. "Gangland style. Could have been a gang initiation. Whitman was ordered to throw down his wallet and he refused. The mugger shot him, got hold of the wallet, emptied the bills and tossed the rest onto the sidewalk."

"It wasn't a mugging," Catherine said.

"We don't know that for certain." Marjorie had walked over and positioned herself in the doorway of Jason's cubicle. "Stranger coincidences have happened."

"Jeremy Whitman saw Mathews and Beckman together in Aspen in June," Catherine said. "It upset him because he believed all the press releases about David and Sydney, the happy couple. He believed in David. So David explained to Jeremy how he had run into an old flame, and that's all there was to it. He had Don Cannon tell him the same thing. In other words, David was determined to convince Whitman he hadn't seen what'd he'd seen."

"Cannon knows who the woman was?"

Catherine shook her head and pressed a shoulder against the bookcase. "David said he wanted to protect the woman's privacy. He didn't give Don her name. And Jeremy didn't know the woman was Detective Beckman until yesterday when he saw her at campaign headquarters. That's when he got scared. He didn't know what to do . . ."

"Let me guess," Marjorie put in. "You tracked him down and convinced him to go to the police."

"He agreed to go with me this morning," Catherine said. "He didn't just happen to get mugged last night. Beckman recognized him and knew he could connect her to Mathews." She drew in a long breath; she would have liked a drink now. A sip of Burgundy. She went on: "The caller recognized Beckman coming out of David's house. Whoever the caller is, she's in danger. The only thing I've learned so far is that she may drive a black BMW."

"You told Bustamante any of this?" Jason said.

"No." Catherine took in another breath and exhaled through clenched teeth. She had wanted to tell him. She had wanted to close the space that gaped between them, but she hadn't wanted to take the chance that Nick would alert Beckman. She hadn't trusted him, she realized. He might stand with Beckman; they were both part of the thin blue line. Ironic, she thought. Beckman was alerted anyway. "I told Jeremy about the witness," she said.

Jason stood up, plunged his hands into his pockets and started patrolling the small cubicle. "Beckman could have seen the witness on the sidewalk. You think Jeremy told her the witness contacted you?"

"Let's assume he did," Marjorie said. "Beckman's top priority has to be finding the witness. Now she's going to worry about you."

Catherine had to turn away. She stared out over the newsroom, the routine chaos of bobbing heads, clicking computer keys and ringing phones. A normal morning, gathering the news from the city, the state, the police, the FBI, the wire services, trying to make the connections and fill in the spaces that the politicians and bureaucrats preferred to leave blank.

Marjorie was going on about how Catherine should take time off, get away for a while. Exactly what she had told Jeremy last night. "I'm going to insist on this," Marjorie said, and Catherine thought about how she should have insisted with Jeremy. "We can't take any chances."

Catherine swung around. "Beckman doesn't know what the witness might have said, and she doesn't know who I've told. We could all be in danger. Now isn't the time to back off."

Marjorie sank back against the glass wall of the cubicle, this new possibility deepening the worry in her eyes. She shot a glance at Jason, who had stopped in mid-stride and was looking at Catherine, as if he had never seen her before. The police reporter, shooting the breeze with the cops, throwing back beer in the cop bars, writing up the reports on murders and robberies and carjackings and gang muggings, never considering the possibility that he might become the subject of one of those reports. Beckman would assume the police reporter and the editor knew everything.

"You could be right." Marjorie faced Catherine. "We need to double our efforts to find the witness. Put a message on your blog. *To the woman who called yesterday, please call back. Very important.* Somebody close to Mathews drives a black BMW. Find out who." She started to back out of the cubicle, then stopped. "One other thing. Find everything you can on Detective Beckman. Jason, that means you. Talk to your cop friends, get them to tell you what they really think about her. Go off the record, if you have to. We need to know who we're up against."

Jason started fumbling with the small black case attached to his belt. "I gotta take this," he said, extracting his cell and clamping it against his ear. "What?" he said. "When?" He stood rooted in place, breathing hard. "I'm on my way." He snapped the phone shut and, still clutching it in his hand, said, "Sydney Mathews is about to be arrested for the murder of her husband. An arrest warrant's been issued."

Catherine felt as if her throat were paralyzed. She couldn't spit out the words jamming themselves together in a hard knot. How can it be? What evidence?

"My contact says they found the murder weapon in the Evergreen house. Ballistics confirmed the two bullets they dug out of the wall and the one in Mathews's chest came from the weapon. He says they've got other evidence to tie her to the murder."

"Well, that changes everything." Marjorie looked from Jason to Catherine. "Seems like we could have gotten ahead of ourselves here. Who knows what motivated the caller to want to implicate a police detective."

"The caller was telling the truth," Catherine said. The tight, clipped sound of her voice surprised her. "Beckman's found a way to frame somebody else, and Sydney's an easy target. She and David were separated, and Sydney could have had a motive to want him dead. It wouldn't have been hard for Beckman to set up—"

"All you've got is conjecture," Marjorie said. "We can't operate on conjecture and anonymous phone calls. The so-called witness could be a crank. We'll have to wait and see how this plays out."

She pivoted toward Jason, but before she could say anything, he said, "I gotta get down to police headquarters and find out what's going on."

After he left, Catherine locked eyes with Marjorie for a long moment, aware of the silence running between them and the sounds of the newsroom muffled by the glass walls. "Beckman knows what she's doing," she said finally. "She'll see to it that Sydney Mathews goes to prison for a murder she didn't commit."

"You want me to believe that?" Marjorie said. "Then find the damn witness."

Catherine sank into the chair in front of her desk, logged into the computer and pulled up her blog. She scrolled to the top of a new page and typed: "To the anonymous caller. Please call again. Very important."

She stared at the cryptic words. The sense of doubt curled like a snake inside her. There was every chance the caller didn't know about the blog. And if she did happen to read today's entry, there was no reason to think she would call back. As soon as Sydney was arrested, the news would be splashed all over the radio and TV. Jason would have it up on the website, and all of it could send the witness into deeper hiding. Would she really want to implicate the police detective who had just arrested the perfect suspect? Catherine doubted it. The woman, whoever she was, was sure to sense that the risk was too great. Detective Ryan Beckman was close to getting away with murder, and she wouldn't hesitate to kill the woman on the sidewalk if she found her. She had already killed the witness who had seen her with David.

"Denver Police Detective Ryan Beckman." Catherine had a sick, helpless feeling as she typed in the key words and watched the list of websites settle into place. Two sites highlighted Beckman's name. The rest had zeroed in on police, detective, Denver, but showed nothing with Ryan Beckman. Catherine brought up the first site, a *Journal* article with her own byline. The headline in bold black type read: "Well-Known Developer Investigated." She scanned through the lines of text, the article coming back to her. *David Mathews, prominent Denver businessman, philanthropist and possible candidate for governor under investigation for the alleged theft of ten million dollars from Kane and Mathews Properties. Senior partner Broderick Kane lodged a complaint with the Denver District Attorney's Office asking that appropriate charges be filed against Mathews. According to Kane, the missing funds were discovered after Kane hired independent accountants to audit the properties managed by Mathews.*

Contacted at his home, Mathews called the accusations ridiculous and without foundation. "I have been a conscientious partner of this firm." He said he has also hired an accounting firm to conduct an audit. "I'm confident we will find all money properly accounted for."

The accusation against Mathews follows a bitter breakup of Kane and Mathews, according to an inside source who did not wish to be named. Mathews had joined the firm five years ago and has been a partner for three years. The funds have been unaccounted for in the last three years. Detective Ryan Beckman said that Kane brought the complaint to the Denver police department. "We take accusations of financial theft very seriously," she said. Both the police department and the district attorney's office are investigating the accusation.

Catherine read through the article again, looking for. . . what? Some insight into Detective Beckman? Some hint of a rogue cop capable of committing murder? The statement was the standard comment on an ongoing investigation: "We take acccusations of financial theft very seriously." Nothing to indicate that Beckman was different from any other police detective. The only thing the article confirmed was that Beckman had been part of an investigation that put her into contact with David Mathews.

Catherine brought up the next site. Here was something: an article from the *Minneapolis Star Tribune* with the headline: "Detective Exonerated." The article was brief: *An internal police investigation has exonerated Detective Ryan Beckman for her role in last August's shooting death of Darnell Clapman. Beckman was among the officers who responded to a hostage call after Clapman allegedly took his girlfriend, Lois Michaels, hostage and was threatening to kill her. When police officers broke into the apartment where Michaels was being held, Clapman pointed a pistol at the officers. Beckman then fired her weapon. In her statement to the investigating commission, Michaels denied that Clapman held her hostage. She claimed they had argued, but Clapman had never threatened her. Michaels said he was in the process of dropping the gun when he was shot. Other officers at the scene corroborated Detective Beckman's statements. The investigation concluded that Beckman had shown exemplary courage in performing her duty as a police officer in the face of danger. "I know guys like Clapman," Beckman said when informed of the exoneration. "He would have killed that poor girl or one of the officers."*

There it was, Catherine thought, the piece she had been looking for. Ryan Beckman, the good officer. Tough, confident, courageous, unafraid to take risks, willing to act, willing to shoot, cool and self-possessed under stress, always in control. The type of person who plotted her way forward, never looking back, making sure to eliminate any threats as she went. Everything had worked out in Minneapolis. There was every possibility she had gotten away with murder because the other officers had stood by her. But she couldn't be sure it would happen again if Jeremy Whitman had gone to Internal Affairs. Or if the caller should come forward.

Catherine sat motionless for a moment. She wasn't that tough. She hadn't been able to shake the nightmares that came with having killed a man, hadn't been able to shrug it off and say, "Well, he would have killed me." There was a piece of Detective Beckman that eluded her, something she couldn't quite grasp. What kind of woman can shoot a man—and go on killing?

She could almost hear Marjorie say: "Take time off. Go Away." What if she did go away? When would the killing stop? After Beckman killed the witness? Then what? Would Beckman go after Jason or Marjorie? She would never be able to return to Denver, Catherine realized. She would always be watching over her shoulder, checking the rearview mirror, jumping at noises in the pipes or the nighttime sounds in her own home, accumulating nightmares.

She typed in a new search for the *Minneapolis Star Tribune*, found a telephone number and called the newsroom. A gruff, impatient voice picked up. "Newsroom," he barked. She said she was calling from the *Journal* in Denver, asked to speak with Larry Burns, then found herself listening to white noise. Burns had been the *Journal*'s police reporter when she started as a general features reporter. She hadn't known him well; their paths had crossed only in the coffee room. Police reports and social events orbited in different constellations. A couple of minutes passed before another voice came on the line: "This is Burns."

"Catherine McLeod," she said.

The line went quiet. Then, Burns said, "Features gal, right?"

"Investigative journalist now."

"No kidding! What can I do for you?"

She told him she was looking into the background of Ryan Beckman, a Denver police detective who had been on the Minneapolis force. "Anything you know about her?"

"Heard the name," Burns said. "Oh, I think she was involved in a shooting, but was cleared. What are you looking for?"

"Why did she leave Minneapolis?"

"Can't say off the top of my head." Burns took another minute. "Look, I'll nose around, talk to some cop friends. I get the feeling this is important."

"You could say it's a matter of life and death," Catherine said.

Burns said he'd get back to her, and Catherine was about to drop the receiver when she saw an incoming call from "Mathews Campaign" on the readout. She pressed the phone button: "McLeod," she said.

"You heard about Jeremy?"

"I heard," Catherine said.

"First David, now Jeremy." Cannon's voice cracked. He took a moment before he said, "You think there's a connection?"

"I don't know," Catherine said.

"Jeremy was a good kid. What the hell's going on?"

"I don't know that either."

The line was quiet for so long, she wondered if Cannon had hung up. Then he said, "I may have something for you. No staffers or volunteers drive a BMW of any color."

"I thought you said you had something."

"Hold on," Cannon said. "The person you might want to talk to is Betsy Kane, daughter of David's former partner."

"Where can I find her?"

"Try her office," he said. Then he gave her an address in Southeast Denver near the tech center.

19

From I-25, Catherine spotted the building stacked alongside other glass and metal buildings on manicured parklike lawns. She took the exit and drove into the tech center. For a moment the building disappeared, then jumped out as she came around a wide curve of sprawling lawns and flower beds. She parked in the lot adjacent to the building, then made her way along the sidewalks, through the glass entry doors and across the marble floor to the elevator. A dinging sound echoed around her and two men in business suits, hoisting briefcases, stepped past the parting doors. Catherine stepped inside. Within moments, she was on the twelfth floor in an office with "Kane Enterprises" on the door and deep blue carpeting, cherry furnishings and abstract oil paintings that screamed "Money."

The receptionist at the computer halfway across the room gave Catherine a raised-eyebrow look. "May I help you?" she said. She had a white face framed by black hair smoothed back into a knot, shoulders squared inside a navy blue blouse, and an impatient look in the way she kept her fingers poised over the keyboard. Catherine gave her name, slipped her business card across the desk, and asked if Betsy Kane were available.

Picking up the card and bringing it close, as if she were nearsighted, the receptionist said, "I don't recall Ms. Kane mentioning a meeting with a reporter." She snapped the card down. "You'll have to make an appointment for a later date. Ms. Kane is very busy."

"Please tell her I'm here about Kane and Mathews Properties."

Catherine realized that the side door had opened and a large man with sandy-colored hair and rimless glasses had stopped in his tracks a moment. He walked over, set some papers on the desk and swung toward Catherine. "Who are you?"

"Catherine McLeod." She fished another card from her bag and handed it to him.

"Mark Talban," he said. "My wife isn't in at the moment." He made a point to study the card. "I suppose you're here because of the murder. We know nothing about that. Kane and Mathews Properties was dissolved on an amicable bases. Old news, all of it."

"We believe we owe it to our readers to shed as much light as possible on Mathews's background," Catherine said. "I can recap the old stories, accusations and counteraccusations, but a current statement from your wife would most likely put the whole ugly business to rest."

"What is it, Mark ?" An attractive woman in her thirties, wearing a gray suit with a short skirt that displayed gym-toned legs, balanced herself in the doorway on five-inch heels. She had blond hair cut short and spiked a little on the top, and a long nose above thin, drawn lips. The silky purple blouse under her jacket showed a little cleavage. Diamonds sparkled in her ears. A blue-carpeted corridor with closed doors stretched behind her.

The man took his time responding. "*Journal* reporter," he said, finally. "Wants to talk to you about Kane and Mathews."

"Oh, my God," she said. Catherine listened hard for a familiar tone, an inflection, anything that resembled the voice on the telephone. "Will the nightmare never end? David gets himself murdered, no surprise, right?" She directed the question into the empty center of the room. "The whole mess has to be regurgitated."

"I suggest you don't say anything else," the man said.

"He's my father, not yours." A tough confidence invaded her tone, unlike the caller's frightened, desperate voice. "I'll say anything I damn well please to make certain his name and reputation remain clear." She nodded at Catherine, pivoted about and headed down the corridor. "You'd better come in," she called over her shoulder.

Catherine brushed past the man and started down the corridor, aware of him closing in behind. "This isn't a good idea," he called, but Betsy Kane had already pushed open a door and disappeared.

Catherine followed her inside a spacious office, almost a duplicate of the reception area except that the oil paintings on the walls were larger and even more abstract. The painting next to the windows on the far wall looked like a sheet of red framed in dark wood. Abstract sculptures that resembled flying steel had been set out on the cherry credenzas and small tables scattered about. A large desk occupied the space in front of the windows, patterns of light playing on the cleared surface. People were different in different situations, she was thinking. Here, Betsy Kane was in charge. But out on the sidewalk, watching a murderer leave the murder scene? How much control would she have felt?

Still it was hard to connect the small, timid voice on the phone with the woman nodding Catherine into an upholstered chair. "What is it you want?" Betsy Kane settled herself into the leather chair behind the desk, leaned forward and clasped her hands together.

"Mathews and your father were partners," Catherine said. She took her notebook out of her bag and unclipped the pen. "You must have known Mathews fairly well." How well? she was thinking. How might this brittle, attractive woman and David Mathews been thrown together over the years? Social events, summer deck parties, July Fourth parties in Evergreen?

"No statement." The woman's husband crossed the office, perched on a corner of the desk and gave Catherine a dismissive wave. "We don't wish to be involved," he said.

"Let me handle this, Mark." The woman didn't take her eyes from Catherine. "I'm happy to give you a statement. You can print this: My father and David Mathews had a successful partnership developing and managing commercial real estate. They created dozens of jobs." She hurried on, not missing a beat, as if she were reading from a teleprompter, and Catherine could sense the hollowness and lack of sincerity, the mouthing of expected sentiments that had no basis. "Kane and Mathews Properties made a positive contribution to the Colorado economy. The misunderstanding that arose in the firm was settled amicably, and my father and Mathews remained close friends. There, does that satisfy you?"

Catherine finished making notes and looked up. This was bullshit. She could have gotten it off the company's prospectus. It had nothing to do with David Mathews or Betsy Kane. "What is your reaction to Mathews's murder?" she asked.

Betsy Kane gave a shout of laughter. "I was shocked, of course. What do you think?"

"That's enough, Betsy." Mark jumped to his feet and faced his wife.

The woman shrugged and sank back in her chair. "Let's go off the record, shall we?" she said, her full attention on Catherine.

"I don't think that's a good idea, Betsy," her husband said.

"Then I'm afraid you have your statement." Betsy Kane started to get to her feet.

"Off the record, if you like," Catherine said. "What can you tell me that might help me to understand why someone wanted him dead?"

"I was shocked," Betsy repeated. "Shocked someone hadn't shot the bastard years ago."

"Don't do this," Mark said, still facing his wife.

Betsy bit at her lower lip a moment and focused on the shiny surface of the desk. "Perhaps you should leave us, Mark. I want to handle this my own way. Someone should know the truth."

Catherine watched the redness move up the back of the man's neck, and when he turned around, his cheeks were flushed, his jaw set. He stomped across the room and slammed out of the office. It could be possible after all, Catherine was thinking. Betsy Kane and David Mathews could have been involved, Mark could have known, and here was a reporter who might entice his wife into spilling the truth. "You didn't like Mathews much," she said.

"Like him? I detested him. He killed my father. Oh, not literally, not in any way that he could have been held responsible."

"Your father's still alive, if I'm not mistaken."

"My father is a vegetable with feeding tubes in his stomach and other tubes stuck in both ends of him. He has twenty-four-hour care just to keep him breathing. The business he spent his life building was gutted and destroyed by a conniving son of a bitch my father had taken into his confidence and trusted. David Mathews was nothing when he came to Denver. He had failed at half a dozen business ventures in Chicago, but he succeeded in marrying the daughter of one of his bosses, and they had escaped to Denver, where Mathews didn't yet have a reputation. With his wife's money, he bought a position in the firm and was so charming—oh, my God, the man could charm a snake—that my father was completely taken in. About two years ago he began to suspect that funds were missing, but he refused to believe David could have anything to do with it. The stress became unbearable. Ten million dollars unaccounted for. It was my father who had to answer to clients. He repaid many of them out of his own funds, desperate to save the reputation of the firm. Oh, David was clever. It took three accountants to uncover the trail of funds he moved from account to account. He took money out of successful properties and put it into his own development projects, all of which were poorly conceived and doomed from the beginning. He shifted money around, budget to budget, different names, different sources. My father finally went to the police and the district attorney. It broke his heart, but he concluded he had no choice but to lodge a complaint and see that David was charged."

"Why did he withdraw the complaint?"

"My father made the mistake of allowing David to have his own accountants audit the books. David was clever. Naturally, his accountants came to completely different conclusions. The money couldn't be missing; it had never been there. The mistakes had been in logging incorrect sums. The police detective who was involved in the case advised my father there wasn't enough proof to bring criminal charges. David's accountants would counter anything the other accountants claimed. At that point, David offered to buy out my father. Five million dollars. You can do the math. David Mathews made off with the other five million."

"You might have brought a civil lawsuit. Other accountants might have confirmed what your father's accountants found."

"You don't understand," Betsy said. "Two weeks after he sold out to that bastard, my father had a stroke. I couldn't put him through anything else; he'd been through enough. So there you have it, all the dirty little background details about the real man our next governor would have been."

"What about the rumors of David's infidelities."

"I wouldn't know."

"A black BMW was seen at night on his block. You drive a black BMW, don't you?"

Betsy Kane brought a fist down onto the desk and got to her feet. "What the hell does that mean? Are you accusing me . . ."

"I'm not accusing you of anything," Catherine said. "It's possible someone other than the killer was at David's house at the time he was shot. Maybe it's the driver of the BMW, I don't know. But I do know that whoever was there could be in real danger."

Hugging herself, the woman walked across the office and stared at the red painting, as if she wanted to make some sense out of the smooth, flat red canvas. There was reluctance in the way she turned back, arms still folded, shoulders slumped. "I told you David was a charming man, the kind you could love and hate at the same time. You covered his campaign. Don't tell me he didn't turn his charms on you."

"He wasn't my type," Catherine said. She was close; she could feel the truth at her fingertips, and yet something was wrong. The scared voice on the phone, the confident woman in front of the red painting made no sense together.

Betsy Kane was quiet a moment, eyes steady, considering her options. "You're saying there's some kind of witness? I find it highly entertaining that a journalist is looking for a witness, but the police aren't."

"How do you know they're not?"

"Two detectives were here an hour ago, asking a lot of inane questions. I gave them the statement. My father and David were always the best of friends."

"Who was here?"

"Excuse me? The detectives, the investigators. Whatever they call themselves. Martinez and Beckman. It was Beckman who took Father's complaint, fell all over herself for David, and convinced my father that filing charges would do no good."

"Had you met either her or her partner before?"

"What's this all about?"

"I'm curious whether you had talked to them when your father made his complaint."

"He handled the matter himself. He was very much his own man. He had no confidence in the police." She gave a little laugh. "Turned out he was right. I don't hold out any hopes they'll solve David's murder. We're still off the record, of course." She walked back to the desk, picked up the phone and said, "Print out my itinerary for the L.A. trip."

She slammed the phone down. "My secretary will have something for you on your way out," she said.

20

Catherine started the engine and rolled down the windows. A cool breeze drifted across the convertible. She spread the itinerary against the steering wheel and read the dates and times. Betsy Kane and her husband, Mark Talban, flew on United to L.A. the morning before David Mathews was shot and returned the following day at 4:31 p.m. "Financial services convention at the Omni Hotel," the woman's secretary had said as she'd handed Catherine the sheet of paper. "Ms. Kane was the keynote speaker that evening. Check the convention blogs. You'll see she gave a wonderful speech, as usual."

Which would have been a few hours before David's murder, hardly enough time to fly back to Denver and be at David's house at midnight. If a BMW was in the neighborhood that night, it didn't belong to Betsy Kane.

Catherine folded the sheet and stuffed it into her bag. The numerals on the dashboard clock read a faint 3:47 p.m. in the bright sunshine.

She put on her sunglasses and pulled out of the lot. She had less than two hours to get back to the newsroom, make a few phone calls, and write up what Marjorie called "all the background information you can find" for tomorrow's edition. She drove around the winding tech center roads out onto the main thoroughfare, writing the article in her head.

She would open with the devastation of Mathews's campaign staff, the empty desks and unswept papers littering the floor as if a tornado had blown through. First the murder of the candidate, and last night, the murder of a staffer. She said the name out loud, Jeremy Whitman. A sense of regret lodged inside her, like a cold, hard object. She could see Jeremy across the table at the Tattered Cover, scared at what he knew and a little drunk. No doubt that was why he had agreed to go to the police with her today, because he was drunk. She should have insisted they get up from the table, march to her car and drive right over to police headquarters. And what would that have accomplished? A drunk trying to remember who he saw last June in Aspen? But he would be alive. It would have accomplished that.

Jason had written about Jeremy's death in today's edition. How the police believed the mugging on a LoDo street had nothing to do with Mathews's murder. She would refer to the article, leaving out the part about the police, and work in a quote from Cannon: "Everyone loved David. I've sent people home to mourn in private."

She had to get a statement from the Colorado Republican Party, although she knew what the spokesperson would say: the party had not yet made a decision on Mathews's replacement. Consulting with the national committee. Making certain the best candidate reaches the governor's office, everyone thinking only of the good of the state, and other boilerplate nobody believed. She would also write the truth: since no other Republican had challenged Mathews for the candidacy, the party would either have to run the candidate for lieutenant governor or select a dark horse. Either way, some poor party member was about to be dumped into the governor's race weeks before the election.

She would have to get the reaction of the Democrats. No doubt, they were ecstatic. Their candidate, running so far behind that she'd had to make an effort to mention him in her articles, had probably leapt ahead in the polls. She would see if any of the pollsters had an update on the numbers.

She would wind up with a brief recapitulation of Mathews's career, including a mention of the theft charges brought and dropped by his former partner, just to remind readers that the popular David Mathews was not the virtuous paragon everyone wanted to believe. She would have to add Betsy Kane's statement on how the whole matter had been settled, how her father and Mathews had remained friends. A few readers might read between the lines and see beneath the surface of Mathews's polished image, but chances were that Edith, his housekeeper, would see only the polished image.

The cell had started ringing as she drove onto I-25. Ignoring it, she worked her way into the fast lane. It rang again. One hand on the steering wheel, she managed to drag the cell out of her bag and flip it open. "Catherine McLeod," she said.

"I have to talk to you," Nick said. His voice was tight against the hum of the traffic.

"I'm on deadline," she said. "We can meet later."

"Now, Catherine."

She took a moment, trying to absorb this unfamiliar tone. "I'm on my way back to the Journal," she said.

"I'll see you there." She was left with a dead line, and a blank feeling inside.

Catherine drove slowly down the narrow ramp into the garage. She removed her sunglasses and blinked into the dim lights as she followed the white line toward the rows of cars nosed against the far wall. Just as she pulled into a vacant space, the driver's door of the black sedan in the next slot flung itself open and a dark-haired man jumped out. Catherine followed the man in her rearview mirror.

"It's me, Catherine," Nick said, and she was aware of the sound of her breath escaping like a deflating balloon.

"You frightened me," she said, getting out of the car and slamming the door.

Nick stood with his arms at his sides, shadows lengthening his face. "Is there somewhere private we can talk?"

She gave him a half nod and headed across the garage toward the banging elevators, his boots clacking behind her. They rode up to the lobby in silence. In silence, across the tiled floor to the reception desk. Nick showed his badge and signed in, and she led the way to the elevators across the lobby. She bit her lip to keep from asking what was wrong. It must be terrible, and she had the feeling—a silly notion, she knew—that if she didn't ask, the terribleness would evaporate. The doors parted and she headed to the right, calling over her shoulder to the receptionist in front of the newsroom that she would be using the conference room for a few minutes. Nick stayed in step beside her.

"What is it?" she said when they were inside. She had never seen him like this; thin lipped, barely controlling the anger that she could almost smell. This wasn't a side of Nick Bustamante she recognized or understood. They were so new together, barely ten months old, still feeling their way.

"I went to the Hudson building this morning." Nick started patrolling the small room, down one side of the table with the chairs pushed in at the sides, hands stuffed into the pockets of his dark slacks. "I asked to see the security videos from yesterday, thinking I might see Jeremy Whitman with somebody in the lobby we'd want to talk to. I saw you, Catherine." He came up the other side of the table.

Catherine sank into the chair at the end. "I met with him last night," she said.

"I know." He was gripping the back of a side chair. "I talked to a couple of guys he was drinking with. They told me he left the bar to meet a reporter. Forty-five minutes later, he returned to the bar and said he'd been at the Tattered Cover, and when I showed photos around there, three clerks identified you and Jeremy, the couple that looked like they were having a big argument in the coffee shop. Why didn't you tell me?"

"I wanted to," she said.

"That a fact? Well, try me now." He yanked out the chair and sat down hard. "What the hell's going on? This is a murder investigation, and you could have important evidence. You think that's something you should have told me about?"

"I didn't think it would do any good." Catherine stared past him down the table. She'd been wrong, she thought. She could have called Nick last night, and he would have escorted Jeremy to the police station. Maybe Nick could have convinced Internal Affairs to take Beckman off the investigation, and if that had happened, Beckman wouldn't have gotten an arrest warrant for Sydney. God, Catherine thought, she had made the wrong choice, and now she was running out of choices that mattered. The man who had seen David and Detective Beckman together in Aspen—lovers in a bar—was dead. The witness who had seen Beckman at David's house after his murder might as well not exist, and Sydney Beckman would no doubt be indicted for murder.

She turned to Nick, aware that he had been waiting for her to say something, the blue vein in his neck pulsing, his mouth and chin rigid. She told him all of it. Aspen and the excuses David had made about how he'd run into an old flame, and Jeremy's inability to disbelieve his own eyes. The phone call from the anonymous woman. Both Jeremy and the witness terrified that the police wouldn't believe them, would shrug off anything they said that reflected badly on one of their own. Detective Beckman would be alerted. She could see in the way Nick's face had started to shut down that Jeremy and the caller had been right.

"Don't pretend it couldn't happen," she said. "Last fall Internal Affairs spiked an investigation into the domestic abuse call at a police officer's home. Spiked it for how long, three months? Long enough for the second call when the officer's wife had to be hospitalized."

Nick let the silence settle between them like another presence. Finally, he asked, "Anyone else see Mathews and Beckman together in Aspen?"

"No one in the campaign," Catherine said. Then she told him that David had been to a fund-raising event in Grand Junction and had insisted upon driving back to Denver alone. Everybody else stayed in Grand Junction, except Jeremy who went hiking near Aspen and, three days later, dropped into the bar at the Jerome Hotel and found David and Detective Beckman.

"I managed to convince him that he and the caller would support each other's stories. With two eyewitnesses linking Mathews and Beckman, Internal Affairs would have to investigate Beckman." Catherine stopped; the image of the tall, gangly young man floated in front of her. She tried to swallow the lump forming in her throat.

"If you believed that, why didn't you take him to police headquarters last night?"

And Whitman would still be alive. Nick hadn't said the words, but they echoed around the conference room as if he had shouted them.

"He was drinking," Catherine said. "He needed to be sober when he talked to Internal Affairs." She could hear the feebleness in her own words, the wobbly effort to excuse herself. She forced herself to go on: "I'd hoped to find the witness today. She may drive a black BMW."

"Along with twenty thousand other people in Denver." Nick spread his hands on the table. "So let's examine what you've got. A caller who's probably a kook. You know how many crazy people call the police in high-profile cases? Admit to the crime or claim their ex-lovers or sisters or bosses did it? All looking for their own fifteen minutes. Whitman could have been mistaken about what he saw. Mathews had a plausible explanation, right? People in his campaign will probably confirm it."

Catherine didn't say anything. Don Cannon would confirm Mathews's explanation. Cannon believed in David Mathews.

"Bottom line, Catherine, Sydney Mathews was arrested an hour ago," he said, his voice still tight. "Her lawyer got her out on bail, but she'll be indicted and she'll stand trial. The murder of David Mathews is solved."

"Do you really believe that?" Catherine could feel the heat in her cheeks.

"What I believe is that you've tried and convicted a police detective on innuendo and an anonymous statement." He drew back, pouring his gaze over her. "There's no evidence any of it is true. Jeremy Whitman could have been mistaken. He could have seen Mathews with a blond woman who resembled Beckman. An unfortunate coincidence. He was murdered in a gang initiation attack. Assaults have been going on all summer, played down, I admit, so people wouldn't stop coming downtown. The point is, the method was typical of gang initiation. As for Sydney Mathews, a search warrant turned up a 9mm Sig 226 Tactical, and ballistics says it's the murder weapon. Hard evidence, Catherine, against your . . ." He lifted his hands. "Instincts."

"Now you see why I couldn't tell you." He didn't take his eyes from her, and she pushed on: "The police would dismiss the whole thing, but Detective Beckman would know that Jeremy could connect her to Mathews. She'd know the witness had called the *Journal*. She could go after both of them and make sure they never talked. Last night she made sure Jeremy could never talk."

Nick got to his feet and kicked the chair back. It shuddered against the hard floor. "Whitman took a .38 bullet, Catherine. You think this is a game? Two homicides that the evidence says aren't related. Just a game to you? Straight out of a movie about the dumb flatfooted detective and the beautiful girl reporter who solves the crime for him? Oh, and another police detective is the murderer. How original."

"Nick . . ." Catherine started to her feet, but he put out a hand, as if to keep her away. He turned and flung open the door.

"What this comes down to is trust," he said, looking back. "Whether you trust me and whether I can trust you. Without that, we don't have anything."

21

“How are things with you?” Dulcie Oldman got right to the point, ignoring the polite preliminaries Catherine was becoming accustomed to when she met with her mother’s people. She could feel the intensity of Dulcie’s gaze boring into her over the rim of a coffee mug. Flecks of light shone in the woman’s dark eyes. She was Arapaho, in her forties, with black hair that brushed her shoulders and tiny silver earrings. She wore a blue skirt and the kind of white blouse that fit underneath a suit coat. A thoroughly modern woman, Catherine thought, with a string of degrees and a position as director of human resources for a telecommunications company. Yet rooted in the past, with black eyes framed in dark, carved features, much like Catherine’s own. Looking at Dulcie was like looking at an image of herself in the mirror.

An hour and a half ago, Catherine had been huddled over the computer in the newsroom, forcing all of her strength and thoughts into writing the background article around Jason’s report of Sydney’s arrest for tomorrow's paper, pulling the curtains in her head to block out everything else—Jeremy Whitman and David Mathews. Nick Bustamante. She had felt herself shaking inside, as if she were being bounced about. How could she have let this happen with Nick? It was not what she wanted, not what she had hoped for. She had wiped at the moisture in her eyes and pulled hard on the curtains in her head and forced herself to concentrate on the story. That was how it had been from the time she had learned to read and write, a little brown girl huddled over a notebook with a pencil in hand, lost in a world of scribbled, imagined stories that made more sense than the white world around her. She wrote the last line, read through the piece and sent it winging electronically twenty feet away to Marjorie's computer. Then she had called Dulcie, the woman she had met at the Indian Center last year when she started looking for the part of her that was Arapaho.

She had finished her own coffee and gotten a refill while she waited for Dulcie's Honda to pull onto the concrete slab in front of the coffee shop. On her way over, Catherine had stopped at the 7-Eleven and bought a can of tobacco, cans of tuna fish and candy bars. She had given them to Dulcie, knowing Dulcie would take them to an elder. The double gift, in the Arapaho Way. Dulcie would have the pleasure of both receiving and giving. She glanced away from the woman across from her. The image of Jeremy Whitman heading down the sidewalk to the bar last night, floated ahead like a ghost, as if she might still run after him, take hold of his arm, insist he get into her car so she could drive him to police headquarters. She should have seen the danger. Anything she had put together, Detective Beckman could also figure out.

"A young man was murdered last night," Catherine managed, the lump so big in her throat, she felt she might choke. "I could have prevented it."

"Tell me about it."

"I should have recognized the danger and warned him. I should have insisted he come with me. I could have taken him home or to a hotel or someplace else the killer wouldn't have known about. He'd be alive this morning . . ."

She broke off and crushed the napkin against her mouth. God, she didn't want to cry. Dulcie was quiet, giving her a moment, and that was something important that she had learned from the Arapahos, the patient, quiet waiting. When she trusted her voice, Catherine said: "He had information about a murder, and he had agreed to go with me to the police this morning. The killer got to him first."

She was aware of Dulcie's hands moving across the table and grasping her own. "You must be a very powerful woman," she said, "if you could have read this killer's mind."

"I should have known." It was a small voice, a remnant of her own, that Catherine heard.

"Nobody has that power."

"Then I should have sensed what might happen." It was Dulcie who had urged her to trust her instincts and not reason them away, as she had learned growing up in a white family, going to white schools. "Listen to your instincts," Dulcie had said. "You'll be surprised how helpful they are in this crazy world."

"I should have felt the danger around him." Catherine said. The tears started, a rush of moisture that blurred her vision and washed over her face. "He shouldn't have died."

Dulcie settled back, her face a calm, unreadable mask. She waited a long while before she said, "What do you feel you should do now?"

"I can't do anything," Catherine said. "It's too late."

"You said the murdered man knew something he wanted to tell the police."

"It belonged to him. Without him, the information is only hearsay."

Catherine twisted the damp napkin in her hands. "There's more," she said. "A woman has been arrested for a murder she didn't commit." She waved a hand between them. "I might have been able to prevent her arrest."

Dulcie was quiet a long moment before she said, "Anyone else involved?"

Catherine felt a sharp prick of pain in her chest, as if Dulcie had laid the point of a knife against her skin. The witness also had information. Information that placed Detective Beckman at the scene of Mathews's murder. And last night Catherine had told Jeremy about the witness. What if Jeremy had blurted out the truth before he died? She saw where Dulcie had been leading her. Detective Beckman, with the resources of the Denver Police Department at her fingertips, would be looking for the anonymous caller.

"There is someone," Catherine managed. "She's in a lot of danger, and I don't know how to find her."

Dulcie sipped at her coffee a moment. Finally she said, "It's been my experience that somebody I am looking for may come and find me."

"How can I count on that?" Catherine wrapped her fingers around her coffee mug. She could hear the terror in the caller's voice. Maybe the caller had left town, left the country. The thought was like a small light flickering in the darkness. But she couldn't count on that either. She couldn't shake the sense that the caller was out there somewhere and that Beckman would find her.

"You also have this information," Dulcie said. She was sitting up straight, gripping the coffee mug, her face still a mask. But behind the mask, Catherine could sense the worry. "You could also be in danger."

Catherine looked away. Traffic stopping and starting out on the street, a couple of high school kids huddled over cigarettes at the corner. She and Marjorie and Jason had talked about the danger this morning, and Marjorie had suggested she take a little time off. As if by some miracle

Beckman would be brought to justice. But Sydney Mathews had been arrested. The case was closed, and things were working out as Beckman had planned.

"I'm a journalist," Catherine said, bringing her eyes back to Dulcie's. "It's my job to get the information." She stopped herself from saying the rest of it: information is always dangerous.

"My grandmother used to tell us a story about coyote and his ways," Dulcie said. "One day a girl went walking out on the prairie alone. She meant no one any harm. She wanted only to walk on the beautiful, open lands. She thought she was alone, but then she realized she had walked up to coyote's den. Inside the den, she could see the bones of the animals and even people coyote had killed. She was very frightened. Just as she started to run back to the village to tell the people, coyote came out of the den, and the girl saw that he had a bow and arrow and he was aiming the arrow at her. She ran as fast as she could, but the arrow flew by her. She veered to one side, and an arrow flew by her again. She veered the opposite way, but another arrow came. She ran faster, dodging one way, then the other, but the arrows always followed, and she realized that coyote was tracking her and no matter which way she ran, coyote would try to kill her. She knew the only way she could save herself was to get behind coyote. Finally she came to a little hill. She ran up the hill and waited. When she heard coyote panting, she ran down the other side and around the base. Then she picked up a rock and climbed the hill behind coyote. Before he could know she was there and could shoot another arrow, she threw the rock at his head, and that was the end of coyote."

Catherine took a moment. A story was always a gift, a thing to be savored. "Thank you," she said.

"Stories have power," Dulcie said. "Grandmother said the story helped to protect our people. We had to be smarter and faster than the enemy.

We had to think the way the enemy thinks to stay ahead. Sometimes we can stay ahead by getting behind."

Catherine followed Dulcie outside and waited on the sidewalk as the sedan's engine turned over and Dulcie backed out of the lot, waved and drove away. She wasn't sure what kind of gift Dulcie had given her. The lump in her throat was still there, and the faint nausea, with coffee slogging about in her stomach, but the story—the rhythm of the words—had been comforting somehow.

The minute she settled behind the wheel of the convertible, the sense of desolation hit her. It had been like a black monster stalking her since Nick had walked out of the conference room and left her alone with the thought of how she might have saved Jeremy. She had tried to hold off the monster while she wrote tomorrow's piece, had kept the monster at bay at the coffee shop, but there was no dodging the monster now. She got out of the car, walked down the shops strung next to the coffee shop to the liquor store, bought two bottles of red wine, then got back in the car and drove home.

Rex was racing around the yard as she pulled into the driveway next to the alley. She swore he could recognize the sound of the convertible because he always raced with excitement when she arrived. She started to press the garage door opener, then caught a glimpse of Rex jumping about and pulled her hand away. There was something different, something more fierce in the way he carried on. The sound of his barking cut through the quiet neighborhood. She hoisted the brown bag with the two bottles in one arm, grabbed her purse and let herself through the back gate. Rex circled her all the way to the back door, barking and yelping. She set the bags on the counter, shook some dried food into his dish and refilled his water, trying to ignore the wine bottle still on the counter beneath the window. The last of the daylight shimmered in the red liquid. She'd forgotten there was still some wine left; it was unusual for her not to finish a bottle. Yet she had spent most of last night at Nick's—a thousand years ago, she thought, aware of the desolation washing over her again, so heavy she felt as if it might drive her into the floor.

She found a wineglass in the drainer next to the sink, unplugged the bottle and was about to pour the wine when something moved out by the garage. She leaned closer to the window keeping her eye on the place. Nothing. A squirrel, perhaps, or a little wind burst that had riffled the clumps of weeds she had been meaning to clean out. She was aware that Rex had stopped eating and lifted his head. When she set her hand on the rough of his neck, she could feel the tension in his muscles. A loud growl started in his throat, and she knew then that she had *felt* someone moving about outside, and so had Rex.

He moved to the door, barking now, but not the happy, excited noise he usually made. Catherine moved to the side of the window and surveyed the yard. The bushes along the fence, the long shadows of the elm tree on the lawn, the petunias and pansies and daisies along the sidewalk, the two pots of flowers she had set out on the cobbled area that passed for a patio. Nothing out of the ordinary. She was imagining things. Everything that had happened had set her on edge, and Rex had picked up on her nervousness. It was so like him; he could always sense how she was feeling.

"It's okay, Rex," she told him. She walked over, patted his head and ran her hand down his back, trying to soothe the bristling hair. "Nobody's there. Just you and me." God, she needed a drink.

She went back to the counter, surveyed the yard again, and filled her wineglass. She wasn't sure when she saw the slight movement at the window of the garage, or if she only *felt* it. Everything happened so fast. She remembered the cork rolling to the floor and stooping over to pick it up. Then the window bursting over the counter, shards of glass falling over the kitchen like a hail of stones, and something invisible but sharp and real and lethal zooming above her. She wasn't sure how she had gotten to the floor, but she was crawling over the tile, sharp pieces of glass embedding themselves in her knees and the palms of her hands, glass floating in the wine that she must have spilled, and Rex yelping and throwing himself against the door. She managed to pull her purse off the counter, then grabbed hold of Rex's collar and dragged him into the dining room and down the hall to her bedroom. She kicked the door shut and threw the lock. Staying low—God, there were windows everywhere, all the curtains opened, the shades up—she pulled the phone off the nightstand and jammed the receiver against her ear. Nothing but the empty, hollow sound of a dead line.

Her hands were shaking so hard, she could hardly grip the cell phone in her purse. She held it tight as she punched in 911.

"What's your emergency?" The voice might have come from another planet.

She gave her name and address, forcing herself to lower her tone and speak slowly. "Someone just tried to kill me," she said.

22

Catherine sat curled on the sofa next to Rex, watching the phalanx of blue uniforms circle through her house again and gather in the kitchen, studying the blown-out window and shard-strewn floor. The officers had arrived thirty minutes ago, the same look about them, cropped, brown hair and bland, serious faces. After a few minutes, they had disappeared out the back door to investigate whatever they were investigating in the yard, and the house had gone quiet for a while. A detective had arrived, not anyone she knew, tall and rangy in a tan sport coat that barely covered the lump of his gun. Then, a grim-faced, dark-haired man in a blue jacket who said he was from the crime lab. They had headed outside with the uniforms, and now she supposed they were also in the kitchen. She dipped her head over Rex and ran her fingers through his soft coat, the dog smell of him comforting and familiar. He licked at her arm.

There was the clack of footsteps on the porch, and Catherine felt herself going tense, as if tension was her natural state and the few moments of calm on the sofa with Rex, police officers swarming about, had been an illusion. She stared at the front door, conscious of Rex lifting his head and following her gaze. She couldn't remember locking the door after she'd let in the officers. She started to her feet as the door inched open.

"Catherine?" Nick pushed the door forward a few inches. She could see a slice of him in the opening, his familiar hand gripping the edge of the door. Then he was striding across the living room. He sat down beside her. "Are you all right?"

Catherine turned a little sideways and looked him square in the eye. "She tried to kill me," she said, bracing herself for the argument, the inane explanation. Crime stats had moved up in her neighborhood, a crazy homeless man had been reported wandering around, muttering to himself. Any explanation that would shift suspicion from Detective Ryan Beckman.

"I'm sorry about this afternoon." Nick took her hands in both of his. She could feel the rough ridges of his palms, and his warmth running through her. "I shouldn't have dismissed what you told me. I guess I'm going to have to learn to trust you." He nodded toward the kitchen. "I never expected anything like this. Thank God, you're safe."

Three officers trailed through the kitchen and into the living room, and Nick let go of her hand and got to his feet. "What do you have?" he said.

"The shot came from the garage." The tall officer with wide shoulders and the beginnings of a paunch over his belt seemed to be in charge. "The window was pushed back far enough for a good view of the house."

"The garage!" Nick said, and Catherine felt his hand grip her shoulder, as if he wanted to protect her from what had already occurred. "My

God, Catherine. You usually park in the garage. The shooter planned to waylay you there, out of sight of any neighbor looking out a window. If you'd driven inside . . ." He stopped, and the pressure of his grip tightened.

Catherine dropped her face into her hands. She had intended to put the convertible in the garage. She had no plans to go out tonight; her plans hadn't gone beyond the two bottles of wine in the paper bag on the passenger seat. But Rex had been tearing around the yard, practically doing cartwheels, barking and yelping, as she'd turned onto the gravel apron in front of the garage.

"Rex tried to warn me," she said. Her voice sounded muffled. "I went into the yard through the back gate."

"You say the shooter had a clear view of the house?" Nick faced the tall officer a moment, then locked eyes again with Catherine. "He also had a clear view of the yard. He could have shot you as you walked to the house."

He, Nick had said. Catherine searched his eyes. So this would be their secret for a while, until there was real evidence to stop Detective Beckman. She looked away. The image of herself walking up the sidewalk, a gun trained on her back. She should be dead now, but Rex had been jumping and racing around her, and she had stumbled along like a drunk, dodging this way and that way to keep from tripping over the dog. *Dodging,* she thought, like the girl in Dulcie's story.

And Rex had been trying to warn her! A chill ran through her at the realization. She shivered and clasped her arms, pulling in around herself. She'd thought Rex had just been glad to see her, but he'd been trying to tell her someone was in the garage. She'd been lost in her own guilt over Jeremy's death. Mourning the end of things with Nick. God, she hadn't seen what was there!

The detective walked out of the kitchen carrying a plastic bag. He held it up in front of Nick. "Lab tech dug the bullet out of the wall. Looks like a .38. I'll get it to ballistics."

"Anything left in the garage?" Nick said.

Two other officers appeared and shook their heads in unison with the detective. "Lab techs didn't find anything."

"Footprints? Fingerprints?" They continued shaking their heads.

Nick gave Catherine a sideways glance. She could read the expression in his eyes: Detective Beckman was a pro. Of course she hadn't left any trace of herself.

Finally the officers grouped together in the living room, the detective warning Catherine to keep her doors locked, call immediately if anything unusual happened. They said they'd keep her posted, then filed out the front door. The pounding of their boots across the porch sent little tremors through the floor. Nick locked the door, then disappeared into the kitchen. She heard the sounds of a broom swooshing across the tile, the gritty tinkling of glass, followed by the sharp thwacks of a hammer.

"Thank you," she said when he dropped down beside her again.

He shrugged, and she felt the weight of his arm slipping around her shoulders. "Serve and protect is our motto. You now have kitchen counters and floor with no glass and a cardboard window. I suggest you get a real window as soon as possible." He went quiet a moment, and she knew he had slipped back into the detective mode. "Jeremy Whitman was shot with a .38," he said. "We'll have to wait to see if it was the same gun. Strange that Beckman didn't get rid of it after last night."

"She was planning to use it again." How many times, Catherine wondered, would Detective Beckman use the gun before she got rid of it? And she would get rid of it. She would not leave any trace.

"You said Whitman had seen Mathews and Beckman together in Aspen," Nick said. "Anywhere else they might have gone together?"

Catherine shifted sideways and stared into his face. "What are you suggesting?"

"That we take a drive to Aspen tomorrow and show some photos around. Stop at other mountain towns they might have been seen in. Can you get a list of mountain towns Mathews went to this summer?"

Catherine nodded. She got to her feet, went into the bedroom and pulled her cell out of her bag. She punched in the number for the campaign headquarters and left a message for Cannon to get back to her ASAP. "It's important," she said.

Then she called the *Journal* and left a message on Jason's voice mail. Someone had fired a gun at her house. She was inside the house and was unhurt. Police are investigating. He would get the police report anyway, but now he would have her statement. Then she switched to Marjorie's voice mail and left a message that she would be out tomorrow working on her part of the Mathews homicide story.

She walked back into the living room and was about to ask him if he would stay the night when he said: "Want me to stay?"

They started at dawn and drove west on I-70, past warehouses and shopping malls and long stretches of industrial buildings etched in the first sunlight, until at last the city fell away and they were in the mountains, winding around the pine-studded slopes, the vast, blue sky overhead. Nick was behind the wheel, steady intensity about the way he guided the sedan with the fingers of one hand. The air conditioning emitted a stream of cool air, but Catherine had rolled down her window a little. She took in a deep breath of the cool pine-scented air. Occasional gusts of wind set the pines and bushes jiggling outside the window. She was glad to get out of the city, as if the mountains rising all around and far vistas could obliterate for a short time the images of Jeremy Whitman lying dead in an alley and Sydney Mathews charged in a murder she didn't commit. And last night—Ryan Beckman waiting in the garage, aiming a gun at her kitchen window, wanting her dead! She pushed the thought away.

"Try not to dwell on it." Nick gave her a sideways glance, and she mustered a smile. He must have been reading her mind. "We'll check the hotel in Glenwood Springs first," he went on, shifting the topic to the e-mail Cannon had sent. Twenty minutes after she had left the message last night, Cannon had called back and she had asked him for a list of places in the mountains where Mathews had stayed this summer.

"You haven't heard the news?" Cannon had said. "Sydney's been arrested. I have to say it wasn't a surprise."

"Why is that?" she'd asked.

"Come on, Catherine. You're the one who asked me about the rumors. Sydney heard the rumors, too."

"You're saying she believed them and killed her husband?"

"The way I see it, she confronted him and they got into one of their big arguments. Look, David was a helluva guy. He had it all, money, power, charm coming out of his ears. Everybody loved him, and that includes every woman he met. Don't try to tell me you were immune because I wouldn't believe it. Sure he and Sydney had some, shall we say, heated discussions over the women around David. I told you how Sydney went ballistic once at campaign headquarters. I guess I always feared one of their discussions could escalate into something horrible. Looks like that's what happened. So what's your piece of this?"

"I'm working on the side story," Catherine said.

"You gonna smear David's reputation?"

"That's not my intention. Can you get me a list right away?"

A loud noise, half cough and half sigh, had burst from the other end. "I wish you and the cops would get on the same page," he said. "They didn't want any lists. What do you know they don't know?"

"Trust me, Cannon. The cops and I want the same thing."

Now she glanced at Nick, staring at the highway, shoulder muscles knotted beneath the blue cotton shirt. She had told Cannon that she and the cops both wanted Mathews's killer brought to justice. Thirty minutes later Cannon had called back and told her to check her e-mail.

Aspen was not on the official list. As far as the campaign knew, candidate Mathews had never stayed in Aspen. No one would have known if Jeremy Whitman hadn't wandered into the bar at the Hotel Jerome.

There were three places where Mathews stayed while campaigning along the I-70 corridor in the mountains, but he covered a lot of territory from each place. From Grand Junction, he traveled the Western Slope, no doubt giving the same speeches to the rotary clubs and chambers of commerce and teachers unions that Catherine had heard him deliver in Denver. Breckenridge put him in the center of Summit County, not too far from the population up and down the Vail valley.

They had agreed to eliminate Grand Junction, farther to the west, on the border with Utah. Catherine knew Nick wanted to be back in Denver by tonight. They would start in Glenwood Springs, then drive over to Aspen and hit Breckenridge on the way home. Westbound traffic was thin, and they made good time, plunging deeper and deeper into the mountains. On the high peaks, the aspen trees had started to turn gold, and a golden blaze spread like bonfires over the slopes. The small towns of Idaho Springs and Georgetown and Silver Plume slipped past. Just outside Georgetown, Catherine pointed out the Georgetown Loop, the high railroad trestle that floated above the valley, like a ghost from another time. A small narrow gauge train was huffing over the trestle, spilling black smoke into the air.

They plunged into the Eisenhower Tunnel and emerged near the top of Ptarmigan Peak. Nick took his foot off the gas as they drove down the steep grade. In Dillon, they picked up a cup of coffee at a drive-through, then kept going, reflections of the pine forests shimmering on the surface of Lake Dillon.

The jazz on the CD, volume low, riffed through the swoosh of air over the window. Nick talked about going fishing in the mountain streams with his father when he was a kid, camping in a tent and cooking hamburgers on a cookstove. The world a simpler place then, he said. He'd asked what she had done as a kid, and she'd gone on about swimming lessons and piano lessons and Girl Scouts. She watched the mountainsides flying past and talked about the white couple who had adopted and loved a five-year-old girl, part Indian—no one was certain which tribe she might have belonged to. It was only last year she had learned she was part Arapaho. Until then she had felt like an apple tree in a pine forest, always trying to be like the pine trees. She laughed at the idea.

Nick gave her a half-second look. "It's nice to hear you laugh," he said.

She wasn't sure why she was going on like this, what it was about this man that made her want to tell him about herself. She took a moment before she said, "What good do you think this will do?"

"We might get lucky and find someone who can connect Mathews and Beckman. You can put another message to the caller in your blog and we can hope she'll get back in contact. In the meantime, I might be able to talk Internal Affairs into reopening the investigation."

"A lot of mights and hopes," Catherine said.

"It's our only shot," she remembered Nick saying. She must have dozed off, because the next thing she knew, they were in Glenwood

Canyon, the spectacular rock-carved slopes jutting above them and the highway suspended over the deep canyon as if it had dropped from space. Beyond the edge of the highway, the white waters of the Colorado River crashed over the boulders. Another thirty minutes and they strolled into the lobby of the Hotel Colorado.

23

The man behind the check-in desk looked like he was in his thirties—sharp nose, blond mustache and shaved head that glowed a sunburn pink under the fluorescent lights. Except for two teenage girls in bikinis trailing bath towels behind them, flip-flops smacking the wood floor, the hotel lobby was empty. Sounds from the gigantic hot water swimming pool outside drifted through the opened doors. The air felt warm and moist.

"Reservations?" The man looked up. He wore a white tee shirt with "Hotel Colorado" emblazoned on the pocket and a small, gold-toned pin that said "Eric." The knotted muscles in his tanned arms bulged below the sleeves.

Nick had pulled open the wallet with his badge and held it up, and in that instant, Catherine saw the man blanch and rock back on his heels. "We're looking for information," Nick said.

Eric shot a furtive glance toward the closed door on the right. "Manager's tied up right now," he said, a nervous, desperate look invading his eyes. He blinked a number of times. "Maybe I can help you." It was obvious he didn't want the police detective talking to the manager.

"I want to confirm the dates David Mathews stayed here," Nick said. He had slipped the wallet back inside his pocket and pulled out a small notepad, which he flipped open. He recited the dates that Cannon had e-mailed this morning. A two-night stay in late June, another two nights in July, four nights in August. Catherine wasn't sure where the pen he was holding had come from.

"Mathews! He's the guy that got murdered, isn't he? I was thinking about voting for him." Eric dipped his head over the counter. "Look, I'd like to help you but . . ." He bit on his lower lip a moment. "I can't comment on guests. Privacy issues, you understand."

"I can talk to the manager," Nick said, starting along the counter toward the side door.

"Wait!" Eric looked as if he'd had to stop himself from grabbing Nick's shirt to pull him back. He tossed another furtive look toward the closed door and started tapping at the keyboard in front of a small screen. "June dates, confirmed," he said, his voice almost a whisper. He continued tapping. "David Mathews here on the July dates. August dates as well." He looked up, relief draining from his face. "That's all I can tell you."

Nick produced the three photographs he had brought from headquarters and set them on the counter. Sydney Mathews, Ryan Beckman and the photo of a blond woman from the police photo lineup. The woman resembled Beckman. "Recognize any of these women?" he said.

"Oh, man," Eric said. "I need this job. The manager finds out . . ."

"This is a police investigation," Nick said. "I can arrange to have the Glenwood Springs police bring you in, and we can continue our chat."

"Jesus!" Eric blew out a gust of breath. He fingered the photos closer and bent over them. "Isn't that Mathews's wife? I saw her picture on TV this morning. She's the one that shot the poor bastard."

"What about the others?"

"Never seen 'em." Eric slipped the photos together and shoved them back. The moment Nick put them in his shirt pocket, Eric broke into a grin. "Hey, I'd remember two babes like that. They never came around this summer or I would've known. I'm here almost twenty-four seven. Management lets me stay in one of the cabins out back. It's a good gig 'til skiing season gets going."

The sedan's air conditioning was going full blast in the parking lot. Catherine said, "Let's suppose David Mathews was cautious enough not to allow his girlfriend to show her face at any of the official stops on the campaign."

Nick backed out of the slot, then looked over and smiled at her before he drove onto the street. "We still have Aspen," he said.

It was a short drive to Aspen, but it took nearly an hour with the SUVs and campers and sport cars with tops down that clogged Highway 82. They passed Snowmass, ski slopes looming above, and crawled into downtown through neighborhoods of Victorian houses with wide front porches and gingerbread trim dripping from the roofs, huddled among century-old pine trees. Nick stopped in a public parking lot and they walked down the sidewalks, hand in hand, lovers on a little vacation, a getaway, Catherine thought. She shivered at the memory thrusting itself upon her again: Ryan Beckman trying to kill her last night. The Hotel Jerome was in the next block: a redbrick building with green trim and beds of red geraniums and petunias in front.

Catherine removed her sunglasses and blinked into the dim light inside. The lobby was filled with overstuffed chairs and sofas arranged around a marble fireplace. Lamps shone on the carved wooden tables and glowed against the deep pink wallpaper. The reception desk was off to the side near a wide corridor that led into the first floor of the hotel. She felt the pressure of Nick's hand on her back, guiding her past the desk and into the J-Bar. Most of the tables were taken, but they found a vacant table next to windows half filled with a view of the geraniums along the sidewalk. When the waiter appeared, Catherine ordered iced tea, and Nick said he would have the same.

"I'd like to talk to you a moment," Nick said when the waiter had set down the glasses of tea. He opened his wallet and held up the badge.

The waiter was tall and spindly with long, rubbery arms and bony knees that protruded through his black slacks. "Sure," he said, eyes locked on the badge.

"How long have you worked here?"

"Five years now," the waiter said. "No complaints. None whatsoever. There some kind of investigation going on?"

"I'm trying to locate someone," Nick said, snapping down the three photos. "Any of these photos look familiar?"

For an instant, Catherine saw the flash of recognition in the man's eyes. His Adam's apple rose and fell like a golf ball in the thin neck. "No," he said. "Never seen any of them."

"You have a pretty good memory, do you?" Nick said.

"Yeah. I got a great memory. Never forget a face. If I'd seen one of them in here, I'd remember."

"You remember seeing David Mathews here?"

"Mathews? He was going to be governor, then his wife shot him?" The waiter swiped the back of his hand across his mouth. "Yeah, maybe I seen him here once or twice. I mean, I didn't know who he was 'til I saw his picture in the paper and found out he was running for governor. I don't follow politics much. Figure they're all crooks. But, yeah, he come in for a beer, couple times this summer."

"Anyone with him?"

"He was always alone." The words shot out of the waiter's mouth. "Never seen him with anybody. A loner kind of guy." The waiter shrugged and started backing away. "Gotta get to work," he said.

Catherine leaned across the table. "He's lying," she whispered, and Nick nodded. "What's next?"

"In a normal investigation? Pay a visit to the Aspen police, explain what we're looking for, get their help in obtaining a search warrant and check the hotel's registration for the names David Mathews and Ryan Beckman."

"We don't know they actually stayed here," Catherine said.

"And this isn't a normal investigation. As far as the DPD is concerned, the investigation is closed. Sydney Mathews will be charged with first-degree homicide." He sipped at the tea a moment, then went on: "I'm on the Whitman shooting that looks like a gang-related mugging. Nothing to do with Aspen or David Mathews's extramarital curricula."

A man with gray, bushy hair sitting alone at a nearby table scooted his chair back and leaned sideways into the corner of their table. "Excuse me." He could have been in his fifties or seventies, Catherine thought, with the sunburned, roughened look of a skier accustomed to the snow and sun, and startling blue eyes framed in deep squint lines. His bushy gray eyebrows spread like tentacles toward his hairline. "Heard you mention David Mathews." He shot a glance over one shoulder toward the spindly waiter delivering a tray of beers to a nearby table. "Better we talk outside," he said.

Catherine got up first and crossed the bar and the lobby into the bright sunshine outdoors. Nick's footsteps clacked behind her. They walked to the corner, away from the windows in the bar and waited. It was a couple of minutes before the hotel door opened and the bushy-haired man strolled out. He walked over, turned the corner, and nodded for them to follow. He disappeared around the next corner, but they found him lounging in front of an art gallery, one boot propped against the brick wall. "Lucky Jameson," he said sticking out a large, freckled hand. "One of Aspen's characters, you might say. Arrived fifty years ago to ski, and never got around to leaving. Still a ski bum, you might say. Let me give you a piece of advice. We got celebrities up the wazoo here. You name 'em, movie stars, politicians, Arab potentates, they all come through Aspen and a lot of 'em own megamansions up there." He pointed with his head in the direction of the Victorian mansions on the West End. "We protect 'em, and they know it. Nobody in the Jerome or any place else is gonna talk to outsiders like you. Don't matter if you're cops."

Catherine started to say she was a journalist, then bit back the words. If people in Aspen wouldn't talk to the cops, they certainly wouldn't talk to a journalist. "Why are you willing to talk to us?" she asked.

"Had a drink with Mathews at the J-Bar end of June, I guess it was. I stop in for a beer in the afternoons like I been doing since the sixties. Silver-haired guy was there all by himself, had city boy written all over him. You know the type. Most of the time suited up with a starched shirt and tie, looking like he was about to jump out of his khakis and Top-Siders. So I said, 'Okay, if I sit down?' and he didn't say no, so I sat. 'Where you from?' I asked, and he says, 'Denver.' Well, guess I could've guessed that, straight out of one of them glass buildings on Seventeenth Street. I wanted to ask him what brought him to town, but it's not what we do around here. Where you from? That's okay. We don't go beyond that. He shakes my hand, says he's David Mathews, like he expected me to know who he was, and I'm thinking, Man, we got the likes of Tom Hanks and Jack Nicholson around here, and I never heard of you. Then he starts talking, like he's so damn lonely, he don't know what he's doing. Plus, you ask me, he'd had a few beers. Says he's running for governor and he hopes I'll vote for him. Goes off, like he's memorized his campaign speech and can't stop himself from delivering it. About that time, I began making excuses to get away."

"What made you stay," Catherine said, because he had stayed. Otherwise he wouldn't be talking to them.

"The fact he was running for governor. The more he talked, the more I realized he had on a big mask, painted to look just like he wanted it to look. Every once in a while, he let the mask slip, and I got a glimpse of somebody else. Started me thinking, who the hell is this guy that wants to run the state? Maybe I don't want him running the state. Something not straight about him, you know what I mean? You get a real sense of people when you're up there on the slopes trying to get 'em skiing. They wear all kind of masks on the lifts, but when they get out on the slopes and look down, that's when they show themselves—the bullies and crybabies and folks so timid they're scared of their own shadows. You get a sense for what's real in folks, and what isn't. Then I seen in the newspaper that his wife shot him, and it made me think she must've known the real guy."

Nick had taken out the photos. He handed them to Lucky Jameson. "Anyone look familiar?" he said.

Jameson tapped the photo on top. "That's his wife," he said. "Saw a picture of her in the paper this morning. Good lookin' babe." He moved the photo to the bottom, stared for a moment at the next photo. He shook his head. "Never seen her around here." He glanced up. "I never forget a face," he said. "It's my business to remember people. I got people come back year after year for skiing lessons."

"What about the last photo?" Nick said.

The man was already looking at it. "Oh, yeah," he said. "That's her."

Catherine felt her heart take a little jump. "How do you know her?"

"She walked into the bar, about the time I was trying to get away.

Mathews practically turned the table over trying to get to her. He led her to a booth in back. Gave me a little nod on the way, said something like it was nice talking to me, and they scrunched themselves together in the booth. I finished my beer and left." He took a moment, looking up and down the street at the traffic inching past. "That wasn't the last time I saw him. Next day, he walks into the bar alone, sits at my table and says, 'Hey, man,' like we're old buddies. 'I was wondering if you could just forget about the lady yesterday.'

"'Your girlfriend?' I said. By then, I knew he wasn't the man he pretended to be. Wedding ring on his finger, hot babe in the booth. He was definitely glad to see her. I expect they didn't waste a lot of time before they moved on to a room somewhere. So he says, 'Let's just say it would be inconvenient for the press to know about the lady.' Then he pushes some folded bills across the table. He'd make it worth my while, he says. I told him to take his money and stuff it."

"Did you happen to see her on TV?" Catherine said.

"Nah." The man shook his head. "Never owned one. I read the papers, read my books. That's how I get informed."

"Why are you willing to talk to us," Nick said.

"Frankly, that jerk offended me. Real low class, you ask me. Anybody with real class knows nobody in Aspen is gonna blow their privacy. No need to bribe people. I sure as hell didn't want that guy in the governor's office. You ask me, he probably got what was coming to him."

24

The sun was low in a copper-plated sky when they drove alongside the Blue River into Breckenridge. Traffic jammed the main street, crowds spilling out of restaurants and shops. People strolled down the sidewalks licking ice cream cones and bouncing to the sounds in their earphones. Groups of diners sat at the outdoor tables and lifted shimmering glasses of wine. There were flowers everywhere, nasturtiums and pansies in baskets that hung from light posts, bright orange clusters of petunias banked in rock gardens that abutted the buildings. On the drive over Vail Pass from Aspen, they had discussed David Mathews. Too smart for his own good, Catherine had said. She'd covered types like Mathews—God, she'd been married to one—certain they had everything under control. Masters of their own spinning universe. Mathews would never have registered at the same hotel as Ryan Beckman. He had stayed at the Hotel Colorado in Glenwood Springs, but she would have stayed somewhere else. When he returned to his room after a banquet of rubber chicken and several thousand dollars pledged to his campaign, she would be waiting.

"Then there was Aspen," Nick had chimed in, tapping his fingers against the wheel. Jameson had agreed to go with them to a notary where he had sworn out a statement that he had seen David Mathews with Ryan Beckman in the J-Bar in late June. It could be enough to reopen the investigation. A slim hope, but it was all they had. "Mathews didn't count on anyone spotting him," Nick said. "No campaign records that he ever stayed in Aspen. Nobody would have known if Lucky Jameson hadn't spotted him and one of his own staffers hadn't blundered into the bar at the wrong time."

"Even then, Mathews thought he was in control." Oh, he was clever, Catherine was thinking. For a man who wanted to be governor, he played a risky game with high stakes. "He must have breathed a sigh of relief that Jeremy Whitman was the one who caught him with Beckman. Whitman idolized him, and Mathews counted on Whitman swallowing his explanation."

"Only he didn't," Nick said.

Catherine had watched the mountainsides flying past, the flashes of gold in the clusters of aspen trees, the deep gorges filled with wildflowers and mountain streams. The image of Jeremy Whitman had unreeled like a movie in her mind. Sitting across the table from her, waving away her offer of a cup of coffee. He had said he was into serious drinking that night. "Whitman was shaken by Mathews's duplicity and hypocrisy," she said. "He had believed in him. He was looking forward to working at the state capitol. It wasn't easy for him to agree to go to the police, but I think, in the end, he wanted Mathews's killer charged. Maybe he thought it was the last thing he could do for the man."

Nick had been quiet for a long period, eyes narrowed on the highway, forehead creased in thought. Finally he had said, "I don't think Lucky

Jameson gave him any worry, even after he'd turned down Mathews's hush money. If we hadn't shown up asking questions, Jameson wouldn't have come forward. It's not part of the Aspen culture."

"Funny," Catherine said. "Jameson is the only one to have seen through David Mathews."

"Except for you." Nick had given her another quick look. "Come on, Catherine. I read your stuff on the campaign. No matter what Mathews said, you found a way to bring in a counterargument. He said he'd lower taxes, and you pointed out how the last two governors had promised the same thing. Never happened."

Catherine had sunk back in the seat and looked out the window. Maybe her journalistic instincts, or some instincts, had kicked in and she had done something right. She hadn't let David Mathews off the hook, and it had bothered him. How many phone calls late at night—three? four?—after an article had run that he didn't like. She had missed the whole point of his speech, he had thundered at her. She should check her notes, write a retraction. He'd been drinking, she was pretty sure.

Nick swung right off Main Street and started up the hill toward the ski area. Log houses, hotels and condominium buildings sheltered in the pines, separated by narrow dirt roads that wound around, disappeared and reappeared farther up the mountain. A half hour ago, Catherine had checked the GPS on her cell. The complex where Mathews had stayed was off one of those roads. "Could be a wild goose chase," Nick said. "If our theory is correct, nobody will have seen Ryan Beckman anywhere near Mathews's condo."

"She's familiar with Breckenridge," Catherine said. "Supposedly she was here for a few days when Mathews was killed. The perfect alibi. Wherever she stayed, she would have made sure someone saw her and could vouch for her."

Nick made another right and shifted into low gear. The car groaned as they started up the steep, narrow road. He slid to a stop in front of a glass-enclosed porch that jutted from a two-story, cedar-framed building. The word "Office" was printed in discreet black letters on the white plaque next to the front door.

A young woman with dark hair and quick eyes stood behind the counter. "What can we do for you?" she said as they crossed the lobby, another comfortable mountain affair with overstuffed chairs, Oriental rugs and a massive stone fireplace.

Nick went through the same routine: holding up the wallet and badge, explaining they were investigating a case, asking if she'd be willing to look at a few photos.

"I don't know." She glanced around, but there didn't seem to be anyone else available. "I guess it's okay. What's this about?"

"We're trying to identify someone." Nick pulled the photos from his shirt pocket and set them on the counter. "Take your time," he said.

The woman shifted her gaze from one photo to the next, then lifted the photo of Sydney Mathews. "You're investigating a murder case," she said, glancing up. "I saw her on TV. Wasn't she married to that guy that got shot? Candidate for senator or something? She got arrested."

"Either of the other photos look familiar?" Nick said. Catherine could feel her stomach muscles contracting. It was always possible Beckman had been spotted at the condos, always possible the man in control had messed up. The woman took her time studying the other photos. Nick had the kind of patience it took to wade a creek, Catherine thought. Slogging forward a half inch at a time while staying upright and balanced.

"No, I never saw them." The woman shook her head. "But I'm pretty sure the candidate stayed with us this summer. What was his name? Matheson or something?"

Catherine waited until they were back in the car, negotiating the ruts and rocks, the engine growling, before she said: "We can check every hotel or condo that Mathews stayed in while he was campaigning, but the chance is slim that we'll stumble on anyone who recognizes Beckman or ever saw them together. Beckman's counting on that. She's got everything figured out. She's ahead of us."

Nick shot her a look that was lined with hope. "She doesn't know about Jameson's sworn statement," he said.

Ryan sipped at the lukewarm coffee she had drained from the bottom of the container and stared at the black text on the computer screen. The downtown lights danced in the black windows at the end of the detective's area. The only sound was the faint hum of traffic on Thirteenth Street. She had told Martin to go on home, she'd write up the report, compile what they had on Sydney Mathews. The black widow, they had taken to calling her. Very rich, now that her husband was dead. What Martin didn't know, and she hadn't told him, was that the widow had been richer than David by millions, before she had met the man. All that would come out when the DA dug up the couple's financial records. It didn't matter. The motive was much simpler, more primitive. Sydney had put up with her husband's philandering long enough. They had argued, and she had shot him. The phone calls from the Denver house and the Evergreen house proved Sydney and David had talked to each other eight times over a two-hour period the night he died. Fortunately, the calls had ended by eleven o'clock, which allowed plenty of time for Sydney to drive to Denver. And ballistics had confirmed that the gun hidden away in Sydney's desk drawer was the murder weapon.

It was beautiful.

Except for Catherine McLeod. It should have been a simple matter to take care of her last night. The instant she got out of her car in the garage, she would have been dead. But she didn't pull into the garage, and that was a miscalculation on her part, Ryan realized. When Ryan had driven down the alley, she had spotted the tracks leading from the gravel apron into the garage and deduced that McLeod usually parked in the garage. Still, Ryan could have shot her in the yard, if it hadn't been for the damn dog yapping and jumping about and McLeod zigzagging all over the place. Another perfect chance muffed with McLeod framed in the kitchen window, and all Ryan had to do was pull the trigger. She had missed, and the thought of failure burned like a hot coal inside her. Now McLeod knew she was a target. Ryan would have to rethink the hunt.

She had run into people like Catherine McLeod before. Something different about them, edgy and distrustful, operating on instincts that defied logic, yet seemed to work out. She had gone after murderers and bank robbers and rapists in Minneapolis, and within minutes she knew when she was up against one of those intuitive types. Survivors, was how she thought of them. They could outrun bullets. But eventually they stumbled, let go of their survival instincts, and that was when she had gotten them.

She finished typing the times of the phone calls between the Evergreen and Denver houses and pressed the print key. "We've worked out an agreement," David had told her. "Sydney will stay with me through the campaign."

"What about after the campaign?" Ryan had asked. The memory of that last conversation at David's house stoked her anger. She could feel the heat rising in her chest, warming her cheeks.

"Listen, Ryan." He had used that irritating, condescending voice, as if she weren't quite up to his mental capacities or his social standing. She had wanted to smash in his face. "You and I both have to move on."

Strange, she didn't remember actually pulling the trigger. She was certain she had no intention of shooting him. She had wanted him to open his eyes and look at her. She had wanted him to listen to her. Then he would have understood there was no room for Sydney, no need for any other women. She would be enough.

She got up, stepped outside the cubicle and collected the sheets the printer had spit out. There had been a few glitches. Last night at McLeod's house was the worst, but in the end, things would work out. Sydney and her stupid phone calls, the murder weapon in the desk drawer—the grieving widow would be tried and convicted.

Jeremy Whitman could have posed a problem, but she had taken care of him. Now there was only the woman out on the sidewalk and Catherine McLeod who knew too much for their own good.

She thumbed through the printed sheets. Another possible glitch, she realized. Motivation. If Sydney Mathews had killed her husband out of rage or jealousy over his affairs, the district attorney might want to produce evidence of David's affairs. Some eager investigator could start looking for the women. God, there was always the chance an investigator might stumble onto her! She clamped her eyes shut against the possibility. There was nothing to link her with David. Except for the woman on the sidewalk, and sooner or later, an eager investigator could stumble onto who she was.

She had to find the woman and silence her. Then she had to take care of the reporter. Catherine McLeod, persistent, dangerous, and clever.

Ryan started back to her cubicle, then stopped. There were footsteps out in the corridor, coming closer. Nick Bustamante working late on the gang angle in the Whitman murder, she suspected. She wondered how much his girlfriend might have told him, then pushed that thought away. Years ago she had taught herself to focus on threats that were real, not those she imagined. She was capable of imagining a lot of crazy things that never happened. If Bustamante had anything solid, he would have gone to Internal Affairs. Which meant his girlfriend didn't have any solid evidence. Not yet.

Martin rounded the corner into the detective's area. "Figured you'd be working late," he said. He looked ruffled and tired, a late-in-the-day beard shadowing his chin. "You okay?"

"Why wouldn't I be?"

"Look, we're close to winding up this case. You should take some time off, try to relax. I'm worried about you. This is a big case, but it's not, you know, personal."

Ryan gestured toward the file in his hand. "What do you have?"

"ID and address from Mathews's Internet provider," he said, handing her the file. Ryan made herself look away from the questions in his eyes. "Full name is Kim Gregory," Martin said. "The address is registered to an escort service. Morningtide LLC."

"Lovely," Ryan said.

25

"Shot at? You were shot at and all you had to say was that nobody was hurt? Then you take off. You're out of contact for twenty-four hours? What the hell is going on?" Marjorie rose from behind the desk, cheeks puffed out and red, and for an instant, Catherine had the image of a big red balloon about to explode. It was true. She had turned off her cell yesterday; the story was developing. She had nothing she could write about. She sank back in the chair.

"I'm here, and I'm okay," Catherine managed. She could tell by the way Marjorie rolled her eyes that she knew it was a lie. She was on edge, every nerve raw and flayed—Marjorie probably saw that as well. Catherine had tried the last two nights to put the shooting behind her, block it out of her mind, but even with Nick—the warmth and strength of him beside her—she had lain awake, replaying every minute in her mind, watching a jerky black-and-white film over and over again in slow motion. Had she parked in the garage . . . God, had she parked in the garage, she would be dead.

"You're off this story," Marjorie said. "The police have the killer. She'll be tried and no doubt convicted. Jason will handle the story from now on."

Catherine took a moment before she said, "An innocent woman standing trial for murder, an innocent young man shot to death in LoDo, and another innocent person in danger. I have to keep going. I'm the only one the caller has contacted."

"Which doesn't mean anything." Marjorie sat down hard, rolled in close to the desk and leaned forward. "You've put messages on your blog, but she hasn't called back. My guess is she's left the state, maybe the country."

Catherine had started shaking her head before Marjorie finished. "She doesn't want Beckman to get away with murder. Maybe she was in love with David. I heard the anger in her voice."

"What you heard was fear," Marjorie said. "Frankly I detect the same thing in your voice."

"Look, Marjorie," Catherine said. "It won't do any good to take me off the story."

"Excuse me?"

"Beckman knows I know about her. Do you really believe she'll drop the whole matter if I stop writing about David Mathews? I don't want to go through life looking over my shoulder, wondering if Beckman's waiting in the garage every time I drive home. Let me stay on the story. I'll find the witness. I'll put another message on the blog." Catherine got to her feet, took hold of the doorknob and waited.

Finally Marjorie gave a reluctant nod, and Catherine let herself out into the newsroom. An eerie silence blanketed the cubicles; heads suddenly tilting toward computer screens. A second ago, she knew, every reporter had been watching the confrontation through the glass partition of Marjorie's office.

Catherine rounded the corner into her own cubicle, dropped onto her chair and stared at the phone. Where are you? Who are you? Why won't you call? The mixture of inevitability and futility clamped around her like a vise. She pounded a fist on the desk; the keyboard skidded sideways a little. Case closed, according to the police. Killer apprehended, evidence handed over to the district attorney, an immense legal juggernaut running down Sydney Mathews. And she had to locate an anonymous caller who, as Marjorie said, had probably left the state, relieved to put the whole affair behind her.

The phone rang, and Catherine felt her heart jump. The readout said unknown. She grabbed the receiver. "Catherine McLeod," she said, pressing the cool plastic against her ear. She could hear her heart pounding.

"Catherine?" It was a man's voice. "Just getting back to you on Detective Beckman."

It was a moment before her thoughts stopped racing and she settled on the name: Larry Burns from the *Minneapolis Star Tribune*. "What have you got?" she said, tucking the receiver under her shoulder and placing her fingers over the keyboard, willing her heart to stop thumping.

"You understand I don't have access to the police personnel files, but I talked to a couple of superiors. Detective Ryan Beckman, two awards in marksmanship, honored for showing restraint and good judgment in one incident, and for bravery in the line of duty in another."

Catherine bent over the keyboard, and the clack of the keys punctuated the recital of Beckman's record. "What were the honors about?" she said.

"She was a rookie, out on patrol, when a drunk threatened her with a knife. Instead of shooting him, she talked him into dropping the knife. Then, a year before she left the force, she shot a man to death in defense of her partner. The victim had refused her partner's order to drop his weapon and Beckman fired. She was exonerated by both the police and DA investigations. Received a commendation for bravery."

Catherine kept typing. Great! She thought. Detective Beckman, a hero.

"Seemed to affect her, though," the voice on the line went on. "Not the shooting itself, her superior told me, but being suspended during the investigation. She acted like she had been unfairly treated, like they should've given her a parade or something. Anyway, the superior thinks that's why she started looking to relocate in another city."

"I owe you, Larry." Catherine wasn't sure what the information meant, or if it meant anything, except that Beckman wasn't afraid of facing another human being and pulling the trigger.

"There's more," Larry said. "Everything Beckman's former superiors had to say was more or less the official line, the only thing they could say. The same stuff that was in the newspaper. But I have a couple of good drinking buddies on the force, and they filled me in on the unofficial line. This isn't for publication, you understand. I promised 'em."

Catherine had stopped typing. "It's background," she said. "I'm working on a story that could involve Beckman, and I'm trying to understand what makes her tick."

A loud guffaw filled the line. "From what these guys said, that is the million dollar question. The shooting she was involved in, they say, could've been avoided."

Catherine started typing again: "The guy holding a gun on her partner was a kid, twenty years old. The partner said he was talking the kid down when Beckman fired the shot. Another half second, he said, and he would've had the kid's gun. Of course, nobody knows that, and the partner might have ended up dead. She was hailed as a hero in the press—and I have to take my share of blame for that. Beautiful, brave female detective! People loved the story. Beckman had followed standard procedure and was exonerated, but her partner asked to work with somebody else. Other guys that worked with her, they said she was trigger happy, quick to flare up, irrational. They didn't trust her."

"So that's why she left," Catherine said. The Denver police department would have looked into her background; they would have gotten the official version of events.

"Then there was the domestic abuse case. Really made the guys mad." Larry exhaled a long puff of air that sounded as if he were blowing out a candle. "Two of the guys I spoke with got a call to Ryan's house about 2:00 a.m. one morning. Nobody there but Ryan and her husband. She'd been married three or four years to a guy who owned a software company. Made a lot of money, and they lived in a fancy neighborhood."

Catherine typed in the words: domestic abuse. Strange how you never know what might turn up in someone's background. It had never occurred to her that Ryan Beckman could be the victim of domestic abuse.

"The call was hushed up, kept out of the news," Larry said. "I sure didn't hear anything about it. That was another thing that ticked off the guys. If there had been a domestic abuse call on one of them, they would have been suspended. Big investigation. Bottom line, they could have lost their jobs. Real double standard operating here. Of course the brass thought of Beckman as a hero and didn't want to tarnish her image."

"Hold on." Catherine had stopped typing. She sat back, gripping the receiver against her ear. "Are you telling me Beckman was the perpetrator?"

"She sure wasn't the victim," Larry said.

Catherine thanked him and hit the off button, a new image of Detective Ryan Beckman forming in her mind. Aggressive, ruthless, violent, accustomed to skating on the edge and taking risks, implacable and dangerous.

She tapped out the number of Nick's cell phone. He picked up on the second ring. "You okay?" he said.

"I'm okay," she said. Maybe 75 percent okay, she was thinking, as long as she managed to push away thoughts of Beckman hiding in the garage, shooting through the kitchen window. She asked if Nick had taken the statement to Internal Affairs.

"Just came out of the meeting," he said. "They'll look into Jameson's claim he saw Mathews and Beckman together, send investigators to Aspen to talk to him. But . . ."

"But? Jameson's statement should be enough to take her off the case and assign other investigators."

"It's pretty thin evidence," Nick said. She felt a prick of annoyance at the patient tone he adopted, as if she were too blinded by her own agenda to comprehend the facts. "Jameson could be mistaken. A lot of beautiful blond women surface in Aspen. And the case against Sydney Mathews is pretty tight. She had possession of the weapon, and she'd been in contact with her husband numerous times by phone before he was killed. They had been seen arguing in public."

"It's circumstantial, Nick."

"She was officially charged this morning."

"Oh, my God," Catherine said. "Where is she?"

"Bonded out. Reporters all over the place, pushing microphones at her and her brother. They got away in a limousine. What about your caller?"

Catherine said she was about to put another message on her blog. "I'll call you the minute I hear anything," she told him before hanging up. She felt limp and powerless, the way her people must have felt in the Old Time, she thought, knowing a horrible incident had occurred that would set off horrible repercussions, and there was nothing they could do about it.

She brought up the blog and started typing. "A message to the woman who called two days ago. Urgent. Please call back immediately. New facts have emerged. You are not alone."

Forty-five minutes later, Catherine guided the convertible on the dirt road that wound through the rocky, pine-studded slopes to the Evergreen house. An SUV was parked in front, but no sign of other reporters or TV trucks. The "No comment" that Sydney's lawyer had probably shouted to the crowd of reporters at the courthouse must have deterred them, for which she was grateful. She had taken a chance coming here, hoping Sydney would agree to see her before the woman's brother ordered her off the property.

She parked next to the SUV, hurried up the steps to the front door, and lifted the heavy, brass knocker, letting it fall against the wood. The house was enveloped in quiet. No sounds of traffic or bustle of people. Even the wind sighing in the pine trees and the distant chirping of a bird seemed part of the mountain quiet. She listened hard for some movement inside, some hint of a human presence. Nothing. She pounded the knocker against the wood, thinking that maybe she should have called, convinced Sydney that it was in her interests to see her. Instead, she had taken a chance Sydney would think that whatever had brought the *Journal* reporter all the way to Evergreen must be important and she would let her inside.

She knocked again. Still nothing, not the slightest sound of disturbance. What a waste of time and effort. Sydney had probably gone home with her brother, wherever he lived. Catherine was about to start down the steps when the door opened with a loud whooshing sound. "What do you want?" Wendell Lane stood in the opening, a fist curled over the doorknob. He looked disheveled and angry, tie loosened at the neck of his white shirt, face reddened as if he'd spent hours in the sunshine.

"I have some information for Sydney," Catherine said.

"You have something to tell us? Well, that's a switch, a reporter giving away information."

"It's important," Catherine said. "Is she in?"

"She has nothing to say to you or any other bottom-feeding reporters. None of this mess would have occurred if the media hadn't piled on, demanding a solution. My sister was railroaded to satisfy people like you, so you can write your story and move on to the next big story. The truth means nothing to you. Just the story, any story will do, and all the better if it's a racy story about a decent human being like my sister."

"Enough, Wendell." Sydney moved like a shadow behind her brother's shoulder, then stepped around him. "What is it you want to tell me," she said.

"This isn't a good idea," Wendell said. "Landon said not to talk to the press." He looked back at Catherine. "You're trespassing. I insist you leave immediately."

"Let me handle this," Sydney said. Then, nodding at Catherine, "You'd better come inside."

26

Catherine followed Sydney Mathews into the living room that sprawled across the south side of the house. It seemed fixed in time, as if nothing had changed. All plush upholstery, carved mahogany tables, paintings of mountain landscapes on the walls, and Oriental rugs on the polished wood floors, static and immobile. Slats of sunshine fell through the mullioned windows. "What is it you have to say," Sydney said, wheeling about.

"First," Catherine began, "I want to say how sorry I am . . ."

The woman threw up both hands. "Save your pity."

"I told you, this isn't a good idea." Wendell's voice came from behind.

"Let me handle this," Sydney said, looking past Catherine's shoulder. Then she drew in a long breath, clasped her arms around herself and said, "This whole thing is a farce, a rush by the police and DA to solve the murder of a prominent man, who happened to be my husband. All based on the worst kind of innuendo and circumstantial evidence.

Did we talk on the phone the night he was killed? Yes, many times. Had we argued in public? Did I go to campaign headquarters and give David a piece of my mind after I realized how many rumors were going around about his unfaithfulness? You bet I did."

"This is off the record," Wendell said. "Nothing that my sister insists upon telling you had better appear in the newspaper."

"Wendell, please!" Sydney stared at her brother a moment, then dipped her head toward Catherine, as if they were in a conspiracy together. "I must thank you for setting me straight. Until you asked me—a reporter asking me about David's affairs!—I had closed my eyes and ears, refused to see and hear what was all around me. Refused to *smell* what was around me! I came back from a trip to New York and a whore's perfume was everywhere. In my house! In my own bed! I told myself it couldn't be true, that I was imagining things. Not that David wasn't capable of whoring around. Oh, I knew the man. But not during the campaign, not when he was so close to his dream of the governor's office. I couldn't believe he would jeopardize his dream by taking such risks. As soon as word got out, and obviously you were trying to chase down the rumors, he would have been ruined. It was only a matter of time. So I went to campaign headquarters to tell him that if he wanted to ruin himself, he would not take me down with him. I wanted out. I had every intention of filing for a divorce."

"Which is what I advised you to do." Wendell crossed the room and parked himself against the back of a sofa. "You wouldn't be caught up in this if you had filed for divorce and gone to Europe like you intended."

"Why didn't you?" Catherine said.

"It's complicated, isn't it? The relationship between a man and a woman." Sydney started circling the center of the room, picking up a ceramic bowl and turning it in her hands a moment before replacing it on a long table. "I loved David, but who didn't? Everyone who stepped into his light fell in love with him. I loved him even though I knew him. He begged me not to file for a divorce. Begged me to stay with him. Promised he was done with other women, they meant nothing. I agreed to think about it. It would have ruined him if I'd filed for the divorce. Everyone would have believed the rumors. I didn't want to do that to him."

She exhaled a long breath, as if she were letting go of the last energy she possessed, and sank onto the armrest of a large, overstuffed chair. "Ironic, isn't it. We talked on the phone the night he was killed. He must have called me five or six times, and I called him as well. We were working out the details of a reconciliation. There were certain demands I made, and I didn't want any misunderstandings. No more extracurricular affairs. He would not travel anywhere without me. We would spend every night together, which meant, of course, that I wouldn't take any trips without him. It was a small price to pay. When I think about it, the shopping trips were really an excuse not to have to face what was happening in my marriage. Anyway, we had come to an agreement I was satisfied with. I even offered to come to Denver, but he said no. He was very tired and still had some policy papers he wanted to read. We planned to meet for breakfast in the morning. Meet for breakfast and start a new life together."

"All very touching," Wendell said. "I believe Catherine McLeod said she has information for you."

The house went quiet. Catherine felt them both watching her, assessing her. Even Sydney, probably wondering if the *Journal* reporter had found a ruse to get inside the house, get her to talking. "There is someone," she began, "who has sworn he saw your husband with a woman last June in Aspen. They were in the bar at the Hotel Jerome, and it looked like more than a friendly meeting."

Sydney closed her eyes and started shaking her head. "This is the earthshaking information you have for me? A confirmation of the rumors? Please!" Her eyes burst open. "How is this supposed to help me?"

"The man who saw them together has identified the woman." Sydney was still shaking her head, and Catherine held up her hand. "There's more," she said. Then she explained about the woman on the sidewalk and the anonymous call. "The caller said that she saw the same woman on the porch at the Denver house just after she heard the gunshots."

"A woman?" Sydney said. "Oh, my God. Don't tell me I'm the one they claim they saw. I was never in Aspen with David."

"They've identified Detective Beckman," Catherine said.

"What!" Wendell propelled himself over to his sister and took hold of her shoulders, as if he wanted to hold her up, but Catherine suspected he was the one who needed support. "You're telling us that the detective who has all but convicted my sister of murder, the detective is the killer? Why wasn't our lawyer informed? What the hell is going on? My sister is being railroaded. The police are protecting their own detective."

"Internal Affairs was informed this morning. They have a statement from the witness in Aspen, and investigators are on their way there now to question him further. There is always the chance he is either lying or mistaken." She didn't believe it; Lucky Jameson told the truth, she was certain. It only remained for the investigators to reach the same conclusion. "The witness who saw Beckman at the house hasn't come forward. She . . ."

"So, a woman was on her way to meet David." Sydney's tone was low, almost accepting of something inevitable. "That explains why he didn't want me to come to the house. So much dull reading to wade through. He'd be asleep before I got there. No, no. We'll start over at breakfast." She dropped her face into her hands and started sobbing.

Wendell patted at her shoulders, a helpless look about him, as if he were searching for the logical and comforting platitudes that would set matters right, but the words eluded him. Finally he tossed his head back and stared at Catherine. "Outrageous!" he said. He gave his sister's shoulder a final pat and stepped in front of her, as if he could protect her. "The DA has withheld information. I'll have our lawyer—"

"The DA didn't have the information," Catherine said. "Internal Affairs is checking on the witness in Aspen, and the woman who called hasn't been identified. I've been trying to send her a message, and I'm hoping she'll call back. But based on the witness in Aspen, I suspect another investigation will be launched."

"You're damn right it will." Wendell strode into the entry, brushing past Catherine and shouting over one shoulder, "I'm going to call Landon's office right now. He had better get to the bottom of this." A door slammed in another part of the house, sending a little rush of air through the living room.

Catherine waited a moment while the woman slumped on the armrest ran her fingers over the moisture on her cheeks and pulled herself upright. "Thank you," she said "Now I know how the murder weapon got into the desk drawer in David's study. Obviously someone had planted it, but I didn't know who. I never suspected a detective."

"Detective Beckman came here?"

Sydney nodded. "Oh, yes. Hours after David's murder, she and her partner showed up. So solicitous, pretending shock over what had happened, assuring us that the investigation took top priority with the police department, that they wouldn't rest until the murderer was charged. And all the time, all the time . . ." She stopped, as if she might break down again, then seemed to summon a new strength. "They made sure I would be convicted."

"How do you think she planted the gun?" Catherine said.

"It was very easy, now that I think about it. How stupid I was. 'Did your husband have a computer?' Detective Beckman said. We were standing right here." She swept one hand toward an Oriental rug. "'May I see it?'" she said. 'Certainly' I said. 'Be my guest. Go on into the study without a warrant. Look around all you want' or some such idiotic thing. I gave her carte blanche to walk into the study and put the gun in a drawer. I did try to follow her, I remember, but her partner, Martin somebody, jumped in front of me, started asking questions to keep me here."

"How long was Beckman alone in the study?"

"Long enough," Sydney said.

"I'm sorry for what you've been through," Catherine said. She started toward the entry, then turned back. "Would you have any idea of who the witness at the house might be?"

Sydney gave a little strangled laugh. "Since I spent most of our marriage in denial, I was hardly collecting names."

Catherine thanked her and turned into the entry. "Check the escort agencies," Sydney called behind her. "He liked to avoid serious entanglements. Whores are good for that."

The newsroom felt like home, familiar faces looking up from the cubicles, Marjorie bent over the computer screen, Jason clamping a phone to his ear. Driving down the mountains, onto I-70 and into Denver, Catherine had replayed the conversation in her mind. What had she done? Violated confidences? Hardly. Lucky Jameson had sworn out a statement, and Nick had spoken with Internal Affairs this morning. Before the day was over, Beckman herself would most likely be the subject of a new investigation. Sydney's lawyer would have the indictment thrown out on evidence that the lead detective was involved with the victim. A detective with a motive to kill David Mathews, a man who had agreed to reconcile with his wife, a man who didn't like serious entanglements. A man who, even while reconciling, might call an escort service.

She had owed Sydney Mathews the truth, Catherine realized. Since the morning of the murder, the frightened, small voice on the telephone, she had known who the killer was, but she hadn't been able to do anything. She had watched an innocent woman being mowed down by the justice system. The caller might not call back, but at least Sydney Mathews knew the truth.

She ducked into her own cubicle, checked her voice mail. Nothing. Checked her e-mail. A lot of junk, but nothing important. She typed in "Escort Services Denver" and ran her eyes down the sites forming on the screen. Twenty-two pages of sites. This would take all day, she thought, and what was she supposed to say when she called a service? "Hello, I'd like to speak to the woman in front of David Mathews's house the night he was killed?"

The phone started ringing, startling her. Larry with another Beckman story he'd remembered, she thought, then she saw the words in the readout: Hotel Francaise. She lifted the receiver. "McLeod," she said.

"I'm the one who called you." The woman's voice was small and tentative, fear seeping through the words, and Catherine was aware of exhaling, as if her own pent-up fear and discouragement had been freed. God, the woman must have read the blog. "Why didn't you do something?"

"I don't understand," Catherine said.

"You didn't run my story."

"I don't know your name. I can't run an unattributed story." She couldn't have run it if she'd had a raft of names, not without bringing libel and slander suits down on the *Journal*.

"It's terrible what they're doing to David's wife. I saw her on TV. I told you who was on David's porch right after I heard the gunshots."

"Listen," Catherine searched for the words, gripping the receiver so hard her fingers felt numb, trying to keep the caller on the line. "There is someone else who can connect Mathews and Beckman. You're not alone. The police will have to believe your story. I'll go with you to Internal Affairs."

"Like hell I'm talking to them. Beckman will hang me out to dry, like she's done to Sydney. And Sydney has money and connections and a high-priced lawyer. None of it mattered. They still charged her. You think they're gonna believe me? They'll say I'm lying to protect my own skin, that I was the one that went to David's house and shot him. They'll never believe me. But they'd believe you if you put the story in the newspaper!" The woman's voice edged toward hysteria. "I thought you'd want justice. I guess I was wrong."

"Wait a minute," Catherine said. "Don't hang up." The line was already dead.

Catherine hit the key for the receptionist's desk. "I was disconnected," she said "Can you get the caller back."

It took a moment before the buzzing noise began. Catherine tapped out a fast rhythm against the edge of the desk.

"Hotel Francaise." Woman's voice, thick accent. "How may I direct your call?"

Catherine jotted down the name, a boutique hotel a few blocks away. "I was just speaking with one of your guests," she said. "We were cut off somehow. Could you ring the room?"

"One moment, please." There was a pause, then the buzzing noise of a ringing phone.

An automated voice came on the line: "I'm sorry, but your party is not available. You may leave a message at the beep."

27

Kim Gregory sat on the edge of the bed and stared at the ringing phone on the table. White plastic, red light flashing, like a wild animal that might spring into action and sink its teeth into her flesh. She pressed her knuckles hard against her mouth. What had she been thinking? Calling the reporter from the hotel? Of course she would get the number and call back. And now Catherine McLeod knew where she was. The light stopped flashing. She waited a moment, then lifted the receiver and pressed the messages button. The automated voice said there was one message. She closed her eyes and listened to the voice of Catherine McLeod: "You are in danger. Beckman knows you've contacted me. She's sure to be looking for you. I can help you, but you have to trust me. I'm on my way over to the hotel now. Please, meet me in the lobby."

Kim propelled herself off the bed, flung the terry cloth robe she'd been wearing into the corner and began pulling on the pair of jeans and pink blouse that had been on the floor. God. God. God. She had to get away from here. She slipped on her sandals, dragged the Louis Vuitton bag out of the closet and started stuffing in her things: blue satin ball gown, short, pink, silk dinner dress, white slacks and sleeveless black top with turquoise beads at the neck. She scooped the pieces of jewelry off the dresser into the bag, then went into the bathroom and shoved her cosmetics into a small bag. Mr. Arnold Winston expected her to look beautiful, coiffured and manicured in designer pieces—he paid the bills, and the clothes and jewelry were hers to keep, one of the perks of her job. There were others: five-star dinners, dancing, hobnobbing with VIPs, riding in limousines with chauffeurs shuffling and bowing, and all she had to do was smile and smile and keep her mouth shut, and spend the week with a bald, lonely man from Atlanta, in town for business meetings and the social events that went with them. He was pathetic in bed, drunk, sick, so tired most nights he fell asleep when his head hit the pillow. None of that mattered. At the end of the week, she was free, with a new Louis Vuitton bag filled with new clothes, a pearl necklace and seven thousand dollars in cash. Two thou for the agency, which would leave her with five. Except there wouldn't be any money this week.

You are in danger. Beckman knows . . . McLeod's voice spun in her head. She should never have trusted her. Trust nobody, Mama had said. She coughed out a laugh at the memory, then jammed the cosmetic bag into the Vuitton, pressed her knee on top and jerked at the zipper. What was she? All of nine years old, she and Mama traipsing from one dusthole, windblown, nowhere town to another. God, they'd pretty much covered Arizona, Nevada, Utah, New Mexico by then, and Mama with her fourth or fifth husband. After a while all the whisky reeking, bowlegged cowboys had blended together. When she was sixteen, she had gotten out. Sayonara, Mama. Adios. She could take care of herself, and she'd done a fine job. South Beach, first. Then Denver. No missteps.

Tread carefully, go with the best clientele, stay safe. Once in a while, even the best pulled a surprise. Big shot from Florida knocked her unconscious in the hotel room a year ago. The agency had banned him, and spread the word to the other agencies. No respectable escort service would do business with him. When she thought about it, and she tried not to think about it, she always felt a stab of pity for the girls on Colfax he was probably picking up when he came to town.

Then there was David Mathews. Call from a local businessman, Ericka at the agency told her. "Want to take it?" There was always danger in taking a local client. Embarrassing later when you ran into each other at a social event, and he could always spread the word: See that woman in the blue dress? Diamond ring? Pearl necklace? Very expensive hooker. Gossip like that could end her career. But she had said yes to David Mathews. She'd read about him in the paper—how his business partner had accused him of theft, how the complaint was withdrawn. Catherine McLeod had written the articles, and Kim had remembered the name.

They had met once at a hotel in Boulder where David wasn't likely to run into a client or friend. What a lonely man, she had thought, talking and talking, pouring out his heart over dinner at a café on the Pearl Street Mall. He and his partner had built a successful business together, plenty for both of them. Why would David Mathews need to cheat him? And his wife threatening to leave him. Not that he would mind, he'd said, but a divorce would be messy, played out in the newspaper and interfering with his long-range plans. He intended to be governor. After that first night, David had become a regular. He always called her cell and told her where and when to meet him. She was never to contact him; it was too risky, he said. They had formed a connection, no doubt about it, the kind of connection she had never allowed before. Trust no one, probably the only good advice Mama ever had.

David's calls were sporadic, but she always knew they would come. Then in the spring, the calls became fewer and fewer, and she'd gotten the sense there was another woman. Not David's wife. Someone more threatening. Two weeks ago, she had decided to send him the e-mail, asking if she would ever see him again, but she changed her mind. She never wrote the message. Somehow she must have pressed "Send" because he had called then. Blown up at her, the only time he had ever raised his voice. She was never to e-mail him! Finally, he had told her to come to the Denver house. They had made plans then for her to come back at midnight four nights ago.

She wasn't sure why the contents of her purse were strewn across the top of another dresser. She brushed the wallet, comb, lipsticks, appointment book, cell, wadded receipts, address book, lighter and cigarettes into the purse, remembering now. Arnold had wanted a cigarette, and she had gone looking in her bag. "Now!" he had bellowed. She had dumped out the contents, handed him the package and lighted the cigarette for him.

You are in danger. She slung the purse over her shoulder, picked up the Louis Vuitton and glanced around the room. The agency would probably let her go: unacceptable to walk out on a client, especially a reliable client like Arnold, who always requested her. Business associates in Denver believed she was his fiancée. What a joke, she thought. What a joke her life was.

David murdered, his wife on her way to prison, the murderer a detective, and she, a whore nobody would believe.

She flung open the door, stepped into the corridor and stopped. The arrow above the elevator was moving. The elevator was two floors below and ascending. Arnold had gone to breakfast with clients this morning. He was due back at any moment. They would go to the Denver Art

Museum, he'd said. She should get her hair and nails done this afternoon. Gala ball at the Hyatt tonight. He wanted her perfect.

She hurried down the corridor away from the elevator, darted around a corner and pressed herself against the wall. She held her breath. The elevator dinged, the doors swooshed open. She could hear Arnold's methodical, padding footsteps coming toward the room. Then the faint click of a plastic key, the pneumatic huff of the door opening and closing. She peeked around the corner, then hurried past the door to the elevator. It would take him a couple of minutes to realize she was gone; he wouldn't believe his eyes—her side of the closet empty, the cosmetics and jewelry cleared away. She pressed the button. A different elevator was on its way down, still five floors above. The first thing Arnold would do—oh, she knew the man—was charge out of the room down to the reception desk and demand to know when she had left. She huddled close to the door, willing the elevator to appear.

From behind, she heard the door open. Then the elevator dinged, the doors parted and she darted into the front corner and jammed her finger against the close-door button. She hit the lobby button. "Wait!" she heard Arnold's raspy shout, the sound of him pounding down the corridor. As the doors slid shut, she glimpsed a slice of his reddened face.

"She called!" Catherine shouted through the half-opened door to Marjorie's cubicle as she headed into the reception area. "I'm on my way to meet her."

"Hey, hold on." Marjorie must have flung herself from behind the desk because she was marching behind her. Catherine could hear the short, quick intakes of breath, the almost palpable excitement. She let herself out of the newsroom and plunged toward the elevators. Marjorie had caught up as Catherine pressed the down button.

"She called? Who is she? Did you get her name?"

Catherine shook her head. "She's at the Hotel Francaise. Let's hope she'll meet me in the lobby."

"Let's hope?" The relief on Marjorie's face dissolved into a look of consternation. "You mean she didn't agree?"

"She's scared," Catherine said. The elevator arrived, and she stepped inside. "I'm afraid she'll run," she said past the closing doors. "I've got to get there before she does."

She drove her car out of the garage into the noonday glare, the sporadic blare of horns and the acrid smells of gasoline and exhaust. Downtown traffic inched along, four lanes converging into one, an accident ahead, red and blue lights flashing. Sirens wailed in the distance. She should have walked, she thought. She could have covered the few blocks faster.

The caller would run. Catherine could feel the truth of it; she had heard it in the caller's voice: remorse, fright, the frantic plunge of her thoughts toward safety. Safety meant not getting involved. And yet, something had led her to call the *Journal* in the first place and to call back.

The hotel was still a couple of blocks ahead. Catherine slid into a no-parking zone, got out and started running, brushing past the lawyers and stockbrokers in wrinkled suits, careening through a group of young secretaries in cotton skirts that wrapped around their legs, sipping on Diet Cokes and munching burritos. The stop light ahead turned yellow. She kept running even when the light flicked to red, weaving past the traffic that growled and screeched around her. She passed the wide concrete steps to the Denver Center for the Performing Arts, the glass-enclosed roof shimmering in the sunshine, and crossed another street on the yellow light. Another block, and she spotted the tan brick building with curlicue embellishments and awnings at the windows.

She was out of breath, her chest on fire, when she hurried past the doorman who had jumped forward to hold the door. The lobby was small and intimate, with cream-colored tiles on the floor and overstuffed chairs arranged around marble-topped tables. She stopped a few feet inside the door and glanced around the seating area. The chairs were vacant. Apart from two clerks in navy blazers behind the reception desk, no one was around. She heard her heart pounding as she walked over to the desk; she could be too late.

"May I help you?" The woman smiling at her might have been anywhere between thirty and fifty, with shoulder-length, black hair and the stretched-drum look of too many cosmetic surgeries.

Catherine launched into explanation: Twenty minutes ago, she had received a call from a guest. The call had been cut off, and the hotel had tried to ring the guest, but the guest hadn't answered. She pushed her business card toward the clerk. "It's very important I speak with her," she said.

The woman fingered the card a moment. "You're from the *Journal?*"

"The woman who called me is in danger," Catherine said, and the woman's eyebrows shot up. "This has nothing to do with the hotel, I assure you. I do need to speak with her. Would you be good enough to ring the room?"

The hesitation was so long that Catherine was certain the woman would refuse. Her heart was leaping around now, knocking against her ribs. Finally, the clerk said, "I don't know if it's possible. One moment." She picked up the card and disappeared around a wood paneled wall behind her.

It was a couple of minutes before she returned. "Mr. Winston suggests you come upstairs," she said. "Room 814. Elevators on the right."

Catherine made her way to the elevators and rode to the eighth floor, not sure of what had happened. It was possible she was on her way to another room where a telephone call had been cut off, except that the call hadn't been cut off. The caller had hung up.

The red patterned carpeting grabbed at her heels as she walked down the corridor. She stopped in front of the door with the brass numerals "814" above the peephole, held her breath, and knocked. From the other side came a shuffle of footsteps, then the door swung open. The man in front of her was in his fifties, bald with a maze of tiny blue veins across his nose and cheeks, lips parted in a smile that registered somewhere between anger and acceptance. He had bright, intelligent blue eyes. She could feel the heat of his gaze running over her.

28

"So you're the replacement," the man said. "Not bad, not bad at all. I like the ethnic look. What are you? Indian? Hispanic. Hell, it doesn't matter. Bellman bringing up your bags? You'd better come in." He stepped sideways.

"Mr. Winston," she began.

"Can't stand around talking in the corridor." He rolled his shoulders to motion her inside. "Don't need a bunch of busybodies listening in on my business."

"I believe there's a mistake." Catherine remained in the doorway. "I'm looking for the woman who called me a short time ago. I was told she had called from this room, but the receptionist must have made a mistake."

He was still craning his neck and looking up and down the corridor. "Step inside now," he said, his tone low and proprietary, as if she were one of his servants. "I'm not a monster. I won't bite you."

Catherine took another moment before she stepped past him into a suite that looked larger than her house. A living room that resembled the lobby, similar overstuffed chairs with decorative fringe, luxurious-looking sofa, marble tables arranged here and there with bouquets of fresh roses that spilled from crystal vases, a flat-paneled TV against one wall. A wall of windows framed the Daniels and Fisher Tower on the Sixteenth Street Mall. Beyond the double doors on the far wall, she could see the large poster bed, tangled blankets and sheets dropping onto the floor. The door snapped shut behind her. She swallowed hard. Thank God, he didn't throw the lock.

"So Kim called you," he said. "Complaining about what? I was too generous, too many gowns and fancy events for trailer trash like her?"

Kim. The caller's name was Kim. "Is she here?" Catherine said, glancing at the double doors and the closed door across from the bed that most likely led to the bathroom.

"Don't pretend you don't know she ran out on me, the ungrateful bitch. You wouldn't be here if the agency didn't send in a pinch hitter. Or is that why Kim called you? You and she good buddies? You doing her a big favor? Don't even think you're gonna get what I said I'd pay her. I'm cutting way back for the inconvenience. I don't have time to get to know a new girl. What do you like, what don't you like? What do you want to order for dinner? Spare me the hassle. Just keep your mouth shut and do your job. I'll have to look at what you brought, make sure you have the right kind of gown for tonight. Otherwise I suppose we'll have to go shopping. I told you, I don't need the hassle. Where the hell's the bellman with your bags?"

Catherine stared at the man. The whole scenario was starting to make sense. Kim was a call girl on her way to David Mathews's house the night he was murdered. No wonder she refused to give her name and didn't want to get involved. A call girl would be the perfect murder suspect.

"What? You want to check things out first, look me over, see if I'm the type that beats the crap out of girls like you? That the idea? Get the lay of the land before the bellman brings up your bags? Well, spill it out. You staying or you gonna run? I would appreciate knowing before I lay out any more money. I need a companion for an event at the Hyatt tonight. Front row tickets at the Buell Theater tomorrow night. Afterward, little intimate dinner with business associates. You'll look beautiful and keep your mouth shut. You're not in, I want to know now."

"Look, there's been a misunderstanding," Catherine began. "I'm Catherine McLeod . . ."

He waved a hand between them. "I don't give a damn what you call yourself. I'll call you anything I please. You're nothing to me, you understand? I don't need your history or your long, sad stories. I heard enough from Kim to last me a lifetime. This is a flat-out business deal, no more, no less. You in or not?"

"Did Kim give you her real name?"

He turned his head and studied her out of the sides of his eyes. "So happened, I liked her real name. Catherine, I have my doubts about. Maybe I'll call you Kit. Or Kitty. Yeah, Kitty works."

"I'm a journalist with the *Journal*," Catherine said.

The man looked as if she had struck him. He flinched. Then he stepped backward, looking at her straight on, reappraising her, pink lips and blue eyes bulging from his pale face. He reached around and grabbed hold of the back of the sofa to steady himself, and for an instant she thought he might collapse. "What's this all about?" His voice was shaking, croaking. "Some kind of a sting? My business competitors paid off Kim to bring you here?"

"I'm not here to see you," Catherine said. "I assure you, I don't care who you are or what you do. You're not the story. I came here to talk to Kim. She's in danger."

"Danger! Who the hell's she been hanging out with? Drug suppliers? What? She owe them money? She's behind on her payments, so she sold me out to some business rivals? Oh, they'd love to get a story like this in the newspaper. Ruin me in this town. They gave her a wad of cash, she calls you up, and now you're gonna get the Pulitzer bringing down an oil company CEO. How dare that low-class bitch do this to me."

"You can be the CEO of hell, for all I care. I told you, this has nothing to do with you, but if I don't find Kim, she could end up dead."

"Get out." He pushed himself off the sofa and wove toward the door, like a drunk, Catherine thought, or a man with a concussion.

"Where did she go? How can I reach her?"

He opened the door and was nodding her through it. "Get out." He hissed the words.

"Do you understand what I've told you? She's running for her life. What's the name of the agency she works for?"

"I will grab you by your hair and throw you out." The color in his face had ripened to bluish red; a pair of veins pumped in his forehead.

Catherine walked past him into the corridor. The door slammed shut behind her.

The doorman was holding the cab door for a tall, wiry man in khakis and navy blue tee shirt intent on a conversation with his cell phone. Gradually he seemed to grasp the opened door and move toward it, nodding at the doorman and slipping him a folded bill, not missing a beat of conversation.

The doorman closed the door, then opened the front passenger door, leaned inside and gave the driver an address. "Afternoon," he said, turning to Catherine. He had a moonlike face, fleshy and red-hued with jowls that waddled when he spoke, and a thick neck that bulged inside the collar of his white shirt. "May I get you a taxi?"

Catherine shook her head. "I was supposed to meet someone at the hotel a little while ago," she said. "I'm afraid she's already left." The doorman observed her out of narrowed, suspicious eyes. "Attractive woman." The doorman's gaze seemed to soften with a memory, and Catherine hurried on. "Carrying a bag." She wondered if Kim had taken the time to pack.

"I believe so." He nodded, smiling. "She took a taxi."

"Can you tell me where she went?" Catherine saw her mistake by the curtain that dropped over the doorman's narrowed eyes and the offended look he gave her.

"Listen," she said, digging inside her bag for her wallet. "I know this is unusual, and I wouldn't ask if the girl weren't in serious trouble. It's important that I find her. I'm the only one who can help her." She managed to extract a bill, fold it twice and hold out her hand. The exchange was like magic, she thought. The bill next to her palm one instant, and next to his the next. He slid it inside his shirt pocket.

"She was going to the Baker neighborhood," he said, and he gave her an address.

It was good to be driving the BMW, Kim thought, the engine purring around her. Almost comforting, as if she were safe in the leather seats, the cool air blowing over her arms and legs. Those people were safe—she always thought of the drivers of expensive cars as "those people."

Nothing could touch them, rock their world. The fancy cars—black was the richest color; she had always wanted a fancy black car—were only the first layer of safety, and beyond that stretched layers of fine houses, influential friends, exclusive clubs, champagne and caviar and you name it. Oh, she had watched the friends of wealthy men like Arnold Winston slip in behind the wheels of the fancy cars the valets brought around and drive off like princes to their palaces and safe worlds. She had felt like Cinderella at the ball when she was with Arnold, or Harry or Mark or Luke—the names and faces blurred together. David Mathews, oh, yes, for a little while, he had made her feel like Cinderella.

She shook away the train of thought, pulled herself upright and tried to focus on the traffic moving down Speer Boulevard. How had she gotten to Speer? She couldn't remember. She had taken the cab over to Misty's place, picked up the keys, and backed out of the garage—she remembered that. Somehow she must have threaded her way through the side streets and onto Speer.

She struggled to grasp hold of the plan forming like mist in her mind. She had to get out of town. A police detective, a murderer, was looking for her. Detectives had ways of finding people, and sooner or later, Beckman would find her. Beckman had already framed Sydney Mathews. It wouldn't matter what Kim Gregory had to say. Who was she? No one. A high-priced whore with a cocaine habit who probably had delusions. Kim heard the quiet, nervous laughing and realized she was laughing at the idea that whatever she might say could matter.

But it would matter. The truth of it was like a presence in the passenger seat. Beckman wouldn't be after her if it wouldn't matter, and Catherine McLeod wouldn't be at the hotel looking for her now. She had to make a plan. Yes, that was what she had to do. She had to erase her trail and make it harder for Beckman to follow. She had to give herself enough time to get the metal box under the floorboards in her condo.

Twelve, thirteen thousand dollars now, and the few pieces of jewelry she had managed to sneak out of hotel rooms in the linings of her bags. Then she would get out of Denver, drive down to Arizona and look for Mama. She was probably around somewhere. She shoved the idea away. Sooner or later Beckman would locate Mama.

Later she would decide where to go.

29

Kim huddled against the painted blue door, thumb tight on the buzzer. The ringing inside sounded like a bell wrapped in cotton. The small, discreet bronze plaque above the buzzer said Morningtide LLC. There was no sound of footsteps, no sign anyone was here. Just a vacant space like the other vacant spaces in the strip mall, with faded signs for Insurance, Nails, Tarot Readings hanging at odd angles in the dusty windows. She held the buzzer down. Now the muffled ringing noise sounded cracked and worn out. Ericka had to be here; she was always here. Unless she'd gone to lunch, dashed off to soothe some dissatisfied client—God, Arnold had called and complained. She could almost hear him shouting over the phone. Bitch walked off on me! What kind of business are you running? I'll ruin you! No reputable businessman's gonna call you again. You're gonna close up shop and disappear, like that bitch.

"Who is it?"

Kim jumped back, as if a fist had reached through the small metal box beside the door and punched her in the stomach. "Kim," she said. Her voice came back to her, breathless and shaky.

"Wait!" There was a loud clicking noise and the door opened about six inches. Ericka, in her short-cropped blond hair and nose earring and those wide, blue innocent eyes, peered out at her. "What the hell are you doing here? You're supposed to be with Winston. What happened? He turn weird or something?"

"God, Ericka. Let me in!" Kim glanced back at the stretch of vacant asphalt in the parking lot and scattering of cars at the far end where the taco café was still serving lunch. She had wedged the black BMW next to a truck in front of the café. It was almost invisible. Out on the street, traffic streamed past. Beckman could turn into the lot at any moment.

The door started to move, and Kim threw herself past the blond woman into the outer office with the desk no one ever occupied and the two easy chairs no one ever sat in. Ericka ran the business on computers and telephones in the back office. A couple of times when she had gone out of town to settle some dispute with a client, she'd asked Kim to babysit the office, answer the phone, check e-mails. The storefront office and furnishings and girls Ericka occasionally asked to cover for her were nothing but stage props for the landlord or building inspector or nosy cop who happened to drop by. Therapist, was how Ericka billed herself. Trained and experienced in the hard school of the streets. You couldn't put anything over on her, she said. Don't even try. She had seen it all, done it all.

"Start talking." Ericka slammed the door. She made no movement toward the back office. This was a matter she could dispose of easily. If Kim had offended one of the best clients, Kim would be gone. A line of girls waited to take her place: Russians and Ukrainians and Lithuanians and girls from a lot of places Kim had never heard of.

"I need your help," Kim said.

"Where's Winston?"

"I don't know. At the hotel or someplace. For godssakes, can we forget him?" Kim clamped the strap of her bag over her shoulder. "You've got to do something for me right away."

The look on Ericka's face registered somewhere between alarm and concern. "You'd better come into the office," she said, crossing the small space toward the door in back. She flung it open, walked over and sat down behind the desk. "Start at the beginning." She motioned Kim onto the chair a few feet away.

"There's no time." Kim stationed herself in the middle of the office. Behind the desk, a window looked out over an alley littered with debris and, across the alley, the lower floor of a brick building with boards tacked over the windows. A door led to a small bathroom, and inside the bathroom, she knew, a back door opened to the alley. "You have to delete my name from the records," she said.

"Have you gone mad? What have you done? Killed somebody?" Ericka half rose out of the chair and gripped the edge of the desk. She leaned forward. "My God, you killed Winston? What? He knocked you around so you killed him?"

"No. No." Kim realized she was shouting. She stopped and struggled to regain control. This wasn't going the way she had hoped. Beckman could burst in while they were having this stupid conversation.

"You can do it. Just tell the computer to delete my name and all my personal information. No one can know my address or cell number. No one can know how to find me. Please, Ericka. You have to do it right away."

"Let's get something straight. I don't have to do anything," Ericka said. "Besides, why would anyone want to find you?"

Kim felt like she was choking. Her mouth was dry, her tongue flopping against her teeth. "Someone wants me dead," she managed.

"What have you done to my business?" Ericka was still half standing, listing sideways, jaw tight with anger.

"Look," Kim said. "No one can connect me to David Mathews if you delete my name and contacts." She thrust a fist at the computer screen. "It's all in there. You sent me out with him last year."

"The guy that was gonna be governor? He was murdered, Kim. What did you have to do with it?"

"Nothing. I swear to God, nothing. Just get my name out of the computer."

"Why would I do that?"

"Because . . ." Kim struggled with the words bunching in her throat. "I saw the murderer, and she's looking for me. Please, please," she said. The walls had started moving in on her, and for an instant, she felt as if she might pass out.

Ericka jerked herself up straight, picked up a ceramic cup filled with pens and threw it across the room. There was the shattering, clanking noise of broken things that could never be repaired. "I've got the picture now," she said. "HD, bright Technicolor. You've been holding out on me, cheating on me. I fixed you up with a big spender like Mathews, and after that you set up your own assignments." She threw out an opened hand. "Don't deny it! How many more times did you service Mathews? Let's see." She bent down and started tapping on the keyboard. "Two, three times a week—we'll go with three—for the last year. My goodness, that comes to a very nice figure, which you will pay me, you conniving bitch. You really think I wouldn't have figured it out eventually? All those dates you were too tired, too busy, too hungover or coked up, you were off to your little rendezvous with Mathews. Is that when you saw whoever killed him? On your way for a private date?"

"I'll pay you," Kim said.

"You're damn right. No one cheats me. You were nothing, a common streetwalker hopping in cars on Colfax Avenue. I cleaned you up, brought you into the business, gave you an opportunity to pull yourself out of the gutter. Pretty face, good hair and teeth, a great body and a classy look—I thought you had potential. I should have known better. Once in the gutter, always in the gutter."

"Just delete my name, I'm begging you," Kim said. "I can't pay you if I'm dead."

Ericka seemed to consider this, tossing glances across the room, thrusting out her chin and sucking on her lower lip. The silver pearl in her nose pulsed in the light. Kim pushed on. "You've never heard of me. I never worked at the agency. Don't you see? It will protect you, keep you from getting involved. Soon as someone comes around asking about me, you can send them off chasing their tails at other agencies."

For a moment, she thought Ericka was moving toward agreement. Then Ericka said, "Who did you see? How come the murderer knows about you? How come you're being chased?" Then she crossed her arms over her waist and swung toward the windows. "Forget I asked. I don't want to know. I can't get involved in this. I don't need a bunch of cops hanging around looking into the business." She swung back. "I should kill you myself."

"Delete my information," Kim said, "and you won't be involved."

"You think it's that easy? There are ways of getting information back, you know. Nothing's deleted forever."

"I need a little time to get away, that's all."

"You aren't going anywhere until you pay me."

"I told you I'd pay. I'll get the cash and send it to you."

Ericka kept her arms folded, her fingers digging blue holes into her flesh. "Like I can believe a lying cheat like you."

The doorbell rang, a loud clanging noise that reverberated against the walls. Kim froze in place, unable to take her eyes from the woman across the desk. "Are you expecting someone?" She knew the answer by the way Ericka started flailing about, moving one way, then the other, circling back on herself.

She swung toward Kim: "Who have you brought here?"

"You have to do it now. For both of us."

"Both of us." The idea seemed to focus Ericka. She moved to the computer and bent over the keyboard. The doorbell rang again, a long and insistent noise that drowned out the clacking keys.

Kim turned and stared across the outer office to the blue wooden door. The ringing swelled into a screeching noise. "I have to get out of here" She was talking to herself. Ericka was huddled over the screen, punching keys. Beckman could be at the front door, or Catherine McLeod. My God, the reporter wouldn't give up until she got her killed! Why had she ever called her? She should have stayed out of it. So what if his wife took the fall for David's murder? She should feel sorry for Sydney Mathews who'd had everything she'd wanted her entire life? Let her see how the rest of the world survives.

The doorbell rang again, punctuated by the hard sound of banging. "Police!" somebody shouted. It was a woman's voice. Kim lunged past the desk for the bathroom. She grabbed hold of the back doorknob. It froze in her hand. "Let me out of here!" She looked back into the office. "I've got to get out."

"What?" Ericka straightened herself and looked around. Finally she yanked open the center desk drawer, fingered a key and, crowding into the bathroom, jammed the key into the slot. Kim reached around, pushed the door open and burst out onto the hot, dusty concrete slab that abutted the alley. She lunged for the alley and started running, footsteps pounding the hard cement. She rounded the corner, and turned into the far end of the parking lot. Hot coals burned her lungs, her calf muscles were cramping. She had an instant view, like the snap of a camera, down the front of the mall. Beckman was nowhere in sight. Ericka had already let her in!

In a couple of minutes, Kim had backed out the BMW and pulled onto the side street. Avoiding the main streets, she wove through neighborhoods of bungalows and apartment houses and cars parked along the curbs. She was about to turn west onto Speer when she realized the mistake she had made. It was like a black cloud enveloping her, a blunder that could be fatal. She passed the turn, pulled into the vacant place at the curb and dug her cell out of her bag. She punched in the number at the agency. There was no ringing noise; she was calling nowhere. Finally an automatic voice came on: "Please leave your message."

"Don't tell Detective Beckman where to find me. Please, Ericka. She's the one who killed David." She could hear the note of despair in her voice, the futility of trying to stop something probably taking place right now. Oh, she could see Ericka, the upright, legitimate therapist, telling the police detective everything she wanted to know. This would be it, the end of the road, unless she got to the condo, collected her metal box, and got out before Beckman came for her.

30

"Who's there?" The woman's voice in the intercom sounded tentative and scared.

She was at the right place, Ryan thought. You could tell by the tone of a voice before you said anything, asked any questions, whether you had collared the right person, rung the right doorbell. It was laughable, really, the way the guilty almost begged to be caught. But that was because they believed they were guilty, and that was their mistake.

"Denver police," she said. "Open up."

Inside, the clack of footsteps on a hard floor, the tentativeness present even in the footsteps. The woman on the other side of the door knew all about Kim Gregory, she was certain. But the woman would be cagey—she'd encountered the type before. The woman would try to cover up, play dumb, claim she'd never heard of anyone named Kim. She might have to get rough, Ryan thought. Well, so be it. There wasn't time to fool around, play pussyfoot with the taxpaying citizen. Kim Gregory, if she had any brains at all, should have left town by now. Instead she had contacted that reporter. If she did leave town, there would be no peace. Every day for the rest of her life, Ryan knew, she would be waiting for the conscience-stricken whore to show up and spill what she had seen. What difference would it make? David's murder was solved, Sydney Mathews was sure to be convicted. Ryan and Martin would be commended on wrapping up a high-profile homicide in an expeditious manner.

Kim Gregory would make a difference. This morning, Captain Donnell in Internal Affairs had called her in and handed her a statement signed by somebody she didn't know existed. Some fool in Aspen who had seen her and David and made it his business to care who David Mathews drank with in a bar. The whole thing was stupid, which was what she had told him. Mathews had a reputation as a womanizer, she'd said. He could have been with anybody, any blonde. So what if the fool thought she was the blonde? She wasn't anywhere near Aspen that weekend.

"But you had taken off that weekend." Captain Donnell had done his homework, and that had set her a little off balance. What other part of her life had he delved into?

"I was sick." She stopped herself from telling him to check with her doctor. No more lies. She had played it safe that weekend and called in sick. It would check out. She had to be careful and not offer anything that could be contradicted. "I was in bed for two days with my annual cold. Whoever he is"—she dropped the statement on the desk—"it doesn't mean anything."

"You knew Mathews."

"I helped the DA investigate theft charges against him last year," she said. "That hardly qualifies as knowing him."

The captain had retrieved the sheet of paper, slipped it inside a folder and gave her a weak smile, the kind she gave perpetrators to let them know she knew they were lying. She had marched out of the office, head high, shoulders straight. He couldn't prove anything, and they both knew it. Unless Kim Gregory walked into his office. Then, there would be two witnesses to connect her with David, one bolstering the other. The scenario had unfolded in front of her: she would be taken off the case; a new investigation would be ordered, charges dropped against Sydney on the technicality that the detective in charge had been involved with her husband and was seen at his house after he was shot.

She had to make certain that never happened.

The sound of footsteps had stopped, and Ryan leaned toward the intercom. "Open the door," she said. She could hear the shallow breathing on the other side. The woman was standing at the door, composing herself, no doubt, getting her lies together.

The door opened. The woman before her was a surprise: a middle-aged former biker babe, maybe, with a short, stylish haircut, quick eyes and a tiny silver ball in the side of her nose. She looked like she had spent a lot of time sunning herself and drinking fine wines and eating rich foods in expensive restaurants that contributed to what was probably a permanent flush and an expanding waistline. "How can I help you?" she said, and Ryan noted the tentativeness was gone. This was an experienced actress.

"Some questions about a homicide case." Ryan held up her badge and stepped inside. "You're Ericka Frasier?"

The woman nodded, closed the door and led the way into a back office. "I wouldn't know about a homicide," she said, taking the chair behind a computer. That was a mistake, Ryan thought, assuming a subservient position where she had to look up. Ryan remained standing, ready for anything that might happen during an interview, just as the police manuals said. The computer screen glowed a sickly purple.

She glanced around the small office with the cheap desk and folding chairs, the credenza that looked as if it had been dragged out of a Dumpster. Pieces of ceramic and pens and pencils littered a section of the linoleum floor. Ericka Frasier must have noticed what Ryan was looking at because she started going on about how the pen holder had fallen and she hadn't had time to clean up.

Ryan looked back. "One of your girls is involved."

"Girls? I don't understand." The woman's hands flopped above the keyboard. "Are you referring to my clients?"

"Your whores," Ryan said, making the most of her advantage. "One of your whores, Kim Gregory, is involved. We have an e-mail she sent from this office. I need to know where I can locate her."

"I don't understand . . ."

Ryan leaned forward and brought a fist down hard on the desk. The handle of the Ruger she'd slipped inside her belt bit into her hip. The woman looked genuinely startled. She reared backward against the chair and bit at her lip until a tiny drop of blood appeared. "We can do this the easy way or the hard way," Ryan said. "I can arrest you this minute and march you out of here in handcuffs for solicitation, operating a prostitution ring and other offenses I know will come to me. I can get the information out of your computer while you enjoy the accommodations of the Denver jail. Sorry, no court hearings until Monday, so you'll have two and a half days to enjoy the food. Or you can tell me the whereabouts of Kim Gregory."

The woman swallowed hard. "I don't know her whereabouts," she said finally. "She shouldn't have dragged me into this. I run a good business. It's a worthy service and nobody gets hurt. I've never had any trouble with the police."

"That's about to change," Ryan said.

"Okay, so Kim just left here." The woman threw up both hands in a kind of surrender. "I swear I don't know where she went. She said somebody wants to kill her. She knows who shot David Mathews, and now the killer is after her. Is she crazy or hallucinating or something? Is somebody really after her?"

"Her address and telephone numbers. Now." Ryan poked at the computer.

"You'll leave me out of this?" Ericka said. "I don't know anything about what she does on her own time. I'm not her employer. She's freelance. Sometimes she takes jobs from me, that's all. I need your word I won't be dragged into this."

"You're not in a position to negotiate," Ryan said.

Ericka moved forward and started tapping the keyboard. The purple screen disappeared and black text flowed into place. Finally she jabbed at a single key that brought the small printer at the side of the desk coughing into life. After a sheet of paper emerged, Ericka tore it off and handed it over the top of the computer. "I don't give a damn what happens to her," she said. "She should never have gotten me involved."

Ryan studied the sheet. Beautiful. Kim Gregory, age twenty-seven, five foot nine, 120 pounds. And this was ironic: she lived in a condo complex not far from her own. Two telephone numbers. At the bottom, one of those glamorous, touched-up photos that made her look like a movie star, reddish hair, a small sprinkling of freckles, eyes golden brown and full, smiling lips. So this was the shadowy figure out on the sidewalk.

Ryan turned, slipped the gun from her belt and swung back. Ericka Frasier had stood up. She began peddling backward, eyes wide with terror, mouth a perfect O of surprise. She threw out both hands, as if flesh and bones could deflect the bullet that sent her crashing backward against the window, then folding onto the floor.

The addresses were hard to spot, hidden behind the low-hanging branches of the old trees that sprawled over the front yards and the wide, sloping porches. Finally Catherine made out the black numbers next to one of the front doors. The address the doorman had given her had to be that of the three-story, redbrick Victorian next door. She managed to jam the convertible into a small vacant slot at the curb and hurried up the buckled sidewalk. Somebody sat out on the screened porch, bent over a computer. Catherine rapped at the door that jumped against her hand, and a girl, tall with dark hair pulled into a ponytail, in cut-off jeans and a yellow tee shirt, turned halfway around and looked out. Catherine dug her fingers into the leather of her bag and tried to steady her breathing. "Kim?" she called.

The girl got up, plodded barefoot across the porch and opened the door.

"I'm Catherine McLeod from the *Journal*," Catherine said.

"Yeah? What do you want?" Catherine felt her heart sink. The voice was not Kim's.

"I'm here to see Kim," she said.

"Well, you missed her." The girl scratched at what looked like a mosquito bite on her neck. "I'll tell her you stopped by."

"Kim's in serious trouble," Catherine said. "Are you a friend?"

The girl stared at her a long moment, then kicked the screened door open. "Come in," she said. Then she walked over and dropped back onto her chair and motioned Catherine toward a slatted wood porch swing. "You can call me Misty," she said. "What kind of trouble?"

Catherine told her that a murderer had targeted Kim; that she was trying to help her. "It's not safe for her now," she said. "Can you tell me where she is?"

"She didn't say anything to me." The girl shrugged, as if this were a fantasy on TV, not to be taken seriously. "Sometimes the guys we go with—" She stopped, a worried look on her face, as if she had gone too far. "Look, I don't know how much you know."

"I'm not here about what Kim does," Catherine said.

The girl shrugged. "Well, sometimes it can get a little rough, but not so much working for the agency. At least the johns are screened; they're pretty decent. Still, you never know what can happen. She never said anything about any trouble. We always have each other's backs. She would have told me."

Catherine tried again "This isn't about a john," she said. But it was, she was thinking. David Mathews had been a john. "Kim is scared. She's on the run for her life. She witnessed a murder."

The girl sat perfectly still for a long moment, then she jumped up, as if she'd been hit by an electric prod. "I knew it!" she said. "I knew something was wrong. She shows up here, says she needs the keys to the BMW." She shrugged. "We keep each other's cars when we have to stay with a client. I gave her the keys, asked if she wanted some lemonade, but she said she had to get going, like she was driving off to meet some big client she didn't want me to know about. One of my johns, is what I thought, and I was upset, 'cause we don't keep things from each other. We made a pact. Johns don't come between friends. I'm thinking, 'What's up with you, girl?'"

"Where did she go?" Catherine said.

"She said she had to take care of some business."

"If she was getting ready to leave town, what kind of business would she take care of?"

The girl shrugged. "I know what I'd do. I'd get the cash and stuff I've hidden away. Yeah, I'd get that for sure. I mean, how far you gonna go with no money?"

"Where would she hide it?"

"At her condo," Misty said. "Where else? She has a special hiding place, burglarproof, she told me."

Then she gave Catherine the address of Kim's condo.

31

The condominium complex was a series of yellow-sided, two-story buildings that spilled out the tenants by 8:00 a.m., Monday through Friday, and that was a good thing. No one around to tell Detective Beckman when she had arrived and left. The parking lot was empty. Her own space was at the far end of the building, but Kim slid to a stop close to the stairway, slammed out and ran up to the second floor, her footsteps echoing around the hollow stairwell. She had her key out of her bag before she reached her door, and in a second, she was inside. Five minutes was all she needed. She ran into the bedroom, dragged an old fake leather bag off the closet shelf and flopped it onto the bed. Then she began dragging clothes and shoes out of the closet and stuffing them inside the bag. The Louis Vuitton was in the trunk of the BMW packed with the evening gowns and expensive lotions and moisturizers and perfumes from that other life. What a laugh. This was her life; Kim

Nobody Gregory from the dusty, one-stoplight nowhere towns of Arizona and Nevada and New Mexico, wherever Mama had wanted to go.

For the first time in her life, Kim would go where she belonged. The thought surprised her. She had always intended to get as far away as possible from the bare, western towns and never look back. Keep going on and going on, Mama always said. She was thinking that Mama said a lot of stupid things Kim had spent most of her life trying to forget. But when it came down to it, they were her towns, her kind of people, spare, unpretentious and hardworking, not expecting anything. No favors or paybacks, no cozying up to people they hated, no dinners in five-star restaurants with the best wine cellars, no showing off all the time in the hope of gaining some advantage. Kim knelt on the bag and struggled with the zipper a moment. Finally, she opened the top, flung a pair of jeans onto the floor and started over.

She managed to close the bag, then went to the corner, got down on her hands and knees and ripped back the carpeting, a green shag probably older than she was that smelled of dog hair and cat pee, with pink stains of old nail polish here and there. She had pulled a triangle back two feet before she spotted the floorboard with the knothole. Working an index finger into the knothole, she struggled to lever the board upright. The board was stuck. God, probably another leak that had run down the inside wall and swollen the boards. She could smell the acrid odor of mold. The board began to give a little, and she managed to jerk it upright and lift out the metal box.

She carried the box over to the bed and opened it. The black bag with the pearl and diamond necklace from the vice president of some Florida company lay next to the bronze case with the diamond bracelet and ruby pendant from the oil guy with the sour smells of gasoline and aftershave. Beneath the jewelry was twelve thousand dollars, neatly stacked in one-hundred-dollar bills, rubber-banded together. The total savings for six years, a hundred clients—she had lost count—all blurred together, the well-trimmed hair and bulbous noses, the hearty laughs and big, hairy hands. The jewelry was worth another couple thousand. She'd find a high-class pawnshop in Phoenix, not one of those cheap places that tried to give you a few hundred bucks for diamonds.

She closed the lid and slipped the box into an empty shopping bag she had left next to the dresser. She yanked open the bottom drawer and rummaged among the underwear and blouses for the baggie. The plastic felt cool to her fingertips. Hardly enough white powder inside to bother with. Besides, she had been cutting back. She kicked the drawer shut, then opened it again. She took the baggie. Beckman couldn't find the cocaine. It would provide the perfect excuse: a drug addict, holding on to her stash, threatening a police officer. With what? A knife, maybe. All Beckman had to do was get a butcher knife from the kitchen and place it in Kim's hand—after she had killed her. She pulled out the baggie and stuffed it inside the shopping bag.

She would take I-25 south all the way into southern New Mexico, then turn west and drive for Arizona. It could take two days, but she wouldn't stop. She would keep going, keep going. She fixed the strap of her bag over her shoulder, then picked up the fake leather suitcase and the shopping bag. She'd get a job on a ranch looking after horses, out in the wide open desert with the big sky all around. She had always liked horses, and they liked her, at least during that time Mama took up with the seven-foot-tall rancher in Nevada. It would be a good life, working with horses. She would be free.

The soft thud of a car door shutting outside cut into her thoughts, and she realized that, behind her thoughts, like an annoying buzzing noise, had been the sounds of an engine. She froze. She couldn't remember whether she'd thrown the lock when she came through the front door. She had been so preoccupied with getting her things and getting out. So little time. Not even enough time to throw the lock. The truth cut into her like a knife: Ericka would give Beckman what she wanted; even if Ericka had gotten the message, she would still tell Beckman where the condo was. Ericka wouldn't forget that Kim had cheated her.

She forced herself to relax. Another tenant had probably come home early. People found a way to leave the office early on Friday afternoons. If she had ever landed an office job, she was sure she would have spent the days planning to get out. She took in a long breath and started down the narrow hall, the bags banging against the walls.

The blond woman in a blue blazer and tan slacks appeared at the end of the hallway. She was gripping a metallic colored gun, steadying her wrist with her other hand. Odd, Kim thought. She didn't look like the calm detective on TV, framed in the doorway of David's house. This was the disheveled woman with the wild, frantic look who had burst out of David's house and stood under the porch light, blinking into the darkness.

"Going somewhere?" Beckman said.

"I'm going home." Kim heard the sound of her own voice floating ahead, disembodied. "You here to arrest me?" She knew it wasn't true. The last thing Detective Beckman wanted was Kim Gregory spilling her guts at police headquarters.

"Home? That's beautiful." A piece of blond hair had fallen into Beckman's eye, and she tossed her head a couple of times as if she could throw it away. "Where might home be? Rathole on East Colfax? Pimp waiting for you? Gonna beat the crap outta you if you don't get over there?"

Kim clenched her jaws together and gripped the handles of the bags hard to stop the shaking that had started in her legs and crawled up into her shoulders. "I'm done with all that," she said. "I'm leaving Denver, and I'll never come back, I promise. I don't care about anything that happened here; it's none of my business. I've never been one to poke my nose in other people's business. Live and let live is what my mama used to say." She was afraid she might start crying, and she swallowed back the lump of moisture in her throat. She made herself go on: "I'll just be leaving now."

She started moving forward, framing the whole picture: the gun that got bigger with every step, the white hands wrapped around the handle, the wild eyes and grimacing lips that parted over a row of white teeth. A deafening noise crashed over her. Then she was looking down on herself and trying to grasp this new reality of floating up to the ceiling and being down on the floor at the same time, a hot flame shooting through her, the noise still reverberating around her.

Catherine realized she had driven past the neighborhood on I-25 hundreds of times. She had never noticed the three-story yellow buildings that looked like the motel complex they had probably once been. The parking lot was empty. No sign of Kim's black BMW, but that didn't mean she hadn't left the car a block away hoping to fool Beckman into thinking she hadn't gone home. "I'd get the cash and stuff I've hidden away," Kim's friend had said. How long would it take Kim to collect her stuff? Five minutes? She could have left already. Or never shown up. What was the stuff worth compared to her life?

Catherine slowed through the lot, scanning the black numbers on the sides of the buildings. Kim's condo would be at the end of the second building, the condo of any ordinary girl. Except that Kim Gregory was not an ordinary girl. She could identify a murderer. She was on the run for her life.

"Let her be here," Catherine said out loud.

She left the car at the curb and ran up the steps to the second floor. An eeriness pervaded the place, the way her footsteps echoed in the stairwell and followed her down the corridor, as if she had stepped into a wormhole that could suck her into another time or place. She made herself slow down to register the numbers on each door as she passed: 2, 4, 6. Goose bumps pricked her arms; her skin was taut, muscles clenched. She could almost smell the wrongness, the scent of things out of whack. The far-off sound of the highway traffic might have been the hum of a distant galaxy.

Catherine stopped in front of number 8 and knocked. A vacant quiet engulfed her. She knocked again and leaned close to the door. Spider cracks crisscrossed the brown paint. "Kim," she called. "It's Catherine McLeod. Open the door." Still nothing. She had the sinking feeling she was too late. Kim had already left and was on her way to somewhere else, but wherever it was, Detective Beckman would find her.

And Beckman would come after Catherine, too. Eventually, Beckman would kill both of them. The certainty knotted like a rope inside her. It was ironic: the only way she could help herself was by helping the girl who didn't want her help.

She pounded on the door, then took hold of the knob. It turned against her palm. She pushed the door open and stepped into a small living room with a green sofa, shiny with use, a matching green chair, a couple of small plastic tables on spindly legs and a faint odor of dampness and neglect. The kitchen—half-sized refrigerator, microwave, foot-long counter next to a sink—filled the alcove in back. The condo had an unlived-in feeling, with no sign of anything personal, no photos or books or newspapers. A place to stop off, Catherine thought, in between stays at hotels with marble floors and deep, plush sofas and mattresses.

"Hello!" she shouted. "Kim! Are you here? It's Catherine McLeod. I have to talk to you."

Nothing. But Kim Gregory was here, Catherine was sure now. The feeling of wrongness that had overtaken her in the hallway was so strong now, she was afraid she might throw up. A few feet from the alcove was a doorway into the hall that must lead to a bedroom and bath.

"Kim?" She crossed the living room and turned into the hall. The body of a girl lay crumpled on the floor, blood pooling beside her, a bloody trail running up the wall, as if she had tried to crawl to her feet. Catherine found herself kneeling beside her, unaware of how she had closed the space between them. She laid a finger against the girl's carotid artery. The pulse was faint, like an afterthought. Blood bubbled out of the girl's chest.

Catherine got up and ran back into the living room where she'd dropped her bag. She found her cell and tapped out 911, her hand shaking so hard she feared the phone would fly across the room. "Send an ambulance right away." She was shouting. "A girl's been shot. She's bleeding badly." She gave the address and listened to the dispatcher's assurance that help was on the way before she closed the cell and ran back into the hallway.

Down on her knees again, barely aware of the warm, dark moisture soaking through her skirt. She leaned over and told the girl that an ambulance was on the way. "Can you hear me, Kim?" The bleeding was worse than she'd realized.

There was the tiniest flicker of the girl's eyelids, then they started to open, a slow motion, as if someone were pulling the strings. Her lips were pale, parting in the effort of a smile "Catherine," she said.

"I'm sorry," Catherine said. "I'm so sorry."

"Detective Beckman . . ." The girl's voice was raspy and choked. She might have been gargling, spitting up the words. "I told her I wouldn't tell . . ."

"Save your strength," Catherine said. Then she got up and went into the small bathroom for a towel. Dropping on her knees again, she pressed the wadded towel against the black, gushing hole in Kim's chest.

"I had a horse named Ribbon once," the girl said.

"Shhh," Catherine said. The towel was already wet. A siren screamed in the distance.

"We went riding on the desert every day. It was like riding in the sky." The girl's eyes started to close in slow motion, as if puppet strings were being gently loosened.

"Help's almost here," Catherine said. She could hear the sounds of engines cutting off in the parking lot. "Try to hang on, Kim. Please hang on."

32

The doctor in green scrubs came around the corner into the waiting room. Catherine jumped to her feet, her mouth parched and rough, as if something vital had been drawn from her, but the doctor went over to the elderly couple huddled on chairs pulled close together. He leaned over, speaking in the kind of tone she imagined doctors reserved for the worst kind of news. The gray-haired woman let out a small, high-pitched cry, like that of a cat in pain. The old man gripped her hand, helped her to her feet and, wobbling side by side, they followed the doctor across the waiting room and out into the corridor. Catherine could hear the shuffling footsteps as they receded somewhere into the cavernous depths of Denver Health Sciences.

She managed to lower herself back into the cushions of her own chair. The police officer, tall and wiry with pink cheeks, still in his twenties, sat near the door—she was a witness, after all, and the killer could still be looking for her. He hadn't taken his eyes from her. They were alone in the waiting room now, with its rows of upholstered chairs and lamp tables and magazine racks and the soft glow of fluorescent ceiling lights, like a small ship adrift on the whir and bustle, the muffled clanking and knocking and subdued voices of the hospital. She closed her eyes and ignored the pulsing of the cell phone in her bag beside her. Marjorie had been texting and trying to call since she had gotten to the hospital almost two hours ago. "What's happening? We hear there's been another murder. Somebody else shot. Jason's on the story. Where are you? Send me what you know. You okay?"

I'm not okay, Marjorie, she had wanted to text back, but she couldn't text anything. She couldn't call. She couldn't pull her notebook out of her bag and write an update for the *Journal*'s website. *Kim Gregory, witness to the murder of David Mathews, was shot late this afternoon. Before she lost consciousness, Gregory identified the person who shot her as Detective Ryan Beckman, the same person she had seen emerge from Mathews's home minutes after he was shot. Gregory is in surgery at Denver Health Sciences. She is in extremely critical condition. She might die.*

Catherine couldn't write any of it. She would have to rephrase and couch the sentences with "allegedly" and not actually name Beckman who was innocent until proven guilty, and where was the proof? Somewhere beyond the yellowish green walls of the waiting room, a girl was fighting for her life on an operating table, and if she died, the killer might very likely go free. There would be no one to place Beckman at Mathews's house. Even the fact that Kim had named Beckman as the one who shot her would be twisted by some clever defense attorney as the illusions of a dying girl. Catherine had seen the glances that two police officers gave each other at Kim's condo when she told Nick what Kim had said. She had spent twenty minutes telling Nick everything, watching him scribble on a little notepad: how she had gotten the address where Kim had gone, how Kim's friend Misty Somebody had given her Kim's address, and all the while the pair of uniforms had worn plaster faces, but the glances had given them away. Then Nick had followed her to headquarters and stayed with her while she gave a video statement on everything she knew, including Misty's name and address. Finally she left for the hospital. The receptionist in the lobby said Kim Gregory had been taken straight to surgery. Visitors were welcome to wait upstairs. Catherine and the officer were the only visitors.

Whatever she wrote for Marjorie could be nothing but half truths, flimsy fodder for the public's curiosity, crucial parts omitted. Somehow she had crossed the invisible line that separated reporters from the story. She was in the story herself; it was her story. Like a reporter, she had watched it unfold, and yet she had known the truth behind the surface and hadn't been able to do anything. She hadn't been able to help Kim Gregory. She felt diminished and exposed and helpless, as if the waiting room and the chair itself had eclipsed her.

"Catherine?" Nick stood in the doorway, dark and big against the bright light in the corridor. "You all right?" he said, walking toward her.

"Kim's still in surgery." She ignored the question. It had no meaning.

He dropped down in the chair next to her. "I know," he said. "I spoke with a nurse. It could be awhile before they know if she'll make it. Why don't you let me take you home?"

Home. Catherine blinked hard, unable to bring the concept into focus. It seemed ridiculous, the idea that she could go home and go on, as if nothing had happened. "I didn't get to her in time." She blurted out the words, as if she had managed to spit out the stones choking her. This was the truth then: she had been close, probably minutes away from the condo, but she had been too late.

"It isn't your fault, Catherine." She felt the warmth of Nick's hand over her own. "Don't blame yourself. You did what you could. You tried. We don't always succeed, you know. What's important is that we try."

"I couldn't get her to listen to me. I couldn't explain . . ."

"She wouldn't have listened to anyone. She was frightened, and her only thought was to get away. She didn't make it." Nick was working her hand between both of his now. "You're in shock," he said. "You should let me . . ."

Catherine shook her head. "She has no one. I have to stay."

"I left a message for her friend, Misty Lucas. She'll probably come to the hospital as soon as she gets it." He took a long moment before he went on. "It's over, Catherine. There's an APB out for Ryan Beckman. We found her car in a parking lot a half block from the condo. Kim's black BMW is missing. We're sure Beckman's driving it. Every cop and sheriff's deputy in the metro area is looking for her. She won't get far."

"The famous Detective Beckman." Catherine tried to stifle the nervous laugh erupting in her throat. "Rock star detective, expert marksman, honored for bravery. No one will believe she had anything to do with this."

"She finally slipped up," Nick said. "We got a call three hours ago about a shooting in a strip mall. A woman named Erika Frasier shot to death in a back office of the Morningtide Escort Services."

Catherine had shifted around until she was facing Nick. "The agency Kim worked for," she said.

"Looks like the weapon was a .38, the same caliber used to kill Jeremy Whitman, and the same caliber of bullets that we dug out of the wall of your kitchen. We have the evidence. Ballistics will prove the gun was used in all three incidents." Before Catherine could say anything, Nick held up his hand. "There's more," he said. "We've been rounding up gang leaders for the last twenty-four hours, the guys we think gave the orders for a double gang shooting and for the random assaults downtown. Eight so far, and still counting. Guy by the name of Devon Waters is looking at a long prison term and desperate to make a deal. He says

Beckman knew all along who gave the orders for the two murders and the assaults. She held it over their heads, threatening to arrest them unless they did what she wanted. Three days ago she wanted an untraceable gun, and Devon provided a .38 Ruger."

"Three days ago? She'll still get away with having murdered Mathews."

"We don't think so," Nick said. "Beckman signed into the evidence room a few days before Mathews was shot. A 9mm Sig Sauer 226 has been found missing. You hear what I'm saying, Catherine? Mathews was killed with that caliber gun. We'll know by tomorrow if it was the missing Sig." Nick leaned closer; his arm around her shoulders felt heavy and comforting at the same time. "Listen to me, Catherine. Ryan Beckman is going to be charged and convicted of three homicides as well as attempted homicide. It's over now. Let me take you home. I'll have the guys bring your car to the house, and I'll come by as soon as I finish up downtown. We're still interrogating Devon and the others. It's likely to take a few more hours."

Nick got to his feet. She could feel the downward switch of his eyes on her, the patience in his waiting. Finally she looked up. "I'll wait until her friend comes. There's no one else here for her," she said.

He waited another moment, then leaned over, kissed the top of her head and was gone.

It must have been another hour before the tall, broad-shouldered doctor in green scrubs appeared in front of her. He had black horseshoe hair that wrapped around a bald scalp. "You're with Kim Gregory?" he said, and she heard the truth in the subdued, sympathetic tone.

Catherine struggled to her feet. "Is she going to be okay?" she said, but he had already half closed his eyes and was shaking his head.

"I'm sorry," he said. "There was too much damage. Are you okay?"

Catherine realized she had sunk down and was straddling the arm of the chair. She managed to nod.

"Are you a relative?"

"No," she said.

"A friend, then?"

Catherine didn't respond.

"I want you to know we did everything we could," he said, and in his half-closed eyes, she glimpsed a shadow of her own failure.

"Thank you," she said. "A close friend is coming. She'll know what to do about the . . ." She stopped, unable to work her tongue around the word "remains."

The doctor nodded. "Can we get you anything?"

"I'd like to see her," Catherine said. "I'd like to say good-bye."

She glanced at the officer who had gotten to his feet. He gave her a quick nod, and she followed the doctor's broad shoulders and green scrubs down a wide corridor, through a series of stainless steel doors that seemed to swing open on their own and into a small room with a gurney in the middle and a lifeless form under a thin sheet. Out in the corridor, a trolley clanked past, glass bottles rattling. The swoosh of a door opening sounded like a little gust of wind. Chemical odors drifted in the air. The doctor stepped back into the corridor, and Catherine folded the sheet back from Kim's face. She looked at peace, she thought, all the effort she had made in the condo to name her killer—Detective Beckman—was gone, leaving only the pale, clear skin and the colorless lips.

Catherine dipped her own face into her clasped hands. "I'm so sorry," she whispered. She closed her eyes against the tears that were starting. She could hear the girl's voice in her head, the fear for herself, but running through the fear, the outraged demand for justice. She had expected Catherine, a reporter, to write the truth.

It was a moment before she could look at the dead girl again. There must be something appropriate to say, but she couldn't think what it might be. Then she remembered the prayer the elder had said at the wake Dulcie had taken her to. "You'll want to come," Dulcie had told her when Catherine balked at attending a funeral service for a woman she had never met. "Until you know the way in which we send our dead to the afterlife, you won't understand your own people." Catherine had met her at the Indian Center and taken part in the wake—the bowls of beef stew, the plates of Jell-O that had covered the tables, the steady rhythm of the drums and the voices of the singers, the sweet smell of cedar smoke that the elders had wafted through the room, and the prayers.

> *You will not see the sun rise in the east again, nor will you see the moon in all its brightness in the night sky, nor feel the wind on your face nor the earth beneath your bare feet. Today you are going home. May the ancestors greet you and show you the way. May your journey be joyful.*

Catherine lifted the sheet and pulled it back over Kim Gregory's face. The doctor was still in the corridor when she left the room, a quiet, prayerful look on his own face. "I'll see you out," he said.

33

Ryan avoided the main highways. Darkness was falling, streetlights snapping on, lights glowing in the houses she passed. They would be looking for her by now. Somebody would have reported the shooting at the strip mall, and it was always possible Catherine McLeod had told her boyfriend everything Kim the whore had said. The department would want to ask her a lot of stupid questions. Best to stay off I-25, where a cop might spot the black BMW. All kinds of ways to track vehicles—video cameras nobody knew about, unmarked black police cars cruising along as if the drivers were ordinary citizens, state patrol and other busybodies who would insert themselves in the hunt.

She had taken care not to leave any evidence at either the shopping mall or the condo. Nothing to connect her to the shootings of a whore and her pimp, apart from the bullets the lab techs would dig out of the walls. They wouldn't matter, because by then she would have gotten rid of the Ruger. She understood the logical minds of detectives. She had attended the same schools. Start with the obvious, the victim's background and associates, look for the evidence left behind. There was no evidence left behind. Which left the background and the associates. Bustamante or whoever got the cases would quickly link Kim with the escort service—two homicides with the same gun!—and conclude they had been shot by a disgruntled associate or client. Or maybe a gang banger, the kind that could have mugged and shot Jeremy Whitman.

Beautiful. Ryan hit the brake at a stop sign and laughed out loud. She realized she was trembling. She would not lose it! She was still in control. Control. Then she crossed the intersection and passed brown brick bungalows with wide porches shaded by massive oaks and elms. Neighborhoods like this existed everywhere in Denver. Quiet, comfortable, no need for patrolling cop cars. She took a right, then a left onto another bungalow-lined street that the GPS showed running a mile or so ahead without stop signs. Everything was working out as if she had planned it. Anyone who might connect her to David Mathews had been safely taken care of, except for the guy in Aspen, but he was a voice crying in the wilderness with no one to back up the story. No doubt there were blemishes and slipups on his record—drugs, alcohol, DUIs—that she would find. There was always something. It was easy to discredit anyone.

The lights of Speer Boulevard twinkled ahead, a dangerous street. Cops could be everywhere. She stopped at the red light and glanced around, muscles tightening, her forehead damp with perspiration. No sign of any patrol cars. The instant the light changed, she crossed the boulevard and continued north onto another side street. The rush and noise of traffic on Speer receded. She felt like a runner who had passed another marker and settled into her stride, and her hands relaxed on the steering wheel. The panic and uncontrollable shaking that had overtaken her when things started spiraling out of control had given way to an odd, yet comforting exhilaration. She was in control now.

The houses passing by were larger, set farther back from the street, two-stories with gabled windows and wide lawns and flower beds that required gardeners. She and David would have lived in a fine house, the sprawling governor's mansion, a historic mansion, he had told her, the former residence of an old Denver family. Not that she cared. The fact that the house was elegant was all that mattered. He had promised that, after a decent interval in which his people would plant stories in the newspaper that the governor and his wife were having difficulties and he had attended a few state occasions alone that sent the gossipers chirping, Sydney would move out of the mansion. The divorce would be swift, both parties amicable. Another discreet interval, and she and David would marry in a tasteful ceremony at a church in Evergreen. She had selected the church herself, perched on top of a mountain with panoramic views of the surrounding peaks.

She felt as if a movie were running in her head that she had watched many times. All of it familiar, as if it had actually happened. In the garage at the mansion, there would be a BMW, like the one she was driving now, and an expensive SUV, a Mercedes or Lexus perhaps. David would be governor. Chauffeurs and private jets and trips to Japan or India or Europe, wherever she and David had wanted to go. All to spur the state's economy. No kids, though. David didn't want children, and she had taken steps when she was twenty-two to insure she never had any.

David. David. She could feel the control beginning to slip. She sat forward, pulling herself up straight and clasping the steering wheel hard. All the dreams, all the plans they made—the movie in her mind—he had tossed aside, as if they were nothing. Tossed her aside, like trailer trash from the backwoods of Minnesota. She had tried to explain that she had gone far, earned the respect of her superiors and bosses, taken home medals and honors. She was somebody!

But it was finished. She couldn't turn back time, say the things that would have convinced David but didn't come to her until he had crumbled onto the floor. What a fool he had been to throw away so much. And yet, and yet—something new had been moving at the edges of her mind since that night: perhaps it was meant to be. David had deceived her; he wasn't the man she had thought. He'd had no intention of leaving Sydney and her money and striking out with a wife as beautiful and accomplished as Detective Ryan Beckman. She had lowered herself to get involved with David Mathews, just as she had lowered herself to marry the software geek who had turned out to be a child-man, groveling, begging her to stay with him. She wouldn't make that mistake again.

She was in perfect control, but that was because she had eliminated most of the problems. Only one left: the nosy, persistent reporter who knew more than she had any right to know and was capable of causing trouble. Ryan glanced over at the bag on the passenger seat. She would use the Ruger one more time before she broke it apart and went on another Dumpster dump. Even if a few pieces were found, the gun could never be traced to her.

Unless Devon Waters decided to shoot off his mouth. She had spotted him in the roundup of gang members getting out of the van behind headquarters this morning, and for a moment, she had felt herself faltering. Devon could link her to the Ruger, swear he had given it to her, that she had blackmailed him, threatened to arrest him for the downtown assaults. But what difference could it possibly make, she had told herself, if a drug-addled homeboy told a preposterous story in a pathetic effort to save himself? No one would believe Devon Waters.

That left the final problem: Catherine McLeod.

Catherine rode the escalator down into the cavernous lobby of Denver Health Sciences, illuminated in the glow of ceiling lights overhead. The officer stayed a couple steps behind her. Next to her, the up escalator was filled with white-faced visitors gripping the black hand rest. A crowd of visitors pressed against the reception counter below while others came and went through the sliding glass doors or stood about looking dazed and lost. She stepped off the escalator and threaded her way through the crowd out into the cool evening, the officer at her shoulder. A long walkway emptied into the parking lot. There was something indescribably sad about the hospital and the little room upstairs with the lifeless form of a girl called Kim lying on a gurney. It had seemed wrong to leave her, and even now, in the parking lot with headlights shooting into the blackness and traffic rumbling in the distance, Catherine had to fight off the urge to return and sit with her a while longer.

She realized she had walked past the convertible. She retraced her steps and crawled inside, and the pink-faced officer leaned over and said he would follow her home and keep a watch on her house tonight. Within minutes she had threaded her way out of the parking lot and onto a side street, guilt and helplessness pulling on her like heavy weights. She shouldn't blame herself, Nick had said. There was nothing more she could have done. She felt numb, as if her hands were floating above the steering wheel. The sky was overcast, and the black night spread all around. Downtown lights looked dim in the distance. The air was suffused with autumn smells of dead leaves and grass and an almost imperceptible sense of the end of things.

She dabbed a finger at the tears that started even though she thought she was done crying. She had stayed in the waiting room until Misty swept in, wearing a long, red gown slit to her thigh, silver heels and carrying a little sequined bag, tears streaming down her cheeks. She had gotten the message on her cell, she'd said, and left what she called "work" as soon as she could. Then she had wanted to know if it was true that Ericka had also been shot to death, and when Catherine told her it was, she sank onto a chair and buried her face in her hands. Her world had collapsed, she said. Her employer and now her best friend dead! What was left for her now? Where would she go?

Catherine had given her a moment before she asked if Kim had said anything about David Mathews's murder, and Misty had shaken her head. No. No. And that explained why Misty was still alive, Catherine had thought. She waited until Misty collected herself, stood up and marched across the corridor toward the metallic-haired woman with black-rimmed glasses who had materialized behind a desk. Kim had a mother somewhere, Misty announced. The name would be somewhere in Kim's things, she was sure. The woman blinked up at the girl in the long red dress and said she would pass the information onto the police. "One more thing," Misty said. "If no one comes for her, I mean no one else shows up, you should call me. I don't want her tossed into some burial pit with a lot of people nobody loved."

Now Catherine turned onto Speer Boulevard and drove toward Highland, past the light-rail tracks with the headlights of the train bearing down, past the lights of downtown and the Auraria campus and across the viaduct, climbing up into Highland. She took Federal Boulevard to the neighborhood liquor store on the chance it might still be open. The neon light in the window was dark, the place shuttered. But there were still two bottles of wine on the counter, she was thinking. She would need a drink tonight.

Ten minutes later she turned into the alley that ran behind the houses on her block, her headlights boring through the darkness and shadows. The headlights on the police car had disappeared, but there was comfort in knowing the young officer was a half block behind. He would see her safely inside. Keep a watch on the house tonight. She could hear Rex barking as the car bucked over the weeds that poked through the concrete and the headlights swarmed across the garages, bushes and utility poles. The dog had an uncanny way of sensing when she was close to home. She felt another stab of guilt. He had been alone all day; she had intended to be home hours ago. Nothing had gone as she had intended.

She had slowed down for the turn onto the concrete apron in front of her garage, aware of the police car's lights jiggling in the alley behind her, when the cell rang. Marjorie calling again, but there was nothing more she could write, nothing she could add to the police report Jason would get. What could she add? That a girl had died because she had failed?

Rex was a dark shadow hurling himself at the chain-link fence, barking and howling. She stopped a few feet from the garage door and dug in her bag. She might as well tell Marjorie there would be no more stories; the story had ended. She yanked out the phone. Bustamante glowed in the readout. She snapped the phone open and pressed the garage button between the visors.

"Catherine, where are you?" Rex was barking so loud, she could hardly hear, but she sensed the tension in Nick's voice, the hard, steeliness of the detective.

"I just got home." In the rearview mirror, she saw more headlights. Headlights streamed into the other end of the alley. The garage door started to creak upward, her own lights sweeping across the concrete floor.

"Listen to me," Nick said. "The BMW's parked around the block. Beckman's at your house. I'm a couple blocks away, and police cars should be pulling up in a few seconds. Drive away now!"

The garage door was almost open, and her headlights bounced off the gun held by the dark figure crouching in the middle of the concrete floor.

"She's in the garage," Catherine managed, the words like splinters working out of her throat. She jabbed at the button to bring the door down. The phone rolled onto the floor as she flipped on the bright lights. The woman in the garage bared her teeth and squinted into the brightness as the door started to fall. There was the noise of tires squealing. At the blurry edge of her vision, Catherine saw police cars careening toward her.

Catherine kept her eyes on the woman in the middle of the garage, like an animal caught in a trap, frenzied and wild, desperate and haunted looking. She held her arms out in front, as if she were bringing an offering of some sort, and Catherine saw the gun coming toward her, the muzzle as large as a cannon. She threw herself sideways, barely aware of the noise of the gunshot crashing over her, the windshield fracturing into a thousand spidery cracks. A sharp, hard pain clamped onto her shoulder. She rammed the gear into forward and stomped down on the accelerator. The convertible shot ahead. She was barely aware of the shouting voices, the boots thudding outside, the garage door scraping the frame of the convertible. Then the convertible bumped over something that seemed to bend and deflate beneath the wheels. Her own face was smashed into the leather of the passenger seat. Not until the car had slammed into the garage wall and the safety bag had exploded out of the steering wheel did she allow her foot to slip off the accelerator, bricks, plaster and wood falling around her like meteors out of the sky. There was no pain now, only a vast numbness that moved through her shoulder and a wet stickiness that soaked her blouse.

She lay against the passenger seat and tried to make sense of what was happening outside—still a reporter, she thought, the objective observer watching the story unfold: footsteps pounding nearer, uniforms crowding around the car, voices still shouting, lights from flashlights as big as torches flooding over her. Rex barking.

"Get an ambulance!" She recognized Nick's voice.

Catherine wasn't sure how long he had been leaning over her, pressing a cloth of some kind against her shoulder. The pain had flared up like a dead campfire and begun moving down her arm and across her chest. She tried to reach for Nick's hand but the gap seemed a thousand miles away.

"Take it easy, Catherine," Nick said. His voice was low and reassuring in her ear. "The bullet grazed your shoulder. You're gonna be okay. Medics will be here in a couple minutes. You following me, sweetheart?"

She had managed to take hold of his hand, or maybe he had found hers, she wasn't sure. She squeezed his fingers and nodded. "I'm with you," she heard herself whisper.

"Beckman's dead," he said. "It's over, sweetheart."